THE PIXEL EYE

TOR BOOKS BY PAUL LEVINSON

The Silk Code

Borrowed Tides

The Consciousness Plague

The Pixel Eye

A TOM DOHERTY ASSOCIATES BOOK

NEW YORK

THE PIXEL EYE

PAUL LEVINSON

This is a work of fiction. All the characters and events portrayed in this novel are either fictitious or are used fictitiously.

THE PIXEL EYE

Edited by David G. Hartwell

This book is printed on acid-free paper.

A Tor Book
Published by Tom Doherty Associates, LLC
175 Fifth Avenue
New York, NY 10010

www.tor.com

Library of Congress Cataloging-in-Publication Data

Levinson, Paul
The pixel eye / Paul Levinson.—1st. ed.
p. cm.
"A Tom Doherty Associates book."
ISBN 0-765-30556-9
1. Police—New York (State)—New York—Fiction.
2. Telecommunication equipment industry—Fiction. 3. Central Park (New York, N.Y.)—Fiction. 4. New York (N.Y.)—Fiction.
5. Squirrels—Fiction. I. Title.

PS3562.E92165P595 2003
813'.54—dc21

2003042647

First Edition: August 2003

Printed in the United States of America

0 9 8 7 6 5 4 3 2 1

TO TINA, SIMON,

AND MOLLY

ACKNOWLEDGMENTS

Phil D'Amato jumped off the page in 2002: Jay Kensinger made a low-budget movie of Phil's first adventure, "The Chronology Protection Case," and Mark Shanahan (assisted by Jay's script and me) wrote a radio play of the story, which was produced by Stage Shadow Productions and performed at the Mark Goodson Theater at the Museum of Television and Radio in New York City. Seeing and hearing Phil come to life inspired me and certainly influenced in unfathomable ways my conception of my forensic detective hero. As Phil lands back on the page in *The Pixel Eye,* I thus want to thank Jay and Mark for bringing so much life to this character.

Thanks, as well, to David Hartwell, my editor, and Moshe Feder, his assistant, for astute readings of the manuscript. Thanks to Christopher Lotts, my agent at the Ralph Vicinanza Agency, and to Stanley Schmidt, editor of *Analog,* where "The Chronology Protection Case" and two other early D'Amato adventures appeared in the mid–late 1990s.

As always, I'm indebted to my wife, Tina Vozick, and our children, Simon and Molly (who are now published and award-winning authors), for their perceptive first readings of *The Pixel Eye.*

And also as always, thanks to the readers of *The Silk Code* and *The Consciousness Plague,* and the viewers and listeners of "The Chronology Protection Case," for their enthusiasm.

CONTENTS

PART I:

Cold Spring

ONE

A cold November wind stalked Central Park. Leaves played the pavement like a kettledrum, squirrels ran for cover. I put my arm around Jenna.

"I don't see any fewer squirrels than usual," she said.

I looked around and agreed. "Birds?"

She pointed to a lone hawk, coasting above. Then to clusters of pigeons and sparrows on the ground. She shook her head. "I'd say they're the same. But maybe you should call in a professional bird-watcher or something."

"I can't believe I'm wasting even my own time on this," I replied. "This has to be a new low in my career—investigating missing animals."

"Are birds animals?" Jenna asked, and snuggled.

"Sure, in the 'animal, vegetable, mineral' sense," I said.

"We can get all three at Sambuca's," she said. "I'm starving."

I took her hand, and we walked toward West Seventy-second Street. "You're going to have mineral water instead of wine?" I asked.

"Why, is wine vegetable?" Jenna responded.

I nodded.

"Maybe I'll have both," Jenna said. "I could have just plain water, too—that would count as a mineral, wouldn't it?"

"Yeah." We reached Central Park West. The restaurant was

just across the street. The wind was even colder on this corner. "I'm getting calamari or some kind of invertebrate," I said. "That way I won't feel guilty about eating a possible subject of my case."

I KNEW, OF course, that missing animals could be a symptom of something much more serious—they could be the first victims of a new germ-warfare salvo, to pick the obvious. I tried to keep this thought in mind as I went in the next morning to see Jack Dugan, just appointed Deputy Mayor for Public Safety, a newly created post in the new administration. But I also recalled the time way back in the 1980s when cats started disappearing on the west side of the Hudson. A Chinese restaurant in need of a free supply of "chicken" turned out to be the culprit.

Jack smiled. "Phil, good to see you!" The same greeting he had been giving me for years. Same slicked-back hair, too—still mostly black, now with some gleaming strands of grey. But his dark blue woolen vest was new, and fit the job. Technically, he was no longer a cop—he was New York City's equivalent of the Secretary for Homeland Security, a position at least as powerful as the police commissioner, maybe more. Technically, I was still with the NYPD—but one of the conditions Jack had set on his appointment was that he could call me in on a case. I didn't object. It wasn't the head of the task force Jack and other brass had been dangling in front of me for years. That position had fallen victim to the reorganizations of "security governance" that seemed to happen in this city every month now. But being the deputy mayor's eyes and legs, and sometimes brains, had its advantages.

He gestured me to a seat. "So what have you got for me?" he inquired.

"I've been on the case just two days."

His smile broadened. "You would have called and cancelled the appointment if you had nothing to tell me," he said.

"The parks commissioner is sure that squirrels are missing," I said. "I interviewed most of his sources—four workers in Central Park, three in Prospect Park, one in Van Cortlandt Park—and they're sure, too. I looked around those parks myself, and Fort Tryon Park as well, and saw plenty of squirrels, but, hey, what do I know?"

"Your take at this point?" Dugan prodded.

I shrugged. "The same as with possible human murders. Without bodies, we have no proof of a crime. And with squirrels, we have the additional problem of no family members to report them missing."

"Other than the park workers," Dugan said.

"Right."

"Didn't Paul McCartney have a song about birds not falling from the sky when they die—they go off and hide someplace?" Dugan asked. "Maybe that's why there are no obvious bodies."

"Elton John," I replied, "and Bernie Taupin wrote the lyrics." But I still had to admire Dugan's command of popular culture. Impressive for a man in his job. "Anyway, we're talking squirrels, not birds. I asked some of the park workers if they'd noticed any reduction in the numbers of pigeons, sparrows, crows, and they said no. I didn't see anything untoward, birdwise, either. I did get hit by a nice, big splat of something from some bird in Prospect Park, but that's par for the course, too."

Dugan nodded. "So at this point it doesn't look like another West Nile Virus thing—no dead crows."

"Right. At this point, it doesn't look like anything at all."

Dugan nodded again. "Let's beat the out-of-the-way places in the parks for squirrel corpses, anyway. I guess we should bring in a squirrel expert—what are they, rodents?"

I nodded. "The squirrels are, yes. The experts presumably are human."

Dugan snorted. "Let's find out where they go to die."

"Okay," I said. "But I'm not sure they go anywhere—I've seen a few dead squirrels just lying on the sidewalks over the years."

"Me, too," Dugan said, "but talk to the experts anyway. And I'll see if I can get the parks commissioner to conduct some kind of squirrel census—presumably they have a rough count of the number of squirrels running around last year, so we can compare and see if the current numbers are lower."

"All right," I agreed, and started to leave. "Oh, one other thing." I reached into my manila folder and pulled out a printout of a news story I had pulled off the Web. It was from the *Bergen Record*, a local New Jersey newspaper.

"See? I knew you had something more for me." Dugan grinned. "What's it say?"

I gave him the single sheet of paper. "Half a dozen hamsters were reported stolen from a pet shop in Teaneck last week. Jenna's friend's little brother works in a deli next door—that's how I first heard about it. Probably has no relevance to our squirrels, but hamsters are rodents, too."

I'D KNOWN MELVIN Kaplan since Junior High School 135 in the Bronx. In those days, he had two hamsters in a cage in his bedroom. They, along with his collection of 1950s early rock 'n' roll 45s, were his pride and joy. By the time he got to college—City College, on 137th Street in Manhattan—he had dozens of hamsters hanging around his one-room apartment off campus. He sold some to pet shops, and used the money to buy more records. He went on to own a pet shop or two. Last I'd heard of Mel, though, he'd decided to indulge his love of music by purchasing The Grace Note in Greenwich Village. He turned it from a jazz-only to a jazz-and-early-rock club. I went down there to see him the next evening. Mel still knew more about hamsters—and rodents in general, I'd bet—than anyone else I knew. He was a little crazy, but weren't we all these days.

The Crows' "Gee" was playing on what looked to be an original Wurlitzer jukebox by the door. (I had just been talking with Dugan about crows yesterday—not the first time in my life that music seemed to come out of the world to reflect what was already in my mind.) Mel was sitting at a table, sawdust at his feet—it was all around the floor of the club—nursing a beer. He looked exactly as I had last seen him, about five years ago—tortoise-rimmed glasses, scanty beard, salt-and-pepper hair. The glasses could have been the same he wore in junior high school, though the present ones did seem to take up a bit more of his face.

"Phil." He smiled and beckoned me over.

"Good to see you, Mel." I shook his hand and took a seat. "Looks like you're doing very well here." The club was about half full. I had no idea whether this was good or bad for a Thursday night.

"Can't complain," Mel replied. "It's a labor of love, anyway. I did okay in the stock market in the last boom, and socked enough away that I don't have to worry."

"Squirreled some away, eh?"

Mel laughed. "What are you having?"

"Ginger ale would be great," I replied.

Mel called out the order to the waitress—blond, bouncy, in a short black skirt. "So you want a little primer on squirrels . . ."

"Right," I said.

"Not really my speciality—hamsters are—but I can tell you what I know about them."

"Good. Then we can also talk about hamsters."

"Okay. Well, you know, they—squirrels—have sort of a schizophrenic role in our culture. Kids love 'em. Adults don't always agree. Some folks call them 'tree-rats' or 'rats with tails.' In some parts of the South, squirrels are called 'tree-rabbits'—I guess folks down there love squirrels a little *too* much."

"They eat them?"

Mel nodded. "And here up north—in fact, everywhere there are birds and bird-fanciers—squirrels are often considered nuisances, because they outwit even the best squirrel-proof bird-feeders. They can jump so far, they look like they're practically flying."

"You think some bird-lovers in Central Park are snuffing squirrels to protect bird-feeders? Pretty extreme." My sister had a couple of bird-feeders in her garden in Brookline, Massachusetts. "They're usually attached to trees in backyards, right?

Mel agreed that vindictive bird-watchers were not likely to blame. "You'd have to kill all the squirrels in New York City—hell, in the whole Northeast—to make a difference, anyway. They breed very quickly. They're everywhere, especially in urban environments where rabbits and chipmunks don't do as well."

The blonde arrived with my ginger ale. She leaned over and put the glass on the table. I thanked her.

"Why do I get the feeling I'm about to enter a Walt Disney movie here?" I asked Mel.

He chuckled. "Hey, life's a demented Disney movie, my friend." He started whistling.

I sipped my soda. "We don't even know that they're dead—just missing, some of them, maybe . . ." I sipped some more. "All right, let's switch to your true expertise—hamsters. A bunch were reported stolen from a pet shop in New Jersey—you hear anything about that?"

Mel shook his head no. "They're cheap as dirt. Can't see the point in stealing them."

"Unless the thieves didn't want to be known, or maybe they were kids."

"I suppose . . ." Mel replied. "But stealing—rather than buying—to conceal who you are suggests some sort of unsavory purpose in getting the hamsters. They're just sweet little creatures, is all."

"I believe you—"

"Never heard anyone say a bad word about them—they're much better liked than squirrels," Mel continued. "Well, I guess you can see where my heart is on this. Hamsters even have their uses in laboratory science—they're much better than squirrels in the lab. Squirrels can get really vicious when caged."

"What kind of experiments—running around mazes like rats?"

"Yeah, that," Mel replied, "and I heard they were being used in some sort of music research up the Hudson—in Cold Spring."

"Music?" I became aware that it had changed in the jukebox. It was playing "Come On Baby Let the Good Times Roll."

"Oh yeah," Mel said. "Hamsters are real rock 'n' rollers. They got great hearing—bad eyesight—and they come out at night. They're nocturnal. They're real gone cats." Mel slapped a rhythm on the table to bring home his point. My empty glass, which I had put back down, provided rattling accompaniment.

I smiled, and realized I was tapping my foot. "And squirrels?"

The song ended with its saxophone flourish. "Just the opposite," Mel said. "Squirrels have great range of vision—they're always scanning the peripheries with those eyes—and they're out all day, except for the siesta they take after lunch."

"So we've got squirrels in the day and hamsters in the night," I said.

Bill Haley and the Comets started on the jukebox.

"That's right," Mel agreed. "Rockin' around the clock."

A DEAD SQUIRREL came to my attention the next morning. It had been spotted by a group of girls on their way to school on the northern end of Central Park.

"I can't believe we're even having this conversation," Ed Monti, the city's medical examiner, groused on the phone.

"My feelings entirely," I responded, "but let's just chalk it up to indulging Dugan."

"I guess one consequence of homicides being down is we have time for the rodent kind."

"So you think this squirrel was deliberately killed?" I couldn't bring myself to utter the word "murder" in these circumstances.

"Well, Rachel Saldana—she performed the autopsy—"

"Right, I know her."

"—Rachel's performed about half a dozen autopsies on squirrels found in the city in the past few days—"

"Is that par for the course? Half a dozen squirrel deaths in New York in a few days?" I asked.

"Yeah," Ed replied. "I checked into that—for this time of year it is, if you take as your territory all five boroughs. Squirrels are rushing around getting acorns for the winter—they're more vulnerable to getting hit by cars, that sort of thing."

"I'm surprised the city even keeps statistics on that sort of thing."

"We've been doing lots of that, quietly, since the anthrax and West Nile Virus business."

"Okay," I said. "But this morning's specimen died of something else?"

"Ketamine and Acepromazine," Ed replied. "Standard anaesthetic cocktail for rodents."

"Ketamine—the date-rape drug?"

"Yeah, but not in these small amounts," Ed said.

"You really researched this."

"Rachel did. The stuff's supposed to put the animal to

sleep, not kill it. Her best guess at this point is that the squirrel received the dose in a dart, fell out of a tree, and broke its neck in a fall to the curb."

"Jeez." I was actually beginning to feel bad for the poor thing. "So some wildlife biologist is getting his kicks taking shots at squirrels now? Last time I looked, they're not exactly selling those darts, or the tranquilizer, on Amazon."

"Could be the biologist's kid—but yeah, I'd say you should check out supply houses, research labs, any place that might carry those drugs. And I'll keep you posted on any new squirrel-cides that show up here."

"All right," I said. "I'm actually off to a research lab right now—Cerebreeze Laboratories, up in Cold Spring."

"Cerebreeze? I didn't know they were into wildlife," Ed observed.

"As far as I know, they're not. They're into hamsters."

I SAW LOTS of squirrels in the trees along the Hudson, through the window of my train. Just as I was looking at two scampering around a naked old oak north of Tarrytown, Dugan called on the cell phone with other squirrel news.

"First survey report is back," he said.

"And?"

"If anything, the current count projects *more* squirrels than last year, but it's statistically insignificant," Dugan replied. "You know, it's not really a census but a sample—they counted about a hundred squirrels in different places, and multiplied to get an overall estimate."

"Just as I was beginning to enjoy the investigation." A train ride up the Hudson was a pleasure any time, including nearly winter. "So what now?"

"Well, let's see how Ed's tranquilizer angle plays out before we pull the case," Dugan said. "If they're being anaesthetized, maybe what's going on is the squirrels are being used for something, then set back loose—that would explain the initial drop based on casual observation—and now there's no difference between this year and last year in the statistical sample."

I smiled. Dugan was definitely getting better with age. "How about we try to capture a few squirrels ourselves, and see if we can find any trace of earlier tranquilizers? . . . We'd have to make sure that we used a different drug than whatever we were looking for. . . ." I half-answered my own question, and mused.

"Well, let's see if Ed comes up with any more cases," Dugan reiterated, "and you let me know if Cerebreeze tells you anything useful. I don't like unexplained bodies, even if they're squirrels."

MY TRAIN ARRIVED in Cold Spring. Jenna and I got up here a few times a year, sometimes by car, sometimes by rail, which for my money was always more fun. An hour up the line from Grand Central, the town had a great gazebo overlooking the river, and some pretty decent restaurants. The antiques shops I could mostly do without—I hated to see old silver dollars at eight bucks a pop, when I remembered collecting them from banks in the Bronx at face value when I was a kid.

This was not the Cold Spring Harbor of genome research fame, located on Long Island. But this Cold Spring had Cerebreeze Laboratories, and a special expertise in at least one interesting kind of rodent. . . .

The lab was about half a mile from the station. I hiked it and enjoyed it—the town still bore a lot of its nineteenth-century dress. The front of the Cerebreeze facility was a big Victorian house, at least a hundred years old, with a wraparound porch and pine columns that bulged attractively in the middle. The house appeared to protrude from a considerable outcropping of light grey granite, guarded by tall locust trees that had already lost their leaves. If I remembered correctly, granite from this area had been brought downstream in the nineteenth century to build the Brooklyn Bridge.

Over the door hung big, rippling wind chimes, of glass or, more likely, crystal. I actually heard them before I saw them, and when I looked more closely, I realized they spelled W I N D C H I M E S T H R O U G H T I M E A N D M I N D . . . Each chime was a delicately chiseled letter. A gust obliged and caused the T I M E to move more distinctly. The sound was vaguely Asian.

The receptionist was a man in his thirties, in a rumpled wool suit. "Dr. D'Amato?—all right," he said crisply, with a trace of an Irish accent. He put a call in to my appointment, and she emerged a moment later.

"Dr. D'Amato?" Now it was her turn to confirm my name. Hers was Jill Cormier—it said so on a lavender name tag that hung high on a clingy sweater. She looked to be in her late thirties—short blond hair, expensively dressed for a scientist, and a big, bright smile.

"Thanks for seeing me." I took her extended hand and squeezed. I had seen her on TV a few times. She was a neuro-musicologist. Like just about everyone I had ever met in person after first seeing them on TV, she looked more vibrant in person. As McLuhan had said, television cools down your image.

"So would you like the tour? And then we can get a bite to eat and talk in our cafe?"

"Sounds good," I replied. We walked through a set of doors into a set of labs—more like a catacomb of labs, all high-tech and gleaming. I assumed they had been carved into the granite.

She explained that her main work was mapping the effect of music on the brain.

"Mapping?" I asked. I pretty much already knew what she meant, but I had found it was always better to hear it in your interviewees' own words.

"Yes, EKGs, CATscans, MRIs, newer peekers, whatever we can bring in to get a look. We want to know, for example, whether the brain responds differently to a major or minor chord, to two-, three-, or four-part harmony."

"Human brains?"

"Well, that's what we're all after, eventually, of course," Jill replied. "But right now it's hamsters—they're easy to work with, and have very keen hearing. We've bred a strain with special musical sensitivity."

I nodded.

She carefully opened a door to one of the labs. "Speaking of which . . ." She gestured to cages, about fifteen or twenty, lining three of the walls. Each cage contained a hamster hooked up with all kinds of wires leading to banks of monitors above.

She walked over to the nearest cage and bid me to follow. Musical notes were playing, softly but clearly, inside the cage.

"That sounds familiar," I said.

"The opening to 'Across the Universe,' " Jill said, and smiled.

"Not a bad way to while away the afternoon," I said, "but pity they don't get Lennon singing."

"Oh, we do that, too—just not in this room."

I put my ear near another cage. " 'Jumpin' Jack Flash'?"

"Yep," Jill responded. "Now take a look at the monitors—see that? 'Across the Universe' is inducing more relaxation—what we might even call contemplation, in humans—than 'Jumpin' Jack Flash.' "

"Fascinating," I said, "though both hamsters look sedated. You're using—?"

"Plain old Valium," Jill supplied. "Sometimes Ketamine, if we want heavier sedation."

"With Acepromazine?"

She regarded me. "No, that'd knock them out—that mix is an anaesthetic. Unconscious hamsters don't respond to music. We need them awake."

I approached a third cage. A Beach Boys song was playing there. I looked at the monitor. This hamster's brain patterns were a lot like the listener's of "Across the Universe."

" 'Surfer Girl,' " Jill said.

"Ah yes. Beatles, Stones, Beach Boys—you have good taste in music. The hamsters are lucky to have you."

Jill's eyes sparkled. "Thank you. But Marty Glick is responsible for the selections."

"And he's . . ."

"Oh, sorry, he's head of this project. He'll be joining us in the cafe."

GLICK SPORTED A neat, angular beard and an argyle sweater-vest in burgundy. I estimated his age as about forty. He knew his music, and more.

"I guess you could say we get our inspiration from Fechner." Glick was explaining the field of neuromusicology.

"The 'psychophysics' guy? He's considered one of the founders of experimental psychology, right?" I asked.

"Gustav Fechner, one and the same," Glick replied. "So you're familiar with his work in just-noticeable differences?"

"More or less—I remember one of my forensic psych professors at John Jay going on about Fechner. He was one of the first to investigate how much more physical energy a sound has to have—"

"Amplitude," Jill supplied.

"Right. If you have two sounds, what's the smallest difference in amplitude necessary for us to recognize one sound as louder than the other?" I asked.

"Exactly," Glick said. "Fechner actually built on an earlier researcher's work in this area—Ernst Weber—but Fechner put it all together."

"That would have been about 1860," Jill added.

"Yes," Glick continued. "And one of the really interesting implications to come out of Fechner's psychophysics—the precise relationship between perception and physical stimulus—was that those just-noticeable differences in loudness, color, brightness of light, what-have-you, are universal. All human beings have the same j-n-d's. But in the twentieth century, this was forgotten in many quarters—lost in the plague of cultural relativism. You know, we can never perceive the world the way someone in the Australian outback can, and vice versa."

I appreciated his passion for the field. "So you're trying to demonstrate a kind of universality here in music?" I asked.

"Yes! You see, some musical snobs have always maintained that the success of the Beatles, the Beach Boys, the whole of rock 'n' roll, was due to radio stations playing those songs over and over again, drilling them into everyone's head. The implication is that anything given that kind of airplay, any garbage, would catch on in the same way. But we aim to demonstrate—scientifically, objectively—that music becomes successful by appealing to universal modes of perception."

"And the hamsters?" I asked. "Do rodents respond to melodies the same way as humans?"

"Well, that's part of what we're trying to find out. . . . If we can demonstrate that hamsters respond in measurably different and consistent ways to different components of music, different kinds of music . . ."

"We of course have much more sophisticated equipment than Fechner did a century and a half ago," Jill added.

"We were very lucky to get funding for a project like this," Glick said. "It wasn't easy, believe me."

I believed it. Much as I loved the Beatles, and the Stones, and the Beach Boys, I don't know if I would have funded a project like this myself. Well, maybe I would have. Aesthetics count for something in this world, after all. "So you have no idea why people might be, ah, kidnapping squirrels from the parks, or stealing a few hamsters from a pet shop?" This was my attempt to get this interview back to my reason for being here, a more serious topic. Serious? I shook my head slightly, then realized I was doing it, and stopped.

"No idea at all, Dr. D'Amato," Jill responded.

"Phil," I said.

"Phil," she said.

"Sorry," Glick said. "Wish we could have been of more help."

"That's okay," I said. "I really did enjoy the tour—thank you for that. You're doing very interesting work."

JILL ESCORTED ME back through the labs and into the outer office, where she said good-bye.

I walked out into the sunlight, and looked back at the wraparound porch. That equipment inside must have indeed cost plenty—hard indeed to believe that Glick and Jill got funding to use it for something like this. . . .

A late-model Ford pulled up. A man in a dark grey suit got out.

I started walking back down to the Cold Spring station.

Just-noticeable differences . . . I wondered if Fechner had ever determined the j-n-d for recognizing a face you had not seen in a long while. . . .

The man in the grey suit. The more I thought about it, I

was sure he was Frank Catania. A lieutenant on the NYPD about ten years ago, more recently with the FBI and Domestic Security and Surveillance.

Did they have an interest in the Beatles and hamsters, too?

TWO

Frank Catania . . . I pulled out my Palm Pilot on the train back to Manhattan to see what I could find out about him. I had access to all kinds of online information these days, with all the recent increases in police interconnectivity. . . .

Yep, my recollections about Frank had been right. He started out NYPD, had a distinguished record with us, then switched to the feds eight years ago, and just last year was given a top-level post in Security and Surveillance.

Okay, so what was he up to in Cerebreeze? For all I knew, he was going out with Jill Cormier, but I was a firm disbeliever in coincidence. More likely, his national security work had brought him to the Cold Spring laboratory. But did it have anything to do with my interest in Cerebreeze? What could the Office of Surveillance in the Department of Homeland Security want with rock 'n' rollin' hamsters?

I was probably looking at this the wrong way—that was the usual reason for things seeming absurd, when they really made sense. But what was the right way?

I tracked down a few phone numbers for Catania on my little screen. One looked like it was his cell phone—the area code didn't look familiar, and that usually meant cell phone. Should I call him on his cell phone now? He was likely still at Cerebreeze. . . . *Hi, Frank, I'm not sure if you'll remember me. We last talked a long time ago, but didn't I just see you walk into Cerebreeze Laboratories about an hour ago, right under that nice tinkling wind chime?* Nah, let me see what I could find out about his work by calling his office instead, and maybe getting a talkative assistant or colleague. . . .

"Special Agent Catania," advised the first voice mail that I reached. Nothing more. No point in leaving a message. Even though we were both on the same side, I'd likely get more from Frank if I caught him by surprise. The other number just rang and rang. I looked at my watch—it was 5:35 P.M. Whoever worked with Frank in his office—if anyone did—was either gone or not answering. Probably gone, given the time of day. I, of course, could try calling some other fed numbers—someone was likely to still be in somewhere—and see what I could find out about Frank's work, but—

My cell phone lost its service. I looked out the window and saw why—we were entering the tunnel after the 125th Street station in Manhattan. "Next and last stop," the conductor said, "Grand Central Terminal." Well, there was really no reason to assume that Frank Catania's business was even relevant to what I was looking into, let alone of urgent importance. I could wait till tomorrow to find out what he was doing in Cold Spring.

I stepped off my train and through Grand Central toward the Lexington Avenue subway line. And just what *was* I looking into, I wondered again, as I boarded a northbound sardine-car, all elbows and briefcases and patent-leather purses, to Eighty-sixth Street. Squirrels and hamsters. Or, more precisely: one assassinated or accidentally killed squirrel, the instrument of death being a rodent anaesthetic; an indeterminate number of squirrels thought to be missing but now apparently not; a handful of hamsters snatched from Teaneck, with no apparent connection to hamsters rockin' their nights—well, days—away in Cerebreeze Laboratories in Cold Spring. I must have smiled to myself, ironically. A sincere-looking lady across the aisle smiled back.

What was I missing? What was I looking at in the wrong way?

Probably nothing.

I got off at Eighty-sixth Street, and quickly walked back to my brownstone. Ralphie Merrit, an eight-year-old who lived next door to us, was sitting at the foot of the inside staircase. "You look so tiny, so far away," he said to me, and laughed. He had a pair of binoculars, backward against his eyes. "See?" He offered me the binoculars, wrong end forward, and laughed again.

JENNA WAS OUT for the evening. I'd worry about dinner later. I put up a pot of Taj Mahal tea, and settled in to read the paper. Just for good measure, I turned on the radio—it was tuned to my favorite oldies station.

I had noticed, over the years, that the universe could either be an active ally or a savage foe in my investigations, but rarely neither. There were some cases in which some force beyond my control seemed to foil and spoil every move I made—hobble me, hinder me, get in the way of everything I was doing. But there were other situations in which the cosmos seemed to serve up answers, good leads, valuable paths, almost of its own volition, when I was otherwise occupied or doing nothing.

Tonight seemed one of the good times. I was just beginning to read an article about new modes of surveillance, when Bobby Vee's "The Night Has a Thousand Eyes" started playing on the radio. And then the phone rang.

"Frank Catania calling Phil D'Amato—is that you, Phil?"

"Yes—Frank—How are you doing?" I turned the radio off.

"As well as can be expected, given the world these days. I understand you've been trying to reach me?"

"Uh, yes, how—"

"At least a few of my phone numbers are so intelligent, they can track down whoever's calling me," Frank replied. "Caller ID/Taller IQ. They do it all on their own."

"Impressive."

"So what did you need to know?" Frank asked.

"Well, I was wondering what brought you all the way up to Cold Spring—I saw you as I was leaving Cerebreeze Laboratories a few hours ago." No point in pretending otherwise. Frank could find out I had been at Cerebreeze just by asking Jill Cormier or Marty Glick.

"I'm driving down the Taconic just south of Cold Spring even as we speak," Frank said. "You feel like a little dinner?"

"You still like seafood?" I asked.

"More than ever," Frank said.

"Good. I know just the place."

FRANK AND I had actually eaten at the Oyster Bar once before, back in the early 1990s. Grand Central Terminal was different then—grungier, more dangerous in terms of muggers, a lot more *terminal*—but also more innocent, like all of New York City then.

The menu in the Oyster Bar that night was pretty much the same, though, and that was a comfort. Every conceivable kind of clam . . .

I ordered the quahogs, tangy and raw. Frank was tamer—he ordered the stew.

"It's all about information," he said, as the food arrived. The service at the Oyster Bar was not fast. We had been talking about the constellations in the baby-blue ceiling of Grand Central, our opinions of the mayor, the seafood on Cape Cod—everything except our reason for meeting. I was happy to get to the business at hand.

"Of course," I said. "Your job is surveillance."

"And it's getting harder and harder," Frank said. "No one plans any attacks on the phone anymore. No one uses e-mail—they know that we're listening in, decoding everything. We won the digital part of the war, but not yet the war itself."

I sucked on a salty clam. "So how are the terrorists communicating these days? Face-to-face?"

Frank nodded. "The old-fashioned way. That's what happens when you wipe out their high-tech capability. They go primitive, underground—and that could be far more worrisome."

"Murder is one of the oldest tech activities in the book," I agreed. "You can murder someone with your bare hands—that's about as low-tech as you can get. Germ warfare is at least half a millennium old—they threw diseased corpses over castle walls in the Middle Ages. And September 11 was just goddamn planes—jetliners have been around since the 1950s."

Frank chewed. "Yeah."

"So . . . how are you combatting low-tech terrorist planning? Just lots of agents in the field, under cover?"

Frank shook his head no. "We don't have anywhere near the number of people for that."

I looked at him, and encouraged him to continue.

He looked back at me, and then at his watch. He took another piece of stew, then pushed the plate away. He wiped his face with a napkin. "I can show you something. It's close by—we don't have to go back up to Cold Spring. You interested?"

There were still two clams on my plate, but this was more important than leisurely dining. "Absolutely," I told Frank. I put one clam after another in my mouth, closed my eyes for a moment, and enjoyed the cold, salty rush.

Frank called the waiter over, and asked for the check.

WE WALKED OUT of the subterranean chambers of Grand Central Terminal onto Forty-second Street and Madison Avenue. A light, glistening rain was falling in the dark. Frank pointed west. "We're going to the Grace Building between Fifth and Sixth," he said. "City University used to have its graduate programs around there. The upper floors still have an odd lab or two." He smiled, slightly.

"Pretty convenient we were eating in the Oyster Bar," I remarked.

Frank's smile widened. "I had a feeling you'd suggest the place—I remember how much you enjoyed your mollusks last time."

The W. R. Grace Building was just a minute away. It was a sleek, striking fifty-story high-rise, set back from the sidewalk on the north side of Forty-second Street, sloping up to the sky like a giant playground slide-upon. I liked it. I touched its cream-colored exterior. I felt protective, almost paternal about it, though I had nothing to do with its construction, decades earlier. I guess I felt that way about all skyscrapers, now. I also took a peculiar joy in striding into them, doing business inside. It felt defiant, dignified, right.

Frank nodded at the security guard as we entered the building, "He's with me," Frank said to the man, bald and bearded, and gestured in my direction. The guard nodded back, and we walked past him to the elevators. No signing in, no display of identification. Frank was obviously well known here, and carried clout.

We took the elevator to the fortieth floor. It was about 8:30 in the evening now, and the place still had a few people in the hall, by the elevator, near the watercooler.

"Doctoral students, most in environmental psychology, if I'm not mistaken," Frank said.

"I saw something on The Learning Channel a few months

ago about the environmental psychology of zoos—how they can be worked into urban life to provide maximum pleasure." Could that somehow be relevant to disappearing squirrels and groovin' hamsters?

Frank grunted, and escorted me through a pair of glass doors, into a long corridor that sported just a janitor with a mop. We proceeded down the corridor past an unoccupied desk to a plain wooden door, with what looked like a scanning device of some sort near the doorknob.

Frank put his palm against the device, and I heard a slight click. He opened the door.

We walked down another corridor. This one was even more spartan than the first, and had an odd, familiar, medicinal odor. No . . . not so much medicinal, I realized as we approached another door. More laboratory, animal laboratory . . . hamster!

Frank opened this door the same way as the previous, and my eyes confirmed my nose. The room was lined with hamsters, just like the room I had visited in the afternoon at Cerebreeze. I looked more closely. This room was about half the size, and the hamsters seemed to be hooked up differently. There were big speakers surrounding each computer screen.

"We meet again, Phil."

I turned around and regarded Jill Cormier. She was more casually dressed now—faded blue jeans that fit her snugly and well, and a denim shirt that also looked good. "You get around," I said, and smiled.

"The times require it," she replied.

"Too bad the two of you know each other," Frank observed. "Deprives me of the opportunity to say 'Jill, meet Phil.' "

"We only met this afternoon," I said.

"Has the same preempting effect on my introduction," Frank said. He looked at Jill. "I thought we might give Phil a little demonstration."

Jill shifted position. She smoothed a crease on her thigh. "You're the boss," she said to Frank.

JILL WALKED US over to one of the hamsters. I noticed that there was a small microphone protruding from the bottom of the computer screen. Jill slipped a keyboard, thin as a wafer, out of her pocket, and ran her fingers over the keys. Subtle color changes rippled through the screen, and the computer made a sound as if it were clearing its throat, except it was more pleasant, almost cozy.

Jill smiled at me. "So, did you enjoy the sweater I was wearing this afternoon?"

I laughed, slightly. "Yes, it was quite becoming."

Jill nodded. "Perfect," she said. She worked the keyboard again.

A computer voice spoke up. "8:49 P.M."

Then I heard another voice—mine, laughing slightly, saying, "Yes, it was quite becoming."

But the voice was distorted in some way—it barely sounded like me.

"Poor recording," I said, and looked at the microphone. It seemed normal.

"Actually, it's miraculous that you're hearing that at all," Frank said.

"You're having problems with the recorder?" I asked.

"Quite the opposite," Frank said.

Jill played my laugh and compliment again. It still sounded strange.

I looked questioningly at Frank and Jill.

"It's not coming from any kind of digital recorder," Jill said.

"Analog?" I asked. "Some kind of antique?"

"Oh yeah," Frank said. "About as analog and antique as it gets."

He was grinning now, as was Jill.

"It's coming from the hamster," Frank said.

I HAD BEEN looking at this the wrong way, I realized, as Frank and Jill sketched out some of the details over tea and coffee in Frank's nondescript little office, just off the hamster lab. What was at stake here was not how the hamsters responded to sounds—not what was going on inside the hamster brains, how they reacted—but what the hamster brains were apparently actually *recording* of the outside world, recording in a way that could now be retrieved, by us. . . .

"You know much about how Alexander Graham Bell invented the telephone?" Frank asked.

"It was in 1876, right? But that's not what you want to tell me."

Frank nodded. "Right on both accounts. Bell figured out how to convert sound waves into equivalent electronic patterns pretty quickly. That was the easy part. . . ."

"Okay . . ."

"But it took him a while to work out the conversion of the electricity—the energy that went through the wires—back into sound, so that the person at the other end could hear it. After all, we can't hear words, literally, in an electronic signal. So decoding—getting the message back into sound—that was the hard part."

"All right . . ."

"We've known for years what part of the brain processes sound—in humans, in animals," Jill said. "And we've also had some good guesses about how, and where, the sound is encoded—"

"Stored," Frank said.

Now I was the one who was nodding in understanding. For I could see where this was going, and it was . . . mind-blowing, literally.

Jill smiled, softly, triumphantly. I had been fortunate enough to see this in a handful of scientists in my life—the quiet shine of satisfaction about an extraordinary breakthrough achieved. "So what we needed was a way to decode the neurochemical storage of sound in the brain—do what Bell did for his electronic signals, or for that matter, Edison did for sound in his phonograph—"

"Edison just stumbled onto that," Frank said.

"Yes," Jill said. "But for my team at Cerebreeze—just three of us, actually—it felt like we were walking through a desert, for miles and miles, not stumbling onto anything. But we broke the braincode, about ten months ago."

"You . . . figured out how to transform what was in the hamster's brain back into sound—that was what we heard when my voice was playing back to us in the lab before?" Seemed incredible, unprecedented, but unless Frank and Jill were just straight-out lying, that's what I had heard.

"They did it with a biochip," Frank said, looking with admiration at Jill. "You know, a chip that runs on DNA-algorithms—much more powerful than our traditional chips. And it was sensitive to some very subtle configurations in the auditory center of the brain—configurations that the traditional equipment was deaf to."

"To coin a phrase," Jill said, still nearly giddy with the contemplation of the accomplishment.

"Yeah," Frank agreed with the sentiment. "We call those neurochemical patterns—the ones that we can now tag and convert back into sound—'murmurform.' "

"Amazing," I said. "And the reason I've seen no announcements about this is . . . ?" But I knew the answer.

"Like I was saying," Frank replied. "Times have changed. New times demand new ways of doing science, new guidelines for integrating—or not integrating—scientific attainment into public awareness."

Jill leaned close, spoke low, her lips practically over my teacup. “My grandfather has an old propaganda sign from World War Two—‘Enemy Ears Are Listening’—ever see it? Tojo, Mussolini, and Hitler, hands cupped behind their ears.” She cupped her own hand around her ear.

“I’ve seen the ‘Loose Lips Sink Ships,’ ” I said. “Pretty much the same point.”

“Right,” Frank said. “It’s going to take a while to develop a force of hamster eavesdroppers. I know that sounds a little ridiculous. But with these decoding, recovery techniques, every hamster’s a goddamn ready-made tape recorder! The possibilities for getting the jump on terrorist planning are enormous!”

I agreed.

“But we need time to get something like this in place,” Frank continued. “And until then—and after we get it going, too—we’ve got to keep this as quiet as humanly possible.”

Jill frowned, slightly. I guessed she was wondering, again, why the hell Frank had brought me in on this.

Her expression was not lost on Frank, either. He sighed, smiled a little sadly. “Take my word about Phil,” he said to Jill. “I know him. He’s worse than a dog with a bone. As soon as I saw he was sniffing around, I knew we’d better cut our losses and deal him in.”

He looked at me apologetically. But he knew better. Like anyone in any branch of the detection business, he knew that what he had just done was tender a bit of praise my way. He smiled, as if he were hearing what I was thinking.

I returned the smile, to both Frank and Jill. “I understand completely, believe me. Don’t worry.”

“Good,” Frank said, and extended his hand.

I shook it. “The last thing I want to do is compromise our hamster ears to enemy ears, or whatever.”

They both chuckled, uncomfortably.

“I *would* like to learn a little more about how you hope to, ah, deploy the hamsters—if you can talk about that—"

"Well, why don't we call it a night, tonight," Frank said. "I've got to get down to Washington tomorrow morning. But we can pick this up next week." He looked at Jill.

She nodded.

"Okay, sure, then just one other quick question," I said. "I assume you're doing with the squirrels visually what you're doing with the hamsters acoustically? Missing squirrels are actually what first got me involved in this—"

"Squirrels?" they both said, and looked at each other again, this time puzzled.

"Uh, yeah, squirrels," I said. "There may be some missing from city parks, and we're looking into the possibility that maybe they're being drugged, with darts."

Frank looked concerned. "I have a strong feeling that I'm going to be the one asking you questions about these squirrels, rather than vice versa."

Great, I thought. If he indeed knew nothing about the missing squirrels, then I knew scarcely more than he.

THREE

A squirrel looked at me the next morning, nervously, for a fast second, as I hurried to the subway. It seemed far less concerned with me than the decayed piece of Crackerjack it was devouring. But I couldn't help thinking: was every damn squirrel a camcorder on feet now, every ear of a hamster a hidden little microphone? Was that the world we would soon be inhabiting?

I slid my card through the turnstile of the East Eighty-sixth Street station, and loped down the stairs to the train tracks. The station looked clean, as far as subway stations and their slightly sticky, sickly white gleam of clean went. No vermin in sight. But I knew there were huge infestations of mice and rats behind the scenes. Most of the time, especially during the day, they had the good sense to stay just beyond the periphery of our vision. But who knew what *their* ears might be picking up of our conversations from the mushy noise of the subway, what their eyes might be picking out. . . .

I shrugged off a shudder, and looked out over the tracks. Nothing moved, except a welcome, distant light of an approaching train. Frank and Jill had claimed no knowledge of squirrel surveillance, and maintained that their hamster programs and procedures would not be easily transferable to the different part of the brain responsible for vision. But they conceded that, if someone did want to develop a way of getting visual recordings out of squirrels, the acoustic work on hamsters was a big first step. And the same had to be true for other rodents.

The train pulled into the station, groaning, shaking, sighing. I looked at my watch. Pretty much on time. I walked over to the second car and went in.

She was right where she had said she would be—on the seat near the front of the car, on the far side. It was a small seat—just room for two—and her canvas bag occupied the empty part. Fortunately, it was well past morning rush hour, and the train was not very crowded. No one was contesting her bag for the seat.

I started walking toward her. The train pulled out of the station, stopped, started again. I lurched forward and backward. I grabbed an overhead hanger and made my way, a chimp among branches, to her corner.

She smiled at me, and put her bag on her lap.

"Thanks for meeting me like this," she said.

"My pleasure, Jill."

"YOU KNOW, WE represent three different interests," Jill said, after I had joined her on the silver-grey seat. "Frank is federal. You're New York police. I'm just a scientist."

I nodded. True enough—though I had learned over the years that there was often a lot more to a scientist than just science. Jill had left a message on *Jenna*'s cell phone, about six in the morning, asking for this meeting, in this gliding place. I had assumed it was all designed to keep away prying eyes and ears, as much as possible—not squirrels' and hamsters'—Frank's.

The train turned a sharp curve, and almost pitched Jill into my lap. She just smiled. "I don't subscribe to everything Frank told you last night," she said, when she had moved back. She smoothed her short skirt.

I nodded again. "How so?"

"I heard something about some squirrel research, similar to mine with hamsters, up in Cambridge." She reached into her canvas bag and pulled out a single sheet of paper, folded. She gave it to me. It contained a street address, a phone number, and an e-mail address.

I knew the neighborhood. "Right off Harvard Square?"

"Yeah," Jill said.

"You think Frank knows about this, and lied to me last night?"

"I don't know for sure," Jill said.

"But *you* lied to me last night, when you said you knew nothing of any squirrel surveillance project—that we do know for sure." I said this amicably enough, to minimize the sting, but I was interested in her reaction.

"Yes, I did," she said. "Because Frank's response took me a little by surprise, and I wanted to think over my options."

"So you and Frank aren't as . . . close on this project as I might have surmised last night," I said.

"There's a lot going on that you don't know about, and probably I don't, either," she said. She shook her head slowly. "I don't even know why Frank brought you into this, so fast. But . . . I just wanted you to know about the squirrels, at this point, that's all. . . ."

She collected her canvas bag, and stood up, suddenly. "I better get to the doors—my stop's next," she said. She walked rapidly to the doors at the other end of the train car.

The next stop would be Grand Central, and that was still at least a minute or two away. But I wasn't about to go chasing her. I watched her as she held on to an overhead hanger and swayed, back and forth, nicely, with the train. She turned and gave me one quick smile, just as the train entered the station. The doors opened, and she left.

I stayed on the train until the City Hall stop, and my meeting with Dugan at the New Muni Building.

"GO RIGHT IN, Dr. D'Amato." Dugan's secretary, Sheila, pointed to the door of his office. It was slightly open.

"Thanks!" I smiled. Sheila had been with him in every job he had, as far as I knew. I walked in.

Dugan was behind his customary cherrywood desk. In fact, just about everything about Jack's office was the same as it had been over the years. The title on the door was, of course, different—Deputy Mayor rather than Deputy Commissioner—and so was the building. The New Muni was shorter, stouter, than One Police Plaza. It was day-and-night compared to the top-hat wedding cake of the original Municipal Building, now known as Old Muni, taken over completely, radio station on the twenty-fourth floor included, by the Department of Homeland Security. But the space within Jack's office, within this New Muni, felt like it always had. Indisputably Jack's.

I took a seat across from that slightly battered, newly lacquered desk of Jack's, right next to the second man in the room. I extended my hand to him. "Long time no see, Frank."

He took my hand and shook it. "Yeah, time flies when you're having a good time."

"But you two did spend a couple of delightful hours together last night—strictly business, of course—right?" Jack asked. "I just want to make sure we're all in the same universe, here."

"It's called joking, Mr. Deputy Mayor," Frank replied, with a smile in his eye.

Jack grinned briefly, then frowned. "I guess I'm not particularly in a joking mood this morning." He passed a folder over to me, and another, presumably the same, to Frank.

It was news to me. I noted that Frank arched his eyebrows in a way that said it likely was news to him, too. I had called for this meeting late last night, in a phone chat with Dugan, after I had returned home. I had suggested that we try to get Frank to attend, and Dugan agreed. I left a message on several of Frank's voice mails, and at least one had apparently been heard.

But the file contained a photo of a pretty, nine-year-old girl. She had been hit by a dart on the east side of Central Park yesterday afternoon. The Ketamine-Acepromazine had been far too little in quantity to knock her out, but she had been hit in the leg, had grown dazed and disoriented, and that had been enough to make her lose her balance. She had stepped onto Fifth Avenue as she was wobbling around, and had come razor-close to being hit by a van that was backing out.

"Jeez," I said. "You think the dart was intended for a squirrel?"

"You tell me," Dugan replied.

I looked at Frank.

He shook his head. "Look, I wouldn't rule anything out, but like I told you last night, I don't know squat about squirrels."

"I wish I could say the same," Dugan said. "They drive the Mrs. crazy—always trying to get at our bird-feeder. And they make an unsettling sound sometimes. Like, I don't know, a whining, a cawing, like a crow."

"Very interesting, Mr. Audubon," Frank said, a bit dyspeptically.

"I think he was birds—John Audubon," I offered.

"Listen, I can't have little girls getting shot by blowguns," Dugan said, in an even worse tone of voice than Frank's. "She could have been *killed*, for crissakes."

Frank looked back at Dugan, and dug in. "I don't have to tell you what kind of enemy we're trying to fight out there, Jack. You've seen—we've all seen—what they're capable of doing to this city. I can tell you one thing. Conduct your investigation into this squirrel thing, into this girl getting hit with a drug dart, if you like, but make sure none of it leaks to the media and points them at us. Make sure nothing you do tangles *our* initiatives. It'll be on your head, believe me, if anything goes wrong. And I'll make sure of that."

Dugan started to reply. He didn't respond well to threats. I interceded—it served no purpose to get Frank any more hostile at this point.

"You know, the dose KellyJane received"—that was her name, KellyJane Mahoney—"looks a little much for a squirrel, if I remember correctly." Actually, I had done some reading on the Web last night, to get more details on some of the things I'd heard earlier that day, but there was no need to expose my recent ignorance here.

"Well, I guess check with Ed Monti on that," Jack replied. "Why up the dose? Wouldn't that risk killing the squirrel?"

"Could be," I said. "I'll also check out the girl—who she is, relatives, friends—just to rule out that she was the target and the squirrels a coincidence."

"All right, makes sense," Jack said. He was still angry at Frank, but he was controlling it pretty well. He also knew that I didn't put much stock in coincidence. "Her father's a dean at the Tolkien School up in Riverdale," he said. "Nothing controversial about that, as far as I can see, but yeah, check it out."

I jotted that down. I was beginning to feel like *I* had been drugged with some sort of dart already, with all of these little details and leads drizzling on me this morning. But sometimes they brought up a useful crop of results.

"I'm sorry I was so aggressive," Frank said to Jack, and extended his hand. "We're all on the same side, we all want the same thing. It's just hard to be calm and courteous when the stakes are so high."

Jack shook his hand.

"WATER, TEA, SOMETHING stronger?" Jack asked me, after Frank left.

"Water is fine."

"Okay." Jack rummaged behind his desk and produced a half-pint of Poland Spring.

"Thanks." I took the bottle and a swig.

"So?" Jack asked.

"I don't know about Frank," I replied, and told Jack about my meeting on the number four train this morning with Jill.

"Well, I'm gratified, at least, that you're seeing fit to share that with *me*," Jack said.

"I have to trust someone," I said.

Jack smiled, briefly, then grew more serious. "Frank was honest with me about what he told you last night—at least, he told me the same thing, before you arrived."

"He could have been lying to both of us. Who knows—Jill and he could both be lying, covering up, either separately or together."

"Yeah," Jack considered, sighed. "I've known Frank for better than fifteen years—ever since he was a rookie detective. He was a good man, back then. No reason to think he's changed."

"Like he said, these are difficult times," I observed.

Jack rubbed his chin. "Check out Cambridge," he finally said. "Check out the little-girl-as-victim angle. Check out anything else you can find out about squirrels, hamsters, decoding of sound in the brain. Check out everything."

"Right."

"And carefully. Frank's right that we don't want to attract attention to this animal-eavesdropping research. If that's what's really going on."

RIVERDALE WAS A lot closer than Cambridge. I could stop there and pay the dean a little visit, if necessary, before heading home. And take the fast train to Boston tomorrow.

But first, I needed to spend a little time in my office, and catch up on accumulated paperwork and a few necessary calls.

I tried Ed Monti. His voice mail informed me that he was in court all day today. I got lucky and reached Rachel Saldana, the squirrel autopsy expert, on the first try.

"You're right," Rachel said, after I had given her the details on the KellyJane drugging. "Thirty-five milligrams is almost twice the dosage used for squirrels."

"What effect would that amount have on a squirrel?" I asked.

"Hard to say—likely nowhere close enough to kill it. Rodents have very resilient respiratory systems—and that's what usually succumbs to anaesthetic overdose."

"So how much Ketamine and Acepromazine would it take to murder a squirrel?"

"More like ten times the usual dosage," Rachel replied.

"All right. So at least we don't seem to be moving into serial squirrel-cide," I said.

"You're lucky there wasn't a worse effect on the little girl," Rachel said. "That's what you should be worried about. Acepromazine hasn't been extensively tested on humans yet, as far as I know."

"They're keeping her under observation," I said.

"Good."

"Anything more you can tell me about either of those drugs?" I asked. "I know that Ketamine is a date-rape favorite, and also used as an hallucinogenic in small doses."

"Yeah. 'Special K,' " Rachel said. "And John Lilly—you know, the dolphin guy—claimed he could talk to aliens while under its influence."

"Just what I needed to hear today. Thanks," I said.

RIVERDALE WAS INDEED a lot closer than Cambridge, Massachusetts, but Cambridge seemed a lot more likely to provide some information about whether some group was anaesthetizing squirrels to get some pictures out of their brains.

I pulled out the piece of paper Jill had given me, and tapped on it with a pencil. *Gnarlingview Laboratories,* it said, with street address, phone, and e-mail. Well, the name certainly spoke squirrel. Gnarly holes in oak trees were typical viewing stands for squirrels.

E-mail didn't make sense. I could receive a reply in five days as likely as five minutes. And I didn't like tipping my hand—I couldn't expect a serious answer to any query unless I said who I was, and as soon as I did that, my correspondents could investigate me, look up my name on the Web, and find out a lot more about me and some of my investigations. If there was anything they wanted to hide, they would stay as far away from me as possible.

Phone had the advantage of getting them by surprise, but that assumed I reached the right person. Otherwise, the person who might tell me what I needed to know could be alerted by the person I had actually reached, and I'd be in the same fix by phone as with e-mail. On the other hand, I had done okay, as far as I could tell, by first phoning Cerebreeze. On yet another hand—I was a centipede, or the hand equivalent, when it came to weighing strategies, I knew that—but yet, on that other hand, why would Jill give me the number of someone who wouldn't want to cooperate? But I had no idea how well Jill knew this person, or how good a judge she was of anyone's willingness to cooperate . . . And, actually, no person's name was on her sheet—just the place, Gnarlingview. I could call Jill, but . . . I tapped the paper some more. . . .

I could catch a train and still get up to Boston before five today. I looked at the paperwork on my desk—all relating to other things. I pulled out a train schedule from my drawer. Yep, there was an Acela-plus leaving Penn Station in about fifty minutes. But what kind of reception would I get at Gnarlingview, just showing up unannounced?

I finally decided on a compromise: travel up to Boston, and call Gnarlingview from right across the street. That old but reliable tack had the advantage of giving me a possible view of anyone who scurried out of the building, after my call. Could be useful—especially if I received a chilly reception on the phone.

I put on my overcoat and headed out of the office. I'd call Jenna from the train and break the news to her about not having dinner together for the second night in a row.

"Up to Boston, for the afternoon," I called out to Libby, our receptionist. "I should be back tomorrow."

She nodded, very slightly. Her way of doing that always left me wondering if she really had heard me.

THE TRAIN TOOK longer than expected—some problem on the tracks near Mystic. The arrival thirty-five-minutes late at South Station was just the beginning. The local T stalled twice over the Charles River. It was dark when I finally approached the street by Harvard Yard. Or maybe, given the end of Daylight Saving Time and impending winter, it would have been dark even if all my trains had been on time.

Gnarlingview's address was actually close to the old Radcliffe part of Harvard, about three blocks from where I was. The evening air was brisk; it was 6:15; I walked quickly. Conceivably someone other than cleaning staff could still be in at the laboratory. If not, I could always get a room at the Harvard Inn, have a good dinner—their food was delicious—and check in on Gnarlingview first thing tomorrow. I could catch the train back to New York, and be in my office by midafternoon.

Gnarlingview loomed across the street. Actually, it looked

too modest to loom—a weak, incandescent light rested on mottled, dusty ivy over old red brick. But considering the effort I had made to get here, it loomed in my mind anyway.

I pulled out my cell phone. A squirrel ran nearby. A scout for Gnarlingview? A few weeks ago, that would have been comical—a scene from Disney's *Song of the South* indeed. Zip a Dee Doo Dah.

Today, that was precisely what I was here to investigate.

THE NUMBER JILL had given me rang four times.

"Hello," a woman's voice answered, in the middle of the fifth ring.

"Hi. I'm Dr. Phil D'Amato, New York City Police Department Forensics. A colleague gave me your number—we're looking into some developments with our Central Park squirrels, and she thought you might be of some assistance. . . ."

No reply.

"Hello? This is Gnarlingview Laboratories, isn't it?" The woman had just said hello, and hadn't said anything about Gnarlingview, so she was not likely a receptionist. But she didn't sound like janitor staff, either . . . I hoped this *was* Gnarlingview—for all I knew, Jill might have accidentally, or deliberately, given me the wrong number—

"Hold on, while I transfer you."

"Okay, but—"

"Deborah Paton," a different voice said. "Can I help you?" The voice was younger, but more in command.

"Yes, thanks." I repeated my introduction. "You are Gnarlingview Labs?" I concluded.

"You're a bit away from New York City jurisdiction, aren't you?"

"Yes, but I was hoping you could help."

"Who did you say your colleague was? I don't believe I caught her name."

She hadn't caught it because I hadn't said it. I didn't like publicizing names in situations like this, especially to faceless voices on the phone. But I didn't see that I had any choice now, if I wanted to get any further.

"Oh. Sorry," I said. "Her name is Jill Cormier."

"Jill Cormier from Cerebreeze?"

"That's right."

"But I thought you just said that you work for the New York City Police Department—Cerebreeze is in Cold Spring. Look, Dr. D'Amato, I'm not trying to give you a hard time. But you call out of the blue, well after our usual hours—I shouldn't even be here now—"

Gnarlingview's front door, which I had continued to keep an eye on, popped open—

"—and you tell me a *colleague* gave you our number," Paton continued, "when she's apparently no such thing—"

A figure emerged. I couldn't quite make out—

"I'm sorry," I spoke as soothingly as possible. "I shouldn't have said 'colleague.' But, obviously, Jill—Dr. Cormier—did give me your number, and it really is important that I see you—"

I caught a glimpse—then a van came between me and Gnarlingview's entrance, and totally obscured my view. The damn thing seemed to be moving one mile an hour—

"All right," Paton said. "Assuming Gnarlingview's not the object of some official government investigation. Because, if so, I'll have to call our attorney—"

"I assure you you're not—I'm New York, as you just said, and we're in Cambridge. This is just a very general fact-finding interview," I said.

"Okay. Let me look at my schedule this week—"

"Actually, I'm right in the area now. Do you think—"

The van finally moved on. No one was in front of Gnarlingview now. I cursed silently. I looked left and right—

"Well, my schedule does look pretty packed the rest of week. How quickly can you get here?"

"I'm across the street," I admitted. I thought I saw someone now, walking away from Gnarlingview, toward the Harvard Square station—

"This whole thing is crazy," Paton said, "but, okay, I can see you for a few minutes now."

"Thanks, I'll be right there," I replied, and started walking across the street.

The figure I had seen was now too far away for me to have any chance of conclusively recognizing.

But, jeez, something about him, something in the nuance of his walk, reminded me of someone I had seen *entering* a lab, another lab, just yesterday.

Frank Catania.

FOUR

My eyesight wasn't as sharp as a squirrel's, so I couldn't be sure about Frank. But presumably my reasoning was a little better. I might as well see, now, what I could get out of Gnarlingview. I could look into what Frank was doing here, if the distant figure was Frank, tomorrow.

The door of Gnarlingview Laboratories was dark, massive oak, with a cast-iron knocker. It clacked plangently when I used it.

A big-boned woman with short, grey hair and a suit the same color opened the door. She looked to be about fifty.

"Phil D'Amato," I said, and extended my hand.

She accepted it. "Deborah Paton." Her voice did sound young. "My office is right down the hall."

The walls had pen-and-ink drawings and etchings of various river scenes. The only ones I recognized were the Hudson and the Charles. They looked to be mid-nineteenth century. "W. H. Bartlett?" Dave Spencer—late coroner and dear friend—had been an avid collector. I still missed him, just about every day. . . .

Paton shrugged. "Not my interest." She escorted me into her office and offered me a plain pine chair. "I was frankly more interested in *this.*"

She picked a piece of paper off the top of her desk and gave it to me. It had my picture, in smeared blurry color. It looked like it had been taken off the Web, but I couldn't quite place the page.

"Checking out my bona fides? Quite sensible." After all, I could have been someone else who had swiped the info Jill had given me. No reason a laboratory should want to let someone in off the street, with no prior appointment, without some sort of ID.

"Oh, we were confident it was you, about thirty seconds after our receptionist got off the phone. Voice recognition analyses can be processed very quickly nowadays."

Not that quickly, at least as far as I knew. "And the voice you matched to that, to make the ID?"

"You're all over the Web, Dr. D'Amato—realaudio, feelaudio, zealaudio, every format."

I nodded. That was true enough. I looked back at my picture. "So this . . ."

"Wasn't primarily for identification purposes, no."

I looked up at Deborah Paton. She also had grey eyes, keen and penetrating. The contrast between the color picture of me and her grey suit, hair, and eyes was striking, almost jolting—like I was real and she was black-and-white TV. Something was very peculiar about this place, or some piece of it, but I couldn't tell which piece. . . .

Paton continued: "Suppose I told you—hypothetically speaking, mind you, there would be no way to prove this just on the basis of that picture you're holding in your hand—but suppose I told you that it came from a squirrel that looked up at your face not twenty minutes ago, as you were talking to us on your cell phone, on the other side of the street?"

I ALMOST LAUGHED. The fact that it was almost laughter, and not flat-out, full-throttle belly laughter, was another indication of how far I'd already gone on this matter—which still seemed to verge on the ridiculous, but lately less so by the minute.

"How would you control it—get the squirrel to look where you wanted?"

"Child's play, Dr. D'Amato—we've had that technology on rats for a few years now. Remote devices send signals to a little unit strapped on the back of the rodent, attached to wires in the pleasure center of the brain, and to parts of the brain that simulate pressure on the left or right whiskers—and we get the animal to move this way or that. We've souped it up a little for squirrels—that's the easy part."

I considered. I had indeed read about such devices a few years ago. "I may have seen a squirrel run by me," I finally said. "But I'm certain I would have noticed any protruding wires." And, for that matter, how could a squirrel run at all, out in the street, hooked up the way I had seen those hamsters?

"Oh, there are many more than one out there, Dr. D'Amato. And surely you've heard about cranial implants?"

"So you're saying you embedded wireless transmitters in their brains, to give you images of what they see?" Was that what was going on with the squirrels back in New York? I looked again at the blurry printout of my image. Paton was right that it proved nothing.

"We don't do the surgery at Gnarlingview," she replied. "We field the implanted squirrels, and collect and collate the images they send."

"How far can the squirrels range?"

"Not very far, at this point. About a quarter of a mile from our receivers is maximum."

"Why are you telling me all of this?" I was always suspicious of information suddenly given so easily. The only question was when was the best time to make an issue of it. Sometimes it was better to let the talk continue, unchallenged. This conversation felt different.

"Please understand, Dr. D'Amato, that this is a much . . .

deeper . . . project than you realize, and probably I realize, as well. It's a safe bet that I don't know everything, and an even safer bet that I'm not going to tell you everything I know."

I nodded.

"I can tell you that there's more than one image-collecting laboratory like Gnarlingview. And we communicate regularly. Early on, a local cop, like yourself—forgive me, I didn't mean to be insulting—"

"None taken, I assure you."

"Well, someone began investigating one of the other labs—"

"When was that?"

"About two years ago."

"This has been going on that long?" I asked.

"Longer," Paton replied.

"Can you say how long?"

"No."

"The name of this other lab?"

"No," she said. "I can't tell you that, either."

"Okay," I said. "So, then, as you were saying . . ."

"Well, this other investigator very nearly brought this whole project out into the open—which no one involved in the project wants—so we all decided, right then, to put into place some safeguards, protocols for what to do when someone gets too close. And one of them is that anytime anyone from any police force begins asking questions, getting ideas about what we're doing, beyond a certain point, we open up and convey some details about the project. Because we're hoping that will help you understand how important our work is. That's something we won't do for the media."

I smiled sourly. "I appreciate the distinction. But what you say doesn't exactly inspire confidence that you're telling me anything like the truth—in contrast to just a good story to satisfy my curiosity and take me down a misleading path."

"I know that," Paton said quietly, with what seemed like sincerity.

"What more can you tell me? How many cities, squirrels, are involved? What kinds of images are you getting?"

"Well the images are mostly what you think—faces, trees, buildings."

"Still photos or motion pictures?" I asked.

"Ours aren't in motion. Most of the images are ordinary, just what you'd expect. Sometimes we get something bizarre—there's still a good deal of noise in the decoding from the brain. Not as much as with the hamsters, but enough to sometimes distort our data. Most of our work here is actually focused on further reducing that visual noise, keeping it to a minimum. The goal, of course, is first to have images, then reliable images, then legally reliable images. Imagine the benefit to national security of having millions of extra eyes, inobtrusive, fleet of foot, that can not only see for us, but send back recordable images of what they see."

"I can understand why you'd want to keep this from the media," I said. "The civil liberties people would go ballistic if they knew what you were doing." And, actually, I had a few mixed feelings about this, too. Safety and freedom—how to have the first, so you can protect the second, without stepping on the second? No simple question.

"Oh, we've heard from them already," Paton said. "One of the participating labs was, in fact, burned to the ground late last year."

Another indication of how long this has been going on, I thought.

"Don't try to recall if you heard anything about that," she added, "because you wouldn't—no one knew it was a lab."

"I see," I said. The profile of these researchers was so low, they could be everywhere—like the squirrels they were conscripting into service. And I hadn't even asked her, yet, how the hamsters tied in. Was there some kind of master plan for animal surveillance, with squirrel and hamster work apportioned? Were there other animals in this low-profile unit? "Any chance I could get a look at the equipment—the screens that receive the images?"

Paton gave me a strange look. "I wouldn't recommend it. It wouldn't be safe."

"Not safe?"

She shook her head no and looked at her watch. She looked at me again. Her face had the closest to a smile I had so far seen on it. Still had a ways to go. "Gnarlingview Laboratories will go up in smoke, literally, in about four minutes, Dr. D'Amato. I suggest you do as I do now, and leave." She vacated her chair, walked to the side, and opened a door I thought was a closet. "This is the fastest way out—I suggest you take it."

I stood up. "You received some sort of alarm?" No, I realized. Her expression said something else. Jeez . . . "You set it!? Why?"

"Protocol, Dr. D'Amato, protocol. Everything I told you is true—we don't mind a little information getting out. But we just can't risk anything more yet . . . We can't leave any proof . . . Now, please, we don't want you to get hurt. Leave now." She turned around and walked quickly away.

I thought for a second, then ran after her.

I felt cold air, then turned a corner—the front door was open. I was approaching it from a different angle, but it was the same door I had entered.

I looked at my watch—probably a minute left to the explosion, or whatever it was, if she was telling the truth. I thought for another second. Should I risk going back down the hall, for a quick glimpse of the equipment?

No, not worth it—I had no real idea even what I was looking for.

I dashed out the door. Deborah Paton was standing next to a dirty grey van—grey hair, grey eyes, grey suit, now grey van. She looked at me for a split second, nodded, and entered the van. It sped away. I couldn't be sure, but her face may have looked relieved when she saw me on the doorstep.

I ran down the stairs and across the street. I turned around just in time to see Gnarlingview Laboratories go up in lacy orange flames.

THE FIRE WAS intense. The flames licked the air and cackled. But fire engines arrived a moment later—just as I completed my 911 call. They had probably been tipped off beforehand—another part of Paton's "protocol"? I didn't see how they could have arrived so quickly otherwise, unless the firehouse just happened to be around the corner. I could check into that later.

The firefighters appeared just in time to see the small building crumble into itself. Presumably no one died—the receptionist was the only other person I had seen inside, and her desk had been empty when I left—but I could barely bring myself to keep looking at this scene, anyway. I was glad to see the red brick buildings on either side of Gnarlingview—or where it had just stood—seemed unscathed.

I turned away. I realized my eyes were tearing. But not just from soot. The sight of a burning, crumbling building did that to me, even if the building was small. . . .

A squirrel ran by me. I sighed. Where are your images going to now, I wondered.

Maybe to some other laboratory like Gnarlingview? That would have to be within about a five-block radius, based on what Paton had told me about transmission distances. I looked around. It would take me a week or longer to carefully search every structure in this area for another Cerebreeze or Gnarlingview. And who knew if she had been telling me the truth about that—had she been telling me the truth about anything?

I pulled out the paper with my picture on it. Could some specialist in pixels discern that this was my face as seen by a squirrel? I hadn't had a chance to ask Paton if her decoding process enhanced the image in any way.

I held it high above my head, to see if the angle looked like what a squirrel might see, looking up from the ground at my head. Maybe—

A sudden cloudburst interrupted my gaze. Icy droplets hit my face, my analysis, my paper, before I had a chance to put it into the relative safety of my jacket. The soggy mess that I managed to quickly fold and shove into a pocket would now likely be of no use.

Was that part of the "protocol," too? Call upon the rain to erase the last bit of evidence?

No, that was just nature, and its penchant for adding insult to injury.

But keeping fire and rain apart, distinguishing between technology and nature, was no easy task, especially when the subject was a cyborg breed of squirrel supposedly outfitted with a device that transmitted visions from its brain.

I made my way slowly back to the T, in the downpour.

THE SUN IN New York the next morning was up like a sweet piece of candy. But the day gobbled it pretty quickly.

Jenna showed me an article in *The New York Times* before she left to teach her course on the genome at Princeton. It was actually from yesterday's paper. It wasn't on the front page, and I'd missed it on the trains to and from Boston.

There were articles like this a few times a month. Jenna

called it to my attention because I had told her about what Deborah Paton had told me about civil liberties advocates setting fire to one of the animal labs last year.

"Well, looks like she was at least telling the truth about that, anyway," Jenna said. "Though I wouldn't put it past her people to have set that fire, too, and maybe she got the idea to put the blame on civil liberties defenders when she was reading this very article!" Jenna didn't care too much for Deborah Paton, seeing as how she had almost killed me.

Jenna shook her head, blew me a kiss, and walked out the door.

I turned to the article. CIVIL LIBERTIES GROUPS HEIGHTENING PROTESTS ABOUT NEW SECURITY MEASURES, the headline read. FEDS FEAR FANATICS MAY RESORT TO VIOLENCE, the subheadline added. The text of the article noted that several possible cases of arson in the past year were under investigation.

"Civil liberties fanatics" would have been an oxymoron just a few years ago. Now . . . now, lots of things were upside down, in the tense new world terror had brought into being. . . .

Well, at least no one had been killed in these protests, as yet, according to the article. And there were no fatalities—no human fatalities, so far—in this rodent eavesdropping business I was looking into, either. A welcome rarity for a case I was working on—

The phone rang.

I knew it was Dugan, even without the benefit of Caller ID. He was my most frequent provider of bad tidings, and something about this day felt like it was going in that direction.

"Your name came up in an assault-case report that just showed up on my screen," Dugan began, without introduction.

"Oh? I didn't know you still took such an interest in assaults. Someone famous, important?"

"No, not as far as I can see," Dugan replied. "The report

was forwarded to me because I put your name on a short list of folks who, when their name appears in any report, it's automatically copied to my attention."

"I'm honored."

"Well, I know how busy you are, and this helps me keep abreast of what you're doing. Don't worry, we're not spying on you."

"I'm not worried." Because I knew the Department had been doing things like this for years. "As long as your informant wasn't a hamster . . . Anyway, how did my name come up?"

"Interview with the waitress," Dugan said. "She was asked if anything different, out of the ordinary, had occurred in the business in the past few weeks—you know, standard question—and she said the only thing she could think of was a visit to the club by an old friend who was a forensic detective with the NYPD—"

"Club? I don't recall . . ."

"Hold on a second," Dugan said. "Let's see—yeah, here it is. The Grace Note?"

"Jeez . . . Mel—"

"Yeah," Dugan said. "Melvin Kaplan. He's in Beth Israel now, in critical condition. He was beaten pretty badly as he was leaving The Grace Note the evening before yesterday—that would actually be very early yesterday morning. Nearly lost his life."

FIVE

The only reason that Mel was still alive, Dugan had told me, was that a group of construction workers had made a wrong turn on their way to the Lower Manhattan Reconstruction Project. They came upon Mel being beaten. His attackers fled. The MDs had said the one or two more punches or kicks that Mel had not received might have well made the difference.

But the difference was still frighteningly slight—I could see that as soon as I walked into Mel's intensive care room at Beth Israel. The charts confirmed it. His chances were no better than fifty-fifty.

The question I had to face immediately was whether the attack on Mel had been triggered by our earlier meeting. The answer was likely no—people were still randomly, savagely attacked in this city, though thankfully much less often than in the heyday of personal lawlessness in New York City, back in the early 1990s. But it made sense to start with the assumption, anyway, that what had happened to Mel was in some way connected to our meeting, to what I was investigating, because if that was the case, then everyone involved, including Mel, was still in a lot of danger.

Okay . . . if Mel was assaulted early yesterday morning, that ruled out Deborah Paton or anyone I had met for the first time yesterday as the source of the assault. That left Frank Catania and Jill Cormier. I had talked to Jill on the train a few hours after Mel's beating, and then Frank right after, in Jack's office. They would had to have been cool customers to talk to me like that if they had played a role in Mel's beating. . . .

Could either "one" have given any flicker of expression, anything that could now tell me, in retrospect, that they knew about the attack on Mel?

Impossible to say—I knew Frank better than Jill, but neither one well enough to make subtle judgments about their facial and body language.

Had I even mentioned Mel to either of them?

I looked at him now, lying in bed, lying so close to death. The nurse on duty had told me that one of his employees—a waitress, blond—had been keeping watch here over Mel and had gone out about ten minutes ago to grab a coffee in the cafeteria. I debated whether to wait for her or look for her in the cafeteria. I decided instead to leave—I could talk to her later.

I walked out of Mel's room and called Dugan on my cell phone. The damn thing beeped instead of placing the call. I looked at the readout on the tiny screen—wonderful, no service!

I beckoned the nurse. "Two things," I told her. "First, please call this number." I wrote the number of Dugan's receptionist on my card and gave it to the nurse. "Say I'm requesting immediate twenty-four-hour security for the patient. And needless to say, please keep a special eye on his room until the officer arrives."

"Sure," she replied. "Like in *The Godfather*, right? I promise I won't let anyone in who shouldn't be here."

"Good. Thank you." I looked at her and smiled. Her name was Heather Digby. She had strawberry hair and spunk.

"And assuming all of that comes under the first thing, the second is?" she asked.

"Second thing is, see if you can rig up some sort of CD with a little speaker in Mr. Kaplan's room. Play some 1950s rock 'n' roll. Who knows, it might help."

Now Nurse Digby smiled.

"Hey, I'm serious," I replied, but still smiling.

"Oh, I'm a great believer in the therapeutic power of music," she said. "My grandmother plays Mozart every time her tomatoes get attacked by aphids. She swears it's better than insecticide."

"What does she do to keep squirrels away from the birdfeeder?"

"Nothing. She's live-and-let-live when it comes to squirrels."

FRANK WAS THE more likely suspect—especially given his possible appearance at Gnarlingview yesterday, and even though he was with law enforcement—but I decided to check out Jill first. There was certainly something peculiar about the way she had told me about Gnarlingview. It was probably nothing, but if I could remove her from contention, I could then concentrate completely on Frank.

I toyed with going up to the Grace Building, but decided that Cerebreeze was a better bet. I caught the next train up the Hudson to Cold Spring. The place lived up to its name this time: my blood ran cold when my train pulled into the station.

Four state troopers and several plainclothesmen were carefully questioning everyone in sight. The questioners were heavily armed.

I introduced myself to one of the troopers and showed him my badge. "What's going on here?" I asked.

He pointed up Main Street. "A laboratory went up in smoke a little ways from here. We're looking for arsonists leaving Cold Spring."

"Cerebreeze?" I thought of that fine Victorian porch, colonnades and all—a shame if it was now just a hunk of carbon against the granite.

"Yeah, that's right. How'd you know?" He looked at me more carefully.

"Case I'm working on," I replied. "Any casualties?"

"None so far," the trooper responded. His nameplate said *Roger Petrowski.* "The lab was warned just beforehand, and everyone got out."

"Where are they now—the folks from the lab?"

"Uhm, I think some of them are in Henry's—up the street—getting a bite to eat. Hey, Richie—," Roger called out to one of his associates, a few feet away, "some of the Cerebreeze people are in Henry's, right?"

Richie nodded.

"Yeah," Roger turned back to me. "Henry's—four or five blocks straight ahead, on Main Street. Left side of the street from where you're facing. You can't miss it."

"Okay, thanks," I said, and started to leave the station.

"Oh, Dr. D'Amato—" he called out after me.

"Yeah?" I turned around.

"The feds have some interest in this." He pulled a card from his pocket. "You probably should call this guy if it turns out the case you're working on has any connection to the fire."

"Thanks." I smiled and took the card. I looked at it. I lost most of my smile. "Did, ah, Agent Catania give you this himself?" I asked.

"Not to me. Hey, Richie—"

Richie turned to us again.

"Did you see the guy who left these cards?" Roger asked.

"I didn't see him," Richie replied. "One of the plainclothes guys gave them to us." He looked around. "I don't see him here now."

"That's okay," I said to Roger and Richie. "No problem. I'll just walk up to Henry's now."

A THIN TINSEL of rain tilled the air.

I walked up the hill to Henry's.

The inside was dark and sawdusty. It reminded me of Mel's place.

It took my eyes a few seconds to adjust.

A woman, about twenty, greeted me. "Lunch?" She wore a nice-looking apron over jeans.

"Yes."

She walked me into a room with about a dozen tables. About half were filled, none with anyone I recognized.

I hesitated for a moment, then sat at a table near the window. I might as well have something to eat here, collect my thoughts, and then resume my search for Jill.

"Anything I can get you to drink? And then the waitress will be over for your order."

"Yeah, a glass of grape juice—the purple kind—if you have it. And in an actual glass, if possible." The only way to drink grape juice was in a glass. It conveyed the crispness of the juice perfectly.

She nodded. "I think we can accommodate you."

I watched her walk away, black string of her apron framing her waist.

I turned my attention back to the patrons. . . .

Ah, one table did have someone who looked familiar in its assemblage of four. The face was half-obscured by some guy with a big bald head who kept leaning in. I had missed it the first time. . . .

I walked over to the table. "Marty Glick?"

He looked up at me, uncertain for a second, then smiled. "Phil D'Amato! Don't tell me you're a regular at Henry's! No, you must be here because of the fire. . . ."

I nodded.

"Sit down with us, please," Glick said.

I complied.

"This is George McLeary." Glick pointed to the bald head, who nodded. "Jim Purse." Glick pointed and Purse nodded, too. "And Mariel Baker." She nodded at me, and scowled slightly.

"All of you . . . work for Cerebreeze?" I wasn't sure whether to use the past or present tense.

A waitress appeared with my grape juice. "Ah, here you are," she said, and placed it on the table.

"Thank you."

"And your order? Oh, have you seen a menu?" There had been one at my first table, but I hadn't looked at it. "Tell you what—here's one." She pulled a paper menu from her pocket. "And I'll come back in a few minutes, after you've had a chance to decide."

"Thanks," I said, appreciatively.

"Grape juice," Glick observed. "Antioxidants."

"Maybe antiviral, too," McLeary added.

"That, and I love the taste," I said.

Glick nodded, then sighed. "Yes, we all work for Cerebreeze—we're going to figure out a way to make sure that work continues, don't you worry. What happened today is just a setback—temporary, that's all. You know the whole story?"

"Just the bare bones," I replied. "I heard everyone made it out okay?"

"Well, the animals didn't," Glick said, somberly.

Been a bad few days for rodents and people who love them, I thought. "You have any idea why someone would do this? Other than just another lunatic at large?" I had no idea if Glick knew about Gnarlingview. "I mean, the motive couldn't be to stop your work—I can't see anyone getting that upset about hamster responses to rock 'n' roll." According to Glick, that was the sum total of the hamster research at Cerebreeze—mapping the effect of music on their little brains. Of course, his colleague Jill, at Frank's urging, had just hours later shown me hamsters in more provocative pursuits—eavesdropping—at the Grace Building. I saw no advantage in letting Glick know about that demonstration, at least not in the present circumstances.

"My uncle thinks rock 'n' roll killed jazz," McLeary offered. "He hates rock with a passion." He laughed.

No one joined him—except me, a little, silently. I had to admit that rock 'n' roll always seemed to evoke anger from some people, especially authorities, ever since its inception in the 1950s. Amazing that there were still people around who felt that way.

Glick stroked his beard with his thumb.

My waitress came back for my order.

I still hadn't looked at the menu, but I didn't want to hold her up. "You have any kind of grilled chicken?" I asked.

"On focaccia, with provolone and tomato?"

"Perfect."

She nodded, and left.

"We know exactly why someone would do this," Glick spoke up, gravely.

I looked at him.

"They goddamn called us," he continued. "We've been getting threats for months, but we didn't take them seriously."

"Who?" I asked. "Who's been threatening Cerebreeze?"

"Animal rights groups," Glick spat out each word. "They thought it was unfair to the hamsters to keep them cooped up in our labs for our acoustic mappings."

"So it's better for them to be incinerated?"

"Welcome to the world," McLeary said. "You seek to improve life by destroying it."

So now I had another factor to contend with. In addition to civil liberties fanatics, possible terrorists, and one or more government groups, maybe rogue, maybe not, who might or might not be working together, I also had to consider animal rights extremists. I bit into my chicken. I had found over the years that a surfeit of suspects, such as what I now seemed to be encountering, was usually the result of some of the real bad guys lying, making up suspects, to throw the investigation off track. So who was lying to me?

Glick gave me details on the calls Cerebreeze had been receiving. He hadn't paid much attention to them, because they seemed vague, crankish. Now he knew better.

"Did you report them to the police?" I asked.

"Every one of them. We at least did that," he replied. "But the sources of the calls were untraceable—public telephone booths from Baltimore to Boston."

"They don't have booths anymore," Mariel Baker added, unhelpfully. "Just phones on stalks, like metal lollipops." She flexed her face, as if she had something distasteful on her tongue. "And even those will be gone soon—it's all cell phones now."

"Whatever," Glick said.

"Were they all from the same person?" I asked. "The threatening calls?"

Glick smiled ruefully. "We're good at tracking voices. They didn't give us their names, or mention any affiliation. But we're certain each call came from a different person—a different man."

"How many?"

"Five—before today," Glick said. "Five in about four months."

Seemed like pretty specific tracking for someone who was

not paying much attention to the calls, but I let it pass. "Did, uh, Jill know about the calls?" This felt like a good way to bring her into this conversation.

"Jill gave Phil a little tour the other day," Glick said, in response to the questioning expressions on the faces of the other three at our table. "Yes, she did," he said to me.

"Is she around? I'd like to talk to her."

"No—I mean, I'm sure she'd like to talk to you, but she's been out the past two days."

"Do you know where she is?" I asked. "I mean, assuming that's not revealing something personal or none of my business. It's not urgent that I talk to her, but I'd like to if I could."

Glick looked like he was mulling over his options. "She lives off Park Avenue—in the sixties, brownstone she inherited from her mother. Right down the street from Central Park."

WELL, AT LEAST that explained why Jill chose the Lexington Avenue line as the place for our brief, rolling meeting, I thought later, as my commuter train edged slowly down the east bank of the Hudson on the last leg of its journey back to Manhattan. That Lexington Avenue line ran practically right under her apartment.

But she was already on a subway travelling southbound when we met at the Eighty-sixth Street station. So she did . . . what? Catch an earlier subway northbound, just so she could meet me on a subway travelling southbound, to disguise where she really lived? Or maybe she just hadn't slept at home the night before—well, there was nothing particularly odd about that.

I shook my head to clear some of the complexities. It seemed as if everyone's stories were fraying around the edges—Frank's, Jill's, Glick's, that Paton woman's—everyone's. As I replayed them in my head, they sounded increasingly like alibis, and not very good ones.

Whom could I trust? Mel. But he was in the hospital, struggling to survive. Rachel Saldana. But her expertise was animal anaesthetics, not really near the core of what I needed to better understand now. The rodent dope was at most just a means to an end: the sound bites and snapshots from rodent brains.

I couldn't trust any of the major players, was the answer. Well, what else was new . . . that's the way it always was with these peculiar cases that I seemed to trip over like packages left near my doorstep in the dark, pouring rain. Except this time, the stakes seemed both more trivial and a lot higher. More trivial, because I was seriously thinking about squirrels. Higher, because of the possible terrorist connection. Well, maybe those stakes were not really higher than in some of the cases I had investigated before, but they certainly had the potential to be more immediately deadly, for more people. The hell with Paton and her protocols; when fires and bombs were involved, sooner or later people died.

I sighed. At least I could trust my own mind, the general accuracy of my memory, in this situation—at least, as far as I could tell. That had not always been the case before. . . .

Now my train sighed, as it and the conductor announced our arrival at Grand Central. I walked to the center of the main concourse and admired the keen, soft blue of the ceiling once again. . . .

I stopped, and considered my choices. I basically had two at this point. I could take the Lexington subway line up to Jill's apartment, or I could pay an unannounced visit to the W. R. Grace Building's hamster facilities, right down the street, and see what that shook loose.

More than anything else, I really needed more evidence. I had nothing tangible at all that squirrel visions were retrievable the way Deborah Paton had said. Not only no real evidence, but I had not even seen anything of the sort myself. All I had was Paton's word for it, given in a laboratory that was now demolished, and a literally washed-out digital print of me that could have come from anywhere. And now Cerebreeze was gone with the wind, too. That left the fortieth floor of the cream-colored cutaway building on Forty-second Street, the end of those corridors within corridors, as the only place I had a chance of finding out anything more about animal eavesdroppers—hamsters, not squirrels, and sounds, not images—but that would have to do.

I walked up the Grand Central incline, past the glittering fruit-juice and power-water and flower stands, toward the street.

The light rain had turned to a soft snow. I used to love the snow as a kid—occasions for missing school, mammoth snowball fights, sweet tickles in my nose and throat. Even as a teenager, prowling the neighborhood for girls and smiles and style, I enjoyed how the first snowflakes dressed up the city, giving every street a new white coat.

But now . . . each snowflake felt like a cold teardrop on my face.

I turned up the collar of my now-inadequate jacket, and hurried along Forty-second Street.

SIX

I ducked into the entranceway of the Grace Building. I was beginning to feel like a squirrel myself, returning to places I had visited just a day or two before, scratching around as if I were worrying over newly buried acorns. Except, there was nothing that I had buried in this place. The best I could find is what maybe others had buried—not too deep, if I were lucky.

My first obstacle was the security guard. It would have been too much to ask for him to be the same guard as the night before last. That would have at least held open the possibility that he might recognize me, and pass me right through. . . .

But, no, this guy was a good thirty pounds lighter, twenty years younger, with a reddish-brown, Mexican-bandito moustache. Definitely not the guy from the other night.

I could, of course, just announce myself and display copious credentials, but if he called upstairs with my name, that could well scare off Jill and anyone else who might not want to see me.

I decided to use a technique that had served me in good stead since high school for getting into places I didn't belong: wait until the guard was distracted with a few other applicants for admission, and then see if I could slip by. The nice part of this strategy now was that even if the guard saw me and called me out—if I heard that accusatory "sir" ringing out behind my back—I could turn around and show him my credentials and be no worse off than if I had properly announced myself in the first place.

I hung back, just out of the guard's eyesight, I hoped, and waited for my chance. . . . It was apparently a slow day at the Grace. . . . I frowned. Just a handful of people, not more than two at a time, had come by in the past ten minutes. . . .

Possible salvation in the form of four women finally walked in a few minutes later. Two were especially promising, in low-cut jeans. Let's hope the guard appreciated that sort of thing. . . .

I kept my eyes on the jeans and turned my head as they walked past me. One was particularly inviting, in soft, smooth blue. The crease in the center swished back and forth hypnotically, like a windshield wiper, as she walked toward the guard. . . .

I cautiously emerged, one eye on the wiper, the other on the guard in the distance. He smiled at the approaching women. His face was too far away for me to see clearly, but judging by his general demeanor, this guard seemed to be liking the jeans—or, at any rate, the women—as much from the front as I had been from behind.

I stepped further out, and then I really got lucky. Two men, accountant types in their mid-thirties, entered the hallway. One nodded at me perfunctorily.

The guard was beginning to look at the women's IDs. My guess was they were graduate students—two had backpacks, and I noticed that one had a book in her hand. If I shadowed the accountants right now, just right, this would be my best chance to get by the guard. It would be difficult for even the most conscientious set of eyes to take in the accountants as well as the women, and then me. . . .

The guard's table was in the middle of the hall, with lots of room to one side. One of the women, not in jeans, was explaining something, some kind of problem, to the guard. Good.

"She's a student at NYU," the woman pointed to the one I had been looking at. "Can't you give her some kind of guest pass or something?"

"Yeah, I already said I could," the guard replied. "But I still need to see some kind of ID. That's Grace Building policy. You got anything from NYU?" He turned to the presumed student.

"I left it home," she said, with a hopeful pout.

I felt like blurting out, *Hey, she's okay, she's with me,* but controlled myself.

Meanwhile, one of the accountants was waving to the guard.

Good, neither was reaching for wallets and IDs. They likely knew the guard—knew the guard knew them—and walked by here regularly without showing IDs.

I tried to gauge the guard's field of vision. The key was to stay not too close to the accountants to arouse their suspicion, but at just the proper angle for the two of them to block me out of the guard's eyesight as we walked to the elevators.

We made it past the guard. So far, so good.

The elevators were just a few feet away.

I thought about taking a quick glance back at the guard's table to see what was happening there, but decided not to chance it.

We reached the elevators—

"Sir?" Goddamn it—that voice boomed out like a thunderclap on my back. It was definitely the guard's.

"Sir??" This time it was more insistent. I couldn't ignore it.

I stepped back from the elevators, and turned around—

Excellent—my luck was holding out! The guard was interrogating a grungy-looking guy who had entered the building—a derelict, or doing a good job of impersonating one.

The four women, now past the guard's station, approached

me and the elevators. One of them smiled at me—alas, not the one whose jeans I had been monitoring. I smiled back, anyway, and then returned to the elevators.

The chime rang, and the doors of one opened.

"Phil!"

Frank Catania stepped out.

SOMETHING ABOUT HIM looked a little different. Was it really Frank I had seen scurrying away from Gnarlingview the other night? Yeah, it was him. I could see that more clearly now, looking at Frank right in front of me. And the reason he looked a bit different now, I realized, was that my brain still called up a little of the image I had had of Frank ten years ago, when he worked on our beat. . . .

"Damn, I haven't checked for calls in twenty minutes," Frank said, apologetically. "I was just about to. You tried to call me? Something new crop up?"

Another elevator opened, with no one in it. Frank walked in, and bid me to follow. I hesitated a split second, then complied. I did want another look at the facilities upstairs. I might not get all of what I wanted with Frank by my side, but I could get something else of value: Frank's expression as we walked through the facilities and talked.

The elevator door closed.

"Actually, no to both," I said. "I just wanted another look at the hamsters upstairs, and I was in the area. Had no idea you were here."

Frank nodded. I had no idea if he believed me. His back was to the elevator door. Mine was to the back of the elevator.

I realized that Frank had the physical advantage—he was taller, likely stronger, and who knew what kind of weapon he was carrying.

He smiled at me, slightly, and ran his hand over his jacket pocket.

I must have tensed a little.

"You okay?" Frank asked. "You seem a little uneasy."

"Been all over the place since last we met," I replied. "Just a little tired."

He looked at me appraisingly. If he had any inkling that I had been up at Gnarlingview just after he was, he gave no indication.

The elevator shook to a stop on the fortieth floor. Frank turned his back to me to face the opening doors. I could see by the bulge in his back that he likely did have a weapon of some sort tucked away there. Well, nothing sinister about that—as long as he didn't point it at me. (And it could have been some sort of new telecom device—a vestpocket-top.)

We both walked out of the elevator. He whirled around suddenly.

I jumped to the side.

"What the hell's the matter with you?" he inquired sharply.

"Nothing. I'm just tired, edgy, like I said."

"Well I'm glad you came by. There's something I want to talk to you about."

HE TOOK ME through the corridors within corridors within corridors. He stopped right before the entrance to hamster-land.

"I know you want another look at the hamsters," Frank said, "but can we talk about something first?"

"Sure."

Frank put his hand against a wall. I heard the crack of a receding bolt lock. The surface of the wall now neatly split, like an eggshell right down the middle, to reveal a door—which Frank pushed open.

"Some kind of palm-print operation?" I asked. I knew it was more than that—some kind of virtual wall contraption as well, designed to masquerade as an ordinary wall until the right person put his or her palm in just the right place.

"Yeah," Frank said, and ushered me into a small office. It was the same one Jill and he and I had been in the last time I was here, but this time Frank and I entered through a different door.

He sat behind a small oak desk and bade me to sit in front of it. "Decentralized intelligence," he said. "I've got half a dozen safe offices like this stashed away in a dozen places."

"I like your arithmetic." More places than offices, I guessed, because there were multiple passages to offices, as in the present instance. "You need it."

"It's heating up," Frank said, with no further elaboration.

I knew he wasn't talking about the weather, and not because it was snowing outside. What I didn't know is if I could believe anything that he said.

"How?" I prodded.

"What we don't know is *who*," he responded. "Animal rights loonies, civil rights nuts, terrorists, domestic maniacs . . ." He rubbed his eyes. "It's getting to where we can't tell which, and I don't know if it really matters anymore."

"It matters," I said evenly. "What we're supposed to be doing is smashing the terrorists so our people have the right to be civil rights sticklers and, I suppose, animals rights advocates, too."

"When they blow up our laboratories?" Frank countered. "Three in just the past twenty-four hours?"

"Three?" I didn't say that I only knew of two. Questioning the "three" could mean that I knew of none.

"Gnarlingview in Cambridge last night, Cerebreeze in Cold Spring this morning, and I just got word about Biomage in Philadelphia about an hour ago." He scowled.

"Biomage . . . are they doing squirrels, like Gnarlingview?" I asked.

Frank's expression changed to slight annoyance. "Squirrels? You still onto that? I told you—squirrel vision as a source of usable images is just a cyber-wetdream at this point. Acoustics—hamsters—is what all this is about."

"Cut the shit, Frank." I pulled out my cell phone, and pressed the call-office-and-record mode. Frank recognized the beep pattern—he knew what it meant: our conversation would now be recorded on voice mail that was accessible, erasable, only from my office. Unless the feds were hacking into the most secure part of the NYPD system, which I had no reason to believe. "I saw you leaving Gnarlingview late yesterday," I added.

Frank looked at me very carefully. He finally spoke, softly, precisely. "Okay, so you saw me at Gnarlingview. I have no problem with that. I've got nothing to hide. And it's fine with me if you record this."

"Good," I said tightly.

"And what do you think you saw at Gnarlingview—other than me?" he asked. "Did you see any squirrels hooked up, the way you saw the hamsters hooked up here?"

"No," I admitted. "They were operating with remote implants."

Frank laughed without mirth. "Then you saw bullshit. That's what whoever it was who told you about Gnarlingview handed you, in a big, steaming serving. We're nowhere near embedded, self-sustaining technology in that area yet—we're as far away from that as telephones were from cell phones in the 1930s. Our magic requires wires—old-fashioned, reliable wires—out of the brain and into the machine. Who told you about Gnarlingview in the first place?" he demanded.

I gave no answer. I certainly didn't want to compromise

Jill—until I knew more—and I needed to think about Deborah Paton.

"Okay . . ." Frank made a sarcastic sound. "You want to protect your sources. Understandable. But surely you can tell me if you saw any squirrels with these embeds."

"I saw squirrels," I replied, "outside of Gnarlingview. The whole point of the embeds is that they're supposed to enable the squirrels to run around and surveil without attracting too much attention, right? The transmitting devices are supposed to be in their skulls. So how would I be able to spot them?"

"Meaning, you saw no physical evidence in the squirrels," Frank replied. "But I take your point about the embeds being invisible to casual observation. So, did your friends at Gnarlingview at least show you any squirrel-engendered images? Anything on the screen?"

"They gave me a printout of my image on a plain piece of paper. It got drenched in the rain—I don't have it with me. It's probably too blurred now to be of much use."

Frank made another sarcastic sound. "Not surprising."

"You don't believe me? You think I'm just making all of this up?" I had always found it more difficult to keep my composure with a cop who might have gone wrong than with the more typical suspect.

"Okay, before it got rained on," Frank said, "did your picture really look like something a squirrel might see?"

"How exactly the hell should I know?"

"Look, I—"

Whatever Frank was about to say was interrupted by a pulsating alarm. We both knew what that meant.

"We can stay in this office," Frank said. "It's supposed to be safe from fires and explosions, even radiation. Or we can take a safe corridor down a safe stairway and be out on Forty-second Street in less than fifteen minutes."

I considered. For all I knew, Frank had just set off that

alarm in this office only, as a way of terminating our conversation. On the other hand—

The caterwauling got louder.

"The elevators aren't safe?"

"Obviously not," Frank replied, "or I would have included them in our options."

Again, who knew if I could believe him. . . .

"Let's take the stairs," I said.

WE EXITED THROUGH a third door from his office—this one also invisible, until Frank put his palm to the wall—and down ceramically gleaming spirals of stairs. I felt like we were escaping from some medieval castle. What was that line in the "Weird Al" Yankovic song, his send-up of "Gangsta's Paradise" that he called "Amish Paradise"? *I'm gonna get medieval on your hiney*? Or did that come from Tarantino's *Pulp Fiction—I'm gonna get medieval on your ass. . . .* Who could remember? All I knew is that I was being kicked out on my ass in the middle of what could have been an important interview, and these safe rooms and escape routes and the circumstances that obliged us to construct them were worse then medieval, they were goddamn barbaric.

"You know, Phil," Frank said to me over his shoulder as we hustled down what looked like the last flight of stairs, "you seem to have a habit of showing up whenever one of our laboratories comes under fire. Should we draw any conclusions from that?"

"I haven't been in Philadelphia in a few months," I answered.

"Fair enough," Frank allowed. "So, then, who can you think of who might be a common link?"

I thought again of Jill, who had been here and at Cerebreeze recently, and obviously knew Gnarlingview. I had no idea if she had been to—what was the name of that place?—

Biomage, in Philadelphia. "Well, there's always you."

Frank laughed. It echoed oddly off the tan-orange ceramic. "I'm trying to *protect* these places—it's my job."

He reached the bottom of the stairs and pushed open a door. We walked through and found ourselves in the lobby, almost right in front of the security guard's desk. It was vacant.

And why wasn't the lobby mobbed with evacuees?

Now a security guard—not the one I had maneuvered around on the way in—quickly approached us. "I don't recall you coming in," he said to me. "You been here all day?"

"He's with me, he's okay," Frank said.

The guard nodded. "You hear about the false alarm on the fortieth floor?"

Frank exhaled derisively. "That's why we're down here. What's going on?"

"A couple of rooms up there got the signal—I'm not even sure who was in 'em," the guard replied. "Was a computer glitch, was all."

I looked at Frank. Very convenient.

Frank looked at his watch. "How about we continue our conversation outside," he said to me. "I've got a train to catch at Penn Station in about an hour. We can walk it, if you're up for more exercise."

I considered. No point in trying to get back upstairs—nothing useful I'd be able to learn under these circumstances.

"Okay," I said. We both nodded at the guard and walked out of the lobby.

The snow had turned back into a cold, sloppy rain.

"Damn, I left my umbrella upstairs," Frank said, wiping a raindrop from his cheek.

"I didn't bring one in the first place," I said.

"Maybe we should take a cab." Frank squinted up at the surly grey sky.

"Fine with me. Where are you going from Penn Station?"

"Wilmington—"

An explosion smacked us and our conversation to the ground. I'd been near a tree in Hoboken, New Jersey, once when it was struck by lightning. The crack of energy nearly made me jump out of my clothes. This was worse.

My ears rang. I smelled the smoke. I felt my arms and legs. I seemed to be in one piece. I opened my eyes.

Frank was already on his feet, giving a hand to an elderly woman who seemed more shaken than hurt. Black smoke and flame were pouring out of a taxicab near the curb. I stood, brushed myself off, and extended my hand to a man, about sixty, on the ground.

"Thanks," he said, and stood.

"You okay?"

"I think so."

"Good. I'd recommend you get out of here now, then go see your doctor, just to make sure you're all right."

The security guard rushed out of the building. "Call the fire department," I told him. "Then help us move these people out of here."

I looked at the burning cab. The rest of it could go any minute.

Three or four more people were already on their feet, walking away dazedly. One was still on the ground, facedown. The jeans, the backside, looked familiar . . . Jeez, it was that woman in the soft blue jeans. . . . There was a twisted, broken umbrella under her legs.

I dashed over to her. She was moaning, conscious, alive. I put my hand on her shoulder. "You think you can stand?" I asked gently. She had no injuries that I could immediately see. Let's hope this was just shock.

"Yeah . . . I guess so," she said groggily.

"Okay," I said, and helped her up. "Are your feet okay enough for you to walk?"

She took a tentative, shaky step. "Yeah . . ."

"Good. Let's try to get out of here, then. Take my arm."

We walked away from the cab as quickly as possible.

A firetruck screeched up to the curb just as an EMS truck made a big U-turn and joined us. I could see cops converging on us from several directions.

"I think she's pretty much okay," I said to the EMS worker who strode quickly up to us. "Nothing serious that I can see."

"Thanks," he said. "How about you?"

"I'm fine," I said, and waved off any attention. I pulled out my ID. "Phil D'Amato, NYPD Forensics."

"Okay, Doc, we'll take it from here. But you should probably have someone look at you later today, anyway."

He escorted the woman to the truck. She turned toward me and mouthed "Thanks," with still-trembling lips.

"Well, apparently this was not a false alarm," Frank said to me. He surveyed the mess and shook his head. "I've notified and briefed all the relevant investigating units, fed and city—NYPD bomb squad should be here soon. . . ."

"Good."

"Maybe you'd like to come with me to Wilmington," he added. "You still up for walking? I've had enough of cabs for tonight."

I nodded, and called in to Dugan.

PART II:

Wilmington Station

SEVEN

I had known since the day I started working for the NYPD that this was no nine-to-five job. Not even when it was confined to investigating the kinds of murders, rapes, and run-of-the-mill depravities that the human species was, alas, forever heir to. No, even in those ordinarily awful cases, my job respected neither clock nor calendar, except for the crunching pressure of needing to identify and remove the culprit as soon as possible. And that pressure, of course, overrode personal agendas.

But when you threw in the kinds of twisted things that sometimes came my way—in this case, hamsters as tape recorders, maybe squirrels as cameras—you might as well throw all watches or anything else that kept track of time totally out the window of a speeding train. Anointed hours, appointed times, had no place here.

I looked out the window of my train as it sped darkly through the New Jersey countryside. I had already called Jenna on my cell phone to tell her I would not be home for dinner, maybe not for bed with her tonight, either. I had asked her if she could check on Mel for me and call me if there had been any change for the worse. So far, so good—I hadn't heard anything more from Jenna, and my cell phone seemed to be working. (I also told her that I missed her, and I did.)

Frank was in the cafe car, waiting on line for a sandwich.

I sipped my stale ginger ale—it had been in front of me, poured in a cup, since our train had pulled out of Newark. But I had been so engrossed in thinking about what Frank had told me that I had lost track of the soda.

Wilmington.

According to Frank, it was the site of a massive, secret federal antiterrorism center, a mile beneath the ground, right under Amtrak's Wilmington, Delaware, train station.

I had never heard of it, but then again, why would I? It was supposed to be secret. Frank said there were at least several others around the country, and even he only knew the location of two. Wilmington, and one other place he would not divulge.

"We've been busy," he had said, with no satisfaction on his face. "But probably not busy enough—if the events of the past few days are any indication."

Wilmington Center. A mile beneath an average street, honeycombed with computers and connective power I could barely imagine, Frank said. "It's part of our new swarm strategy. Independent pockets that can work on their own, or join together to process data and then pull apart with no indication that they had ever been connected." In the deep underground, all of them. Immune from planes or anything else thrown against us. Our high-tech version of caves, bunkers. Fight fire with fire.

But telecommunicating squirrels were not part of the picture, according to Frank. Which meant either he or Jill and Paton were lying.

He returned with his sandwich and a coffee. I finished my ginger ale.

"You sure you don't want some?" Frank offered me half of what he had purchased in the cafe—it looked like Alexandrian chicken, a tasty new variation on Caesar-salad chicken, except this was made with feta cheese and a splash of wine.

"I'm fine, thanks." I had gobbled two rolls of sushi in Penn Station while Frank had excused himself to make some calls.

He took a crunchy bite of his sandwich. "I know you don't trust me," he said. "Let's see if we can find a way out of this."

"All right, tell me what you know—" The train swerved sharply, and took our attention. Frank steadied his coffee. I had another second to think about my question, and decided to go ahead with the one I had started to ask.

"Tell me what you know about Deborah Paton," I said. Frank already knew that I had been up at Gnarlingview and had seen him there. I realized there was little if anything to lose by revealing to him that I had seen Paton there.

"I honestly never heard of her," Frank replied. He looked at me and blew on his coffee.

"Bad start, Frank."

"You want—what?—I make up a fancy story? I'm telling you, I don't know her. The only thing that even sounds vaguely familiar is my mother used to watch *Peyton Place* in the 1970s when I was a kid, and my old man hated the damn show."

The conductor announced, in static, crackly *sotto voce*, something about the train soon pulling into North Philadelphia.

Frank finished off his sandwich. "Did you see her name anywhere inside Gnarlingview—on the door to her office, on a nameplate on her desk . . . ?"

I thought about it. "No," I was obliged to concede.

Our train pulled into the station. "North Philadelphia, North Philadelphia," the conductor announced. "Only the middle two doors open. . . ."

Frank waited until the announcement was over. "So maybe your lady was lying when she told you her name was 'Deborah Paton.' "

We suspended our conversation as two bustling families, with at least a dozen kids between them, made "ready" to leave. . . . The doors opened, then closed, and our train moved slowly out of the elevated North Philadelphia station. . . .

"Philadelphia, next stop, in about eight minutes," the conductor's voice crackled out. "We'll be making only one stop in Philadelphia—the Thirtieth Street station. . . ."

I described to Frank the woman I briefly knew as "Deborah Paton." . . . His face was nonresponsive, until I got to the part about the greys.

"Is that significant—that just about everything about the woman was grey?" I asked.

"I'm not sure," Frank said, a little oddly.

"Look, how about you just tell me what you were up to at Gnarlingview," I prodded. "Maybe we can start cutting this Gordian knot that way."

"All right," Frank agreed. "I'll start at the very beginning. . . . I didn't have time the other night."

"By all means."

"From what I know—and, you need to understand, I've been directly involved in this for only about three years, now—Project Bird-watcher began at least a decade ago."

" 'Bird-watcher'?"

"Yeah," Frank said. "Ironically, we haven't done much with birds. But the name was clever, so it stuck—you know, birds watch us, instead of we watch birds? So, 'Project Bird-watcher'—nice reversal of subject and object, eyeball and image—I don't know, you probably know that stuff better than I do."

"You're doing a pretty good job of demonstrating just the opposite. But, okay, 'Project Bird-watcher'—it is a good name. Nice, innocuous name to disguise an incredible development, if it's viable. Brains as camcorders. Marshall McLuhan used to say that the CBS eye—the eye on our TV screen—looks at *us*—"

"McLuhan? The *Annie Hall* guy?"

I nodded.

" 'Medium is the message,' *WIRED*?" Frank continued.

"Yeah."

"*War and Peace in the Global Village*?"

"Right."

"I better look that guy up," Frank said.

"He's all over the Internet. Glad I sparked your interest," I said, a little sourly. Well, Frank had made his point that he probably even knew more about McLuhan than I did.

"Hey, you're the one who mentioned his name," Frank said.

"True . . . so, okay, Project Bird-watcher started with birds, never even thought of squirrels, and wound up with hamsters? How exactly did that happen?"

"No," Frank replied, "I never said we didn't think about squirrels. We've thought of all kinds of things. We did a lot of work with mice the first few years—you know, experiments always start with mice—but we decided against them. People don't like them. We didn't want our operatives turning up in glue traps."

"Or getting dragged in by the cat."

Frank nodded. "Hell, one anthropologist on the team even had a proposal going a few years ago about the Ice Man."

"The guy from five thousand years ago found frozen in the Alps?"

"Yep, the very one," Frank said. "Imagine what sounds and images recovered from *his* brain could tell us."

"Likely not much about his killer," I said. "He was shot from behind with an arrow, last I heard."

"Spoken like a true forensic scientist," Frank said. "But still . . ."

"Oh, absolutely—the possibilities would be enormous. So what happened with that proposal?"

"Nothing," Frank said. "We haven't a clue about how to get anything out of dead brains—even freshly dead brains. But think about what it would do for forensic science, for justice, if we could get even sounds from the brains of murder victims. You'd probably get the goods on half the murderers in this country, maybe more. . . ."

I had to agree—

Frank's phone rang.

The conductor announced that we would be in Philadelphia's Thirtieth Street station in two minutes.

Frank stood, still talking on the phone. He gestured for me to stay seated.

"Okay," he said to the phone. Then he put it in his pocket. "I'm sorry, I have to get off in Philadelphia, alone," he said to me.

I started to object and stand—

"Here," Frank pulled a card from a pocket in his jacket and jotted down some quick notes as the train slowed. "The people in Wilmington are expecting you. Just follow what I wrote on this card."

I looked at Frank, not the card. "We haven't finished our conversation," I said. We had barely started it.

He looked at me.

The train stopped in the station. We both swayed with the halt.

"You'll learn more in Wilmington," Frank said. "And I'm sure we'll be in touch." He broke our gaze and walked quickly toward the door.

I had nothing official to hold him with—not to mention that, given his position, he could just as likely hold me as I him.

WILMINGTON WAS TWENTY minutes later on the train. . . .

The buildings surrounding the station were done up with

neon signage, most announcing the colorful varieties of theater that had taken root all over the place here. The deeply glowing strands looked like they had been squeezed out of tubes of pastel by Picasso, in who knew what ethereal period. . . .

I looked at the card that Frank had given me, for at least a tenth time. I wanted to be sure enough of the instructions that I would not have to consult the card again once I was in the station. Maybe this came under what Jenna and other women had told me was the irrational male antipathy about asking for directions. Looking at written instructions right in front of the place you were headed was a form of asking directions. At the very least, it showed anyone in the area who cared that you weren't sure where you were going.

I detrained and walked downstairs. I looked for a place on the wall that looked like it once had a pay phone, about thirty feet from a group of four Quik-Trak ticket-purchase machines. I spotted the machines easily enough, but nothing on any of the walls that looked like . . . Ah, yes, there it was. I could see a patch on the wall that looked like it might have once supported a pay phone—gone now, a victim, like many pay phones, of the cell phone in every pocket, as that dyspeptic woman in Henry's had noted. The discolored area on the wall had been temporarily concealed by a snuggling teenage couple, who now joined some friends who had just come down the northbound stairs.

I approached my appointed wall as casually as I could. According to Frank, I was expected here. "There's no way I or anyone else can get you in there without a prior verified palm print," he had explained to me about the Wilmington Center facility shortly after we'd boarded the train in New York. So I had put my palm on the screen of his little telecom device, which also served as a camera, and the print had been relayed to some big computer which also had access to the palm prints I and everyone else in the NYPD had given just last year.

"Okay, that's step one," Frank had said, and nodded. "You're confirmed as Dr. Phil D'Amato, NYPD. Congratulations."

"Thanks."

"Now, I've just given your palm print special one-night entrance-clearance at Wilmington. So, assuming no one on the way down slashes your wrists and sews new hands on you, we should both sail right through when we get there."

Right, I thought, now. But I would soon see if my palm print was enough for me to sail right through, all on my own. I looked around the station, then back at the wall—

"Excuse me."

I nearly jumped when I heard the voice. Not that it was familiar, or unfamiliar, or threatening. I just didn't expect it—didn't realize there had been anyone so close.

The owner of the voice looked at me when I turned around and then he smiled, very slightly. He looked to be in maybe his early sixties, stubble of grey hair, stubble of grey beard, and a suit that might have been grey or green or beige; in this light I couldn't tell. Lots of grey, again, but he was otherwise nondescript. I certainly didn't know him.

He pointed to a ticket office, closed, across the station. "This takes two," he said, and turned and walked quickly.

Well, I guessed he was one of the "people" down here who Frank said would be waiting for me. He would have had no problem learning what I looked like—my picture was easy enough to fetch on the Web.

I caught up to him, and matched his pace.

We reached the ticket office. He placed his palm on the door.

Click. It opened.

He entered and waved me in.

He walked to a bare wall and placed his palm on it. "And you've got ten seconds to put your palm right there now, too," he said. "Sorry to be so brusque and secretive, but stations can be targets, too." He walked past me and out the office door, which clicked shut.

I put my palm to the wall. I imagined that if the palm was other than mine, I'd be locked in here, trapped, until someone came to arrest me—

But I heard the familiar click—like the one I had heard earlier today in the Grace Building, and twice in the past minute.

A door cracked open.

I pushed through and entered.

IT TOOK MY eyes a few seconds to adjust to the dimmer lighting on the other side.

I wondered, as a small room came into clarity around me, if the door crack in the ticket office would heal as quickly as the one I had entered on the fortieth floor of the building on Forty-second Street. I assumed it would. The attracting of unwanted eyes was always a problem, even for doors behind closed doors.

I could now see that the room I was in was even smaller than I had thought; in fact, I was not in a room at all, but a chamber of an elevator . . . which began to move down. I looked around. No buttons to press, nothing which even said I was in an elevator. Except I was moving, down, and now with increasing speed. I sat on a simple wooden bench. It hadn't looked especially inviting when I had first entered the "room," but I was beginning to see its appeal. This could be a long ride—what had Frank said, a mile beneath ground-level?—and I might as well be comfortable. . . .

The ride down did take a good few minutes—whatever

"good" meant in these conditions. I used the time to think about some of the underground complexes I had visited throughout the years. Sections of the Smithsonian were a few stories underground, Montreal had miles of walkways below the surface, and, of course, the New York subway with its stained, shiny tiles was an Edwardian city in itself. But my favorite underground facility was actually a place in my imagination, something I had been thinking about for as long as I could remember. Wouldn't it be great if certain locations that only I knew about—buildings, supermarkets, and sure, train stations—had secret elevators that I could take far below the surface, where I could catch underground automatic trains that would take me miles away, to other cities, to deserted clearings in the forest? Wouldn't that be a great way to escape, since no one would know or expect me at the destination points? Odd, I suppose, that the boy who had thought about that had gone into law enforcement. . . .

The elevator landed. The doors opened. I walked out and looked down a long corridor—I heard the elevator doors swish shut behind me. I turned around and noticed there were no elevator buttons on the wall, no niches for palms, nothing I could use to recall the elevator. I suppressed an urge to pound on the outside of what I knew to be an elevator shaft—knew because I had just gone a mile in it down this rabbit hole, I knew that for sure. But I refocused my attention on the corridor. The way out would be down there, even if it was just the procedure for recalling the elevator which had just existed right here. I wasn't quite as sure of that, but what choice did I have?

This corridor was more like the Washington, D.C., Metro than any of the other underground networks I had been thinking about—poured, dark grey, smooth-dried concrete. The ceiling and sides were curved and lit with what I recognized to be new light-emitting microchip tiles. The soft, almost organic quality made me wonder for a moment if this is what hamster burrows looked like from the inside. . . . Nah, I had hamsters on the brain these days. But I wished Mel were here with me, anyway. He seemed like the only expert I could trust about hamsters. I hoped he was okay.

I came upon some kind of junction or terminal on the floor. It looked like the dial of a luminescent watch—twelve o'clock, two o'clock, four o'clock, eight o'clock, ten o'clock were each lit, and attached to a separate foot-conveyor. I realized I was standing on six o'clock, which was unlit.

None of the conveyors was moving. Which one to take? Frank's instructions had ended with the station above.

I stepped on the conveyor to twelve, straight ahead. I didn't agonize, or even ponder too much. Faced with a variety of apparently equal choices, I always plunged straight ahead.

The twelve o'clock numeral glowed more brightly, and my conveyor started moving. I looked at my cell phone, out of an instinct that it might offer a voice or a text that might provide some bearings as to where I was going. It, of course, was flashing "no service."

I put the cell phone back in my pocket and walked doggedly ahead. What an absurd situation: a mile below Wilmington, at the invitation of someone I did not completely trust, walking with the help of a conveyor to who knew where. . . .

The last part of the absurdity was soon resolved, at least somewhat. The conveyor belt ended about two feet in front of a door with no name. But it did have what I was now beginning to quickly recognize as a palm niche. I felt reasonably sure that the door would open in response to my palm and would then vanish, at least to outside observation, as soon as I entered.

I tested and confirmed the first part. I entered. There would be no way to test the second, of course, unless there was a camera on the outside and a screen on the inside with the image the camera conveyed. Or maybe a squirrel . . . no, these tunnels felt too claustrophobic for squirrels. They lived in trees, not warrens. Maybe a chipmunk.

There was no screen on the inside, in any case. Just a small office, weakly lit, with a small desk, and a man behind it who looked familiar.

He swiveled around to face me, and smiled.

"Hello, Phil."

EIGHT

His identity was no clearer from the front than the back. Still, uncomfortably familiar . . .

"Have a seat," he said, and his voice sounded familiar, too. A bit like Dugan's, perhaps? Maybe. Definitely New York.

His shirt and tie, loosened at the top, his jacket, looked like clothing I had seen as well. It was also . . . all grey.

I sat down and looked at him.

Something was wrong about him. That was very clear. I suddenly realized part of what that was: the person in front of me was very *un*clear. Clearly unclear. I squinted. Didn't do any good. Was it the lighting? No, it was more.

"I know, you're wondering who I am," he said. "And why I make you itch." I realized that he had not extended his hand. Okay, definitely not Dugan.

"Is this better?" he asked. He imploded into focus.

Jeez, it wasn't a face I wanted to see—not in these circumstances. I looked around the room for cameras.

"No, this isn't being done live," he said. "I'm the result of at least two dozen images taken of you in the past few days."

I again noted his jacket, his shirt and tie. The first I did have on, right now. The second was crumpled in our hamper back home. The third was on my tie rack, sagging from about thirty monstrosities I never wore.

"My voice is projected from half a dozen speakers you cannot see, to give the impression that it's emanating from this place where you see my face." He pointed to his face, almost touching it with his index finger. "Of course, I can't actually touch my face."

"Okay, you're a hologram," I said. "Is that what Frank lured me down here to see?" I had seen many before. But this one was a lot more realistic, I had to admit. And it seemed to have a good sense of what I was feeling. Well, presumably my responses were not unpredictable, given my situation. I looked around the room again. Even if my image wasn't live—for all I knew, whoever was programming this had a way of changing its clothing, like any computer graphic—there no doubt were hidden cameras in this room, anyway, picking up my facial expressions, my posture, my body language. And microphones, too, to pick up my voice. I looked around, uncomfortably, and then back at the hologram. I looked myself right in the eye. Pupil to pixel.

He didn't blink. He didn't shimmer like any hologram I had ever come across, either. The flesh-finish was matte.

"I can't touch anything," he continued, ignoring my question. "You can't touch me. I can't *give* you anything, except one thing, intangible—information."

"Okay . . . I'm listening." I had been a fan of holograms since way back in the days when the only examples were those in the Museum of Holography, down in Soho, in the city . . . The image in front of me, the image of me, didn't look at all like those Sohoan ghosts. . . .

He shifted a bit in his seat, as if he were the one on edge. "You look uncomfortable," he said. "Shall I change into something more comfortable?"

He grew blurry again, before I had a chance to respond. And then clear. But this time, he wasn't me. He didn't resemble me. But he looked familiar. And the effect was . . . comforting. . . .

"That better?" he asked.

There was a theory that as humanoid images grew more like us, they were loved. Barney, Big Bird, Mickey Mouse. But if they got too close to us—if a face, a voice, was perceived as human, but just a little off—it could be very frightening. Scary, like the smile of a maniac. Upsetting, like a fractured face. The "uncanny valley," Masahiro Mori, a Japanese roboticist, called it—a thin but deep, queasy zone in between nearly human and human. Just noticeable differences again. Except for me, the zone was my hologram. I did like what I now saw across the table. "I wasn't complaining," I replied.

"I'm a composite now," he said.

He was still wearing my cashmere jacket. Grey, as it had been before—not dark brown, like mine—but otherwise . . . he looked like an old friend, but not like anyone I had really known. "What do I call you? Seeing as how 'Phil' is no longer appropriate."

"I have no name," he replied.

"No? Even computer files have names."

He smiled thinly. "I won't exist after this interview," he said. "There would be no point in giving me a name."

"How about I call you 'Temp'?"

"Be my guest."

"Why go through all the trouble of . . . creating you, if you're just going to disappear at the end of this?" I asked.

"Who says it was trouble?"

I snorted. "Look—"

"Okay, I admit it took some doing to create me," Temp allowed. "As I told you, I'm here for one purpose—to give you information. And my very existence should convey one very important piece of information, whatever else I may say. And that information is that our side has a lot more technical know-how than most people, including you, would likely guess."

"Are you and I on the same side?" I asked.

"Yes," Temp replied, "though there is no way I can prove that to you here, in this room. But, think about it: for me to not be on your side, well, that would mean that the person who sent you my way was either an enemy, or not very competent. . . ."

I nodded. All I was really willing to bet money on was that Frank Catania was no incompetent.

"As I said," Temp observed, "one hundred percent proof is not available. Much like one hundred percent security."

"Is there a live person—or people—talking through you to me right now? Or are you a very good program?"

"A very good program. Thank you."

"So everything you're saying to me now—your part in our current conversation—draws on your previous programming, words and ideas stored for you in some virtual file somewhere?"

"Is your DNA-engendered brain really any different?" Temp countered.

"According to Minsky and Skinner and those behaviorist guys, it isn't," I acknowledged. "I read somewhere that Minsky called our brains 'meat machines' . . . But let's not get into philosophic debates about artificial intelligence right now."

"Too bad," Temp said. "It might have relevance to your other interests—the reasons you came here. But, okay, have it your way. Let's get to your question about why I look familiar to you."

"I don't believe I actually asked you that."

"I'm coaxing you. I told you—my purpose is to give you information."

"Okay," I said. "Why the hell do you look so familiar to me—if you don't mind my asking?"

Temp smiled. "Because, as I told you, I'm a composite. And

that composite is made of images of males you know, and my voice of their audio samples, though that may not be as noticeable as my visual appearance. I've been using my composite voice all along—we don't yet have enough of your voice in all of its nuances to replicate it for these purposes."

"And the images and voices were obtained—"

"In a variety of ways," Temp said.

I looked at him.

"Yes," he said.

"To what question?" I asked.

"You were likely wondering if any of the images and sounds were obtained by organic means. So, the answer is yes, some were."

"So Frank Catania was lying when he told me he knew nothing about squirrel images?"

"Frank was telling you the truth."

"Meaning: you are the result of squirrel images, at least in part, but Frank didn't know that?"

"Meaning: I'm not the result of squirrel images at all, as far as I know," Temp retorted.

"So . . ."

"Don't look so surprised," Temp said. "Are squirrels the only animals that can see?"

"No, of course not—"

"Squirrels scampering around wouldn't be a big hit in people's living rooms and bedrooms, would they?" Temp continued. "The lady of the house—probably the man, too—would scream before the squirrel got off a single frame. But a dog on a leash—a leash with an embedded wire—that's an ideal organic camera for the home. People are more relaxed about dogs. Hell, one of my programmers told me that he once went out with a girl who had no problem with a dog in the bed when they made love."

"Charming," I said.

"But true."

"Jack Dugan doesn't have a dog."

"So? One of his neighbors does—a Seeing Eye dog, with a different meaning to the term." Temp smiled at his own word play. "Do you have any idea how many mutts looked at you in the past few days? I doubt it. Most people take dogs for granted, unless they bark in their face."

The smile, I needed to remind myself, was just in some 3-D virtual icon file that Temp could access—no, was programmed to access—when he uttered certain words. If I could believe his digital confessions . . .

"How many different animals do you have on this, ah, video leash?" I asked.

"Just dogs, so far," Temp replied. "The listener-recorder critters are different. The dogs are new—just a few months out of beta testing. But some of this has been going on a little longer than you think."

"Tell me."

WHAT WAS IT with me, that so much of what I investigated turned out to have roots in the deep past? Well, part of it was my fascination with DNA, whose links to the past made seconds out of millennia. And part of it was . . . well, maybe that's just the way the world was, with so much of its existence floating on the surface like lily pads, each with tangled lines penetrating far below into dark, primeval soil. . . .

"What do you suppose those paintings on the caves in Altamira and Lascaux were all about?" Temp was asking. "You ever think about that?"

Lots of times. And this could be no coincidence. He wasn't reading my mind. The data used to construct him obviously went beyond images and sounds, and must have included profiles of my interests and predilections. How else could he have a meaningful conversation with me? "You're saying they were based on some kind of animal vision?" Temp's notion of 'a little longer' obviously went back further than Frank's mice.

"I'm saying they *are* animal vision," Temp replied. "Think of what they look like—almost recognizable as bison, deer, things that we know, but not quite. Somehow always slightly out of focus. You know why? They're bison the way some other *animal* has seen them. The same with a lot of Egyptian art."

"I know it's stylized, but you're saying it's not human?"

Temp nodded.

"Where'd the Cro-Magnon artists get the telecom?" I prodded "him."

"You mean: How did these ancient folk, these prehistoric people, get the images from inside the brains of the observing animals to a place where they could be recorded as art?"

"That's right."

"I have no idea," Temp said.

I looked at him.

He returned my gaze. Eyes that were not really eyes, that could not see, in a head whose mouth was telling me about prehistoric people who figured out how to get what animals perceive—what they see of other animals—out of their animal heads and up on a cave wall . . . I wasn't sure which part of this was the most preposterous. . . . Yet I was indeed having a conversation with this holographic head, in a high-tech cave a mile below the surface at Wilmington. . . .

"Come now, Phil," the head said. "You know that I know you too well to believe that you would reject what I'm saying out of hand, simply because there is no extant technology that has survived from that time. You've spent a decade or more tracking down hunches that perhaps organic technologies of one sort or another existed in the distant past, and are invisible to us now because we no longer think of them as technology. Haven't you? You're on record as saying that DNA is the ultimate technology, aren't you?"

"Something like that, yes."

"Well, then . . ." Temp made an expansive gesture with his matte hands. "Maybe there are other possibilities—"

I jumped up and reached for one those hands, totally on impulse. My hand went right through the opaque image of his.

Temp shook his head and clucked his tongue. "What'd you think—they smuggled in a real person when you weren't looking and lit me up to look like a hologram? Happy now?"

"Look, this is all very interesting," I said, and it was. "But how about you give me the tour now."

"The tour?"

"I'd like to see some of the facilities."

"You're looking at them."

I half-laughed. "I'd like to see some of the equipment you have here—organic, digital, cyber, whatever."

"I told you," Temp responded. "I'm here for just one purpose: to give you information."

"Frank Catania said this was a huge center."

"You feel cheated?"

"Where's the center?"

"Everywhere. Nowhere. The center is distributed. But—okay, maybe you're right. Talking heads can get monotonous. How about this?" Temp dissolved into a Monet painting, an undulating field of wildflowers. None were grey. Debussy's *Claire de Lune* tinkled, softly. . . .

It was mesmerizing . . . "Stop it," I managed to say. "I didn't come for a multimedia concert."

The wildflowers imploded back into Temp. He said, "A concert is a kind of information."

I realized I was breathing heavily.

"Think," he said. "Once you leave, if terrorists somehow find this facility, far below Wilmington, and level it—inside out, from deep down up to ground—what will they have destroyed?"

"An image. Nothing," I replied.

Temp nodded. "End of lesson. I'll be out of here in a second, and so should you. You'll find an elevator to the left, just beyond the door."

HE WAS RIGHT—as I had been about the door sealing, healing, a second or two after I stepped through. Though of course I couldn't be sure it had vanished from the outside view when I had stepped through it, into the room, the first time. It was definitely not there now. I shook my head and wondered about the room itself. The door had disappeared, the occupant disappeared, maybe the room itself was gone now, too. Was it a hologram? No, at least not the part, the chair, I had been sitting on—that was real. Hard-ass proof.

I shook my head again and looked around. Ah, there was the elevator. Just where Temp had said it would be. Was it there when I had arrived? I didn't know—I hadn't looked in that direction.

The elevator's niche took my palm print. The door opened. I walked in, sat down, and soon I was moving up . . . I assumed its destination would not be precisely where I had entered the elevator, in Wilmington Station, above. I had, after all, walked a bit, on a conveyor belt, to get to my interview with the hologram, and I certainly didn't feel as if I were now moving in any diagonal way, just straight up. But I couldn't tell for sure . . . I took consolation in the fact that not knowing the precise vertical trajectory of a mile-long elevator was a lot less absurd than not knowing how much of a room I had just been in really existed. . . .

I thought about perception, illusion, reality. One of my favorite philosophers of the twentieth century, Sir Karl Popper—I was always telling people about him—once wrote that ingestion of food was our most profound, reliable contact with the real world. We actually consume reality, take it inside us, make it part of us, transform part of it into us, when we eat. Touch and any direct perceptions through the body would be second—not as reliable an intersection with reality as eating, but far better than seeing and hearing. (Tasting and smelling, I supposed, were part of eating. Even if considered independently, they'd be closer to reality than seeing and hearing.) So, all in all, I could be reasonably confident in my current kinesthetic sense that I was moving up.

And what about what had happened in the room? Temp had been hologramic—at least, that's what my touch had conveyed, when I had reached for his hand. . . . And my back, backside, and legs had confirmed the reality of my seat—at least as convincingly, maybe more, than the motion I was feeling in this elevator.

I thought a bit about some of the other people I had run into the past few days. How many of them had I literally come into contact with? I had just talked to a pretty convincing hologram of me. Was there any chance that I had talked to other holograms, unknowingly?

I'd broken bread—actually, saltine crackers—with Frank in the Oyster Bar at Grand Central Terminal. He was eating, I was eating, but that was no confirmation of anything, unless we had been literally eating the same cracker. . . . I thought some more. . . . Okay, I'd shaken his hand the first time we'd been in the Grace laboratories. Right after he'd explained to Jill why he was explaining so much to me . . . Okay, Frank was real.

How about Jill? I was pretty sure I'd squeezed her hand the first time we met, at Cold Spring. Yeah, I was sure.

How about that stick-up-the-ass at Gnarlingview, Deborah Paton? Yeah, she shook my hand right before we had walked down to her office.

But she had been a study in grey, just like Temp. What significance did that have? Was she rehearsing for a hologram?

Who else was I overlooking?

I went over the various people again. I'd shaken Mel's hand in The Grace Note—for crissakes, of course *he* was real. I'd known him since we were kids. . . .

Who else?

I thought, again, about my first meeting with Jill. After she showed me the hamsters, she showed me to Marty Glick. Had I shaken his hand? I couldn't recall, one way or the other. Probably I did, I usually do, but I had no recollection of doing so. . . . All right, I'd seen Glick a second time, in Henry's, the day that Cerebreeze had been torched. Had I shaken his hand then? The more I thought about it, the more I didn't think so. Glick and the other guys at the table—and the woman there, too—were eating. I often didn't shake hands with people when they were eating—it sometimes felt like an intrusion—and besides, they had their hands full of hamburger grease, chicken fat . . .

Could Glick, could the other three at his table, have been holograms, like Temp? Glick had recognized me. Henry's would have had to have been outfitted with some pretty serious cameras and projectors for that. . . . Or, who knew, maybe a mouse under a table . . . a goddamn Board of Health violation.

But whose purpose would it have served for Glick and company to be holograms? They had no idea I was coming. For that matter, I still was not clear why Temp was a hologram—why drag me all the way down a black hole in Wilmington just to talk to a hologram, of me or a composite? Surely our government had lots of places to conduct such "light" conversation in New York. . . .

I was missing something about this trip—still looking at something the wrong way. . . .

My elevator slowed—at some place in Wilmington Station, near ground level, I hoped. I shook my head clear. I had no proof about anything concerning Glick. That I was even contemplating the possibility that he was a hologram, given that I had seen and talked to him in a cafe with other people in the middle of the day, seemed ridiculous. Those conditions were nothing like the carefully controlled Lewis Carroll underground I had just popped out of—

And it was indeed controlled. It didn't matter which of the conveyor belts I had stepped upon in that luminescent watchface of a terminal—two o'clock, four o'clock, eight o'clock, ten o'clock, or twelve o'clock straight ahead, they each likely led to a room furnished for hologramic conversation. Temp could have been instantly projected into any of them. . . .

My elevator came to halt; the doors opened; I rose and walked out.

"So, did you enjoy your visit?" Frank smiled and extended his hand.

I shook it. Real. At least I could be sure of that.

NINE

We were indeed in a different part of the station. It seemed deserted, except for Frank and me. He looked at his watch. "A northbound train is due in ten minutes. It's about a five-minute walk to the platform. Let's get going."

I nodded and followed his brisk pace.

"If it were up to me, we'd have the entrances as well as the exits all off-station, like this one," Frank said. "It's crazy to have an elevator to our facilities in any kind of public place, even a locked ticket office."

"So why did they put it there?"

"Trade-off," Frank responded. "It does allow you to enter the facility more quickly, in case of emergency. I'll give them that. But it's controversial—our agents don't agree on everything, by any means. There's a lot of focus on trains as the backbone of our response system. With that in mind, swift access right from the train became the overriding factor. We tend to use it late at night, of course, for regular business. So far, so good."

"How long has the facility been open?" I asked.

"Five weeks."

I shot Frank a glance. . . .

We walked through a door and out into the night. I realized the structure we had been in was actually not part of the station, but a separate little building, across the neon-lit street.

I breathed in the chill. The temperature felt like it had dropped at least ten degrees.

"You never got to tell me what you were doing up at Gnarlingview," I said to Frank.

"Gnarlingview? I would have thought you'd be much more interested in discussing what happened to you down there." He pointed to the street.

"I am. But I'm also still interested in what you were doing in Cambridge."

We reached the station and started climbing stairs.

"I was scanning the place for explosive devices," he said grimly. His breath was white in the cold.

"You didn't do a very good job."

"Obviously not. I didn't do too well at Cerebreeze or Biomage, either. I was just checking further into Biomage in Philadelphia—last-minute lead that didn't pan out."

We reached the top of the stairs. The train was already in the station, doors open.

We walked in. "What were you looking for, exactly?"

"Not the right thing."

We took our seats.

THE CONDUCTOR ANNOUNCED that Philadelphia's Thirtieth Street station would be the next stop. His announcement had an odd kind of rhyme to my ears. This train was a tape, winding in reverse, carrying me back to where Frank and I had started, in New York.

In reverse physically, but not in terms of what I now knew.

Frank spoke: "You can't be party to everything, not yet. Actually, you'll never be. I'm not, either. I doubt anyone is."

I nodded.

"But you're in," he half stated, half asked.

"I'm thinking about it."

"We showed you a helluva lot down there."

"More tell than show, actually. Why did you want me down there?"

"This separation of powers—Army, Navy, Air Force; local, state, federal; CIA, FBI, all the other 'I's—that's what got us into this trouble in the first place," Frank said. " 'Operation Wildflower' is designed to surmount that. We take root where *we* want, anywhere we're needed, not where we're expected."

Not really an answer to my question, but good to know, anyway. I thought about the shimmering field of wildflowers a mile below Wilmington. "And if the NYPD and Wildflower come to loggerheads? You'd expect me to be loyal to whom?"

"No reason it should come to that," Frank replied.

Yeah, but could I report on Dugan if necessary? Could I turn a blind eye to a dead body in New York if some national interest suited it? I supposed yes, but only to save a lot more people from dying in New York—and elsewhere—if I was really sure. . . .

"Our first order of business now is finding out exactly who is behind these attacks on our laboratories, and how they're doing it," Frank said. "We're looking at Forty-second Street almost molecule by molecule. "The NYPD and OWL have identical goals on that score."

"Well, obviously someone from the inside is involved." But I refrained from saying, Who else have you shown your Wilmington facilities to? And I'm not even sure you're telling me the truth, Frank. There's still the question of why you told me one thing and Jill Cormier told me something else about squirrels and Cerebreeze.

"Of course," Frank replied. "But who?"

OUR TRAIN PULLED into Penn Station in Manhattan precisely on time. Late-night trains, I'd noticed years ago, were more likely to be on time than trains earlier in the day—if the late-night trains were not hours off, due to construction or whatever. But there was less minor clutter late at night. A lot like inside my head.

We walked up to the sidewalk. The city, too, looked uncluttered this night. Work on the station renovation—which I hadn't noticed coming in, since I had entered from the other side—was well under way. Moynihan Station, as it would be called, would soon be gleaming in the moonlight. Frank shook my hand, said we should talk tomorrow, and sped away in a cab.

I looked a little longer at the stately columns. I sighed. An edifice from another age. There wasn't even much noisy traffic tonight. The world seemed at peace, and I was in turmoil. No, that contrast was false. The world only seemed at peace at this instant, in this particular place. It was a beautiful illusion. A longer view would show flames singeing the fields of wildflowers. . . . My job was to keep the searing heat at bay, on the sidelines. It could never be eliminated.

I caught a cab. "East Eighty-fifth Street and York." I knew a few people who had moved out of the city in search of safer surrounds. Hadn't been an issue, even a question, for Jenna and me. I had lived in the city all my life, and although I loved time away, especially on Cape Cod, I couldn't imagine being away, anywhere, without New York City to come home to. Something in my system was timed to its pulse.

Jenna said she felt the same way, and I was pretty sure that was true. She had always had a non-native New Yorker's special love for the city—hey, now I've found this place, I'm never gonna leave it—that was even stronger, in some ways, than my born-and-bred-in-the-Bronx kind. We didn't have kids yet, though. I wondered how that would figure in our sense of the city and its safety and appeal. . . .

I tipped the cabbie well. I'd been soaring into the twenty-five percent range lately. I couldn't say exactly why. It wasn't that I had suddenly come into money, or anything like that. It just felt right. These cabbies, in their own way, were the life blood of the city. Red blood cells carrying the oxygen of people. I wondered if cabs were literally red, rather than yellow, in any city. . . .

I buzzed Jenna on the intercom to let her know I was home. I had called her on the phone, on a walk alone to the cafe on the train, and filled her in. I felt like I had been away for weeks. A trip down a hole in Wilmington to talk to a Mad Hatter hologram could do that, I guess. I ran my hand through my hair.

I climbed up the stairs and knocked on the door and she opened it by pulling it back so that she was between the door and the wall and I couldn't see her. She let the door close, slowly, after I was inside. She was wearing one of my beige Van Heusen shirts, partly open. She had nothing else on, except a thin silver necklace.

She gave me that slightly mischievous look. "You hungry?" she asked.

"Oh yeah," I replied, and pulled her, and her necklace, and her shirt, into my arms. I kissed her and scooped her up and carried her—piggyback style except she was in front and kissing me—into our bed. Her hands moved from the back of my neck to the front of my shirt. I recalled feeling a little tired on the train, near Trenton, but that seemed like a long time ago, too. . . .

The warmth and fragrance of her body were a lot better assurance of reality than Frank's damn handshake.

"So LET ME give you a rundown on the day's events," she said later. We were both mostly still not dressed, moved to the kitchen table, she with a glass of chablis, I with a cup of green tea.

"I'm never sure that everything gets through on these cell phones," she added.

I sipped and agreed.

"So, no change on Mel," she said. "The attending doctor I finally managed to reach told me the crucial time is tonight—right now, probably. Lots of things could go one way or the other. They'll know a lot more tomorrow."

I looked at the clock on the wall. Past one in the morning. I had half a mind to put on shirt and shoes and take a taxi down to the hospital. But the other half said, first, You're too tired, and second, You're not likely to find anything more by rushing down there anyway.

Jenna regarded me. "It can wait until morning. You're not going to do anyone any good if you short-circuit on fatigue."

"Okay." I let Jenna and my more reasonable half win, this time. I smiled a little. "I won't risk a short circuit—I'm not surprised you're thinking in those terms, given all my babbling these days about the ins and outs of brains."

"I'm not sure I understand exactly what happened to you tonight in Wilmington," she said.

"I'm not sure I understand, either."

She drank her wine.

"It was in part a demonstration," I continued, "intended to show me how much they could do, at least in deployment of nimble holographic images." I looked at her lips on the wineglass. "You just talked me into that wine."

"Sure." She took a long-stemmed glass from the counter, filled it, and passed it my way.

I tasted the wine and closed my eyes. "They fielded a hologram of me to impress me—to show me as plain as the nose on my face that they can make holograms of anyone."

"Like who?"

"Anyone," I replied. "At this point, the only way I figure I can be sure is by actually touching someone, or—"

Jenna smiled at me through her wine. "So I passed the test."

"Clean off the scale, out of the ballpark."

"What else did they tell you down there?" Jenna asked.

"The dog on a leash—that was something new."

Jenna considered. "Blind people with Seeing Eye dogs could be spies."

Temp had said something similar. "Yeah. Seeing Eye dogs are bred to be friendly, relaxed, don't scare any kids, blend into the scenery. People attend to the blind person—are you comfortable, can I bring you anything, is there something you need? Makes the dog a perfect spy—everyone's looking someplace else. Do we have any blind people in this building?"

"I don't think so."

I nodded, and considered. I was still being blind to some things—

"And you think the people at Wilmington—"

"The hologram—"

"You think the hologram at Wilmington was trying to recruit you?" Jenna asked.

"I don't know for sure. That's what Frank seemed to be saying on the train. Show me how much they can do, give me at least enough inside information to make me feel I've been accepted, and already part of the team. . . . That still doesn't explain why they wanted me down there to make the pitch . . . down that long elevator shaft. . . ."

"You weren't completely swayed?"

"I'm still sympathetic to the goals of the civil liberties people. I can't help it—I've loved the First Amendment, been an absolutist about its enforcement, all of my life. Censorship is cancer—once you let a little in, it can take over and destroy the entire body. I guess invasion of privacy isn't censorship, but I still don't like it—even for good reasons. And yet . . ." I shook my head. "If they're blowing up Frank's facilities, killing people, even just endangering them—they're certainly destroying equipment—and if Frank's work is trying to stop terrorists, then every dendrite in my body also says we've got to support him. And if that includes more invasion of privacy . . . and operating with a law-enforcement group beyond the NYPD . . . I don't know, to save innocent lives . . ." I shook my head some more.

Jenna touched my face with her fingertips. She stood up, walked toward the door, then turned around. Her hair flipped quickly around her neck in a way that I liked. "We can sort this out more in the morning," she said. "I can think of better things to occupy your dendrites now."

I followed her into bed. From time to time, I thought about whether it was wise to share all of my professional life and information with Jenna—how safe it was, for her. But the older I got, the more I believed that in most cases not knowing was more dangerous in the end than knowing. . . .

"Oh," she said to me about an hour later, when we were finally about to use the bed to get some sleep. "I forgot to tell you. A woman called from the medical examiner's office—"

"Rachel Saldana?"

"Yeah, I think that was her name. And she said that two other squirrels turned up, drugged and dead."

PART III:

The Grace Building

TEN

I couldn't sleep. I slipped out of bed and put in a long session on the Web. Squirrels, hamsters, holograms . . . I knew a lot about photography—it was part of forensic science—but I needed to know more about holography. . . .

Eventually I went back to bed. Holograms had a dream-like quality . . . I slept soundly, but didn't dream. . . .

I woke to birds chirping . . . dogs barking . . . cars screeching.

Then the phone rang.

"Here." Jenna passed the ringing phone to me. "You take the phone, I'll take the window."

They were both about the same thing. A bomb had been discovered, Dugan told me on the phone, in the tunnel below the New York Public Library on Fifth Avenue and Forty-second Street. "Big enough to put those lions into orbit, if it had blown." He was talking about the majestic stone lions in front of the library. "But I want you down here a-s-a-p to look at something else."

"Yeah?" That would be right across the street from the Grace Building. . . .

"Preliminary reports say the bomber was a dog," Dugan explained—

"It's a police car," Jenna called out from the window.

"What? A dog was carrying the bomb, Jack?"

"I thought it might have some conceivable connection to your rodent case," Dugan continued. "I sent over a car to pick you up and get you down there."

"It made good time—it's already here." In fact, I thought I'd heard more than one car, but that could have been just echoes bouncing in a brain still empty from sleep. "I'll be right down," I said, and reached for my shirt.

I NEARLY TRIPPED over Ralphie Merrit, the eight-year-old, who was at it again with his backward binoculars at the bottom of our inside staircase.

He turned them toward me. "You still look tiny," he said, and laughed.

"Don't you have school today?"

"Jewish holidays," he replied smartly.

"Oh yeah? I don't think so—not this time of year."

I walked out into the street and the waiting black-and-white. They still called them that, even though they were blue.

The ride downtown was choppy. We were stationary for a good thirty seconds at a clogged intersection at Fifty-seventh Street, sirens blaring and my driver cursing through his open window notwithstanding.

"I sometimes wish I could just blow those cars away with a laser," he turned around and told me. "We'll have you there soon, Doc, don't worry."

I knew how he felt. And I suddenly didn't mind being stuck in traffic, now that we were moving. It put the last piece in place about Wilmington and the hologram. . . .

"Here you go, Doc." We pulled up to Forty-second Street.

I set the hologram aside; time to concentrate on the bomb.

NEW YORK CITY lacked the sheer extent of Montreal's underground walkways, and certainly had nothing as deep as Wilmington Station, but it made up for this with a wide variety of separate underground passages, sprouted beneath buildings like fine networks of venerable roots. The World Trade Center had had one, Rockefeller Center still did, and a walkway below Forty-second Street between Sixth Avenue and the New York Public Library was now under expansion. When completed, it would connect with Grand Central Terminal to the east and the Times Square complex of stations to the west. Plans even called for an eventual connection to the huge facility under Thirty-third Street, via an old passage running down Sixth Avenue. It would not be easy, I supposed, to burrow under Forty-second Street, from the New York Public Library to the Grace Building, with a pair of subway lines already running through there. But new laser technology sped the drilling, assisted by a genetically engineered bacterial "cream" that digested some of the bedrock. "Drillcream"—a little went a long way. . . . If the Feds were involved in this, they would want their labs on the fortieth floor, accessible via these passageways. For all I knew, this had already happened.

Dugan was waiting for me right next to one of the lions. We walked through several checkpoints and flights of stairs. He had no need to show badge or credentials. Every cop knew the new deputy mayor. Some in the library shook his hand.

"How'd the dog get past all this in the first place?" I asked. I could see that the checkpoints had been in place for a while. The city was very careful with all new construction.

"Probably got here some other way," Dugan replied. "Some other tunnel that we don't know about, or knew fifty or a hundred years ago and forgot. Lots of underground doohickeys crisscrossing the city—closed up years ago, abandoned, not on many maps, not in anyone's awareness. My uncle George was a subway engineer, and he used to tell me— Ah, here we are. Close call, close call."

A group of bomb squad people were huddled around a sedated St. Bernard dog.

A big guy with a beard looked to be in charge. He had a bit of a hangdog expression, himself. Dugan called him over and introduced us. His name was Gabe Nebuch.

"It was a small device, strapped around the pooch's neck," Nebuch explained. "We got it off and disabled just in time."

"Around its neck?" I asked.

"Yeah," Nebuch replied. "Why? You expected something else?"

"I don't know. I guess with what I've been hearing about telecom devices inside the brain, I thought the bomb might be—"

"Don't even *think* that," Dugan interjected.

Nebuch agreed. "A bomb *inside* the skull? We'd never spot it in time. Not to mention that even if we somehow did suspect it, we'd have to slaughter the poor animal to get it out."

"Glad to put what actually did happen down here in such a favorable light," I commented.

"How would a bomb even fit inside a skull?" Dugan wondered. "Wouldn't leave much room for brains."

"There've been rumors for a while that terrorists have been developing really tiny bombs with triggering devices that run on molecular chips," Nebuch advised.

Dugan winced.

"But, well, like I said, we got it in time, this time," Nebuch advised. "The bomb was external . . . still haven't the vaguest how the animal got in here, though."

"Who made the ID in the first place?" I asked. "We were in nelucky on that score, too."

Nebuch nodded. "One of the construction guys had to take a piss, went looking for the Johnny-on-the-spot or the Port-A-San or whatever they call them here—Johnny-on-the-spot is the only name I ever really liked—and wandered down here by mistake. He saw the St. Bernard and realized it didn't belong here."

"He made the call to security. One of their guys used to work with the bomb squad in Boston," Dugan picked up the account. "The Boston guy noticed the suspicious device around Fido's neck and called in Gabe and company."

"We got it off with fourteen minutes to spare," Nebuch concluded. "Close. Like I said." He looked at his watch. "The fed contingent will be here in five minutes. I'm due to brief them."

"You did good." Dugan clapped him on the back.

I agreed, and looked at the dog. "I'll get its coat sampled for human DNA. Maybe its trainer got sloppy and patted it."

"With our luck, he probably wore gloves." Dugan glowered.

"At least the dog wasn't a hologram," I said.

Dugan looked at me quizzically.

Nebuch laughed heavily. "As long as a hologram can't carry a real bomb, we're okay."

Dugan looked even more confused.

"I've got a whole bunch of things I need to talk over with you," I explained. "But first I need to check something out."

Dugan nodded. "You know where to reach me."

"Yep." I shook both men's hands, and left.

When I reached the street, and my cell phone was fully up, I called in to my office and requested the DNA team for the dog. Then I focused on Jill Cormier. Before I went any further on this, I needed to resolve the contradiction between what she and Frank had told me about squirrels.

I THOUGHT I understood, now, why Frank had invited me down to Wilmington. Not to dazzle me with my own hologram. I had indeed been looking at that the wrong way around, like Ralphie Merrit had been looking at me with his inverted binoculars. What I had read last night about holograms . . . getting stuck in traffic on the way down here . . . Holograms required a lot more information to construct than flat photographs. Of course they did—they were three dimensional images, in motion. Even photos, in the early decades after their invention, required subjects to sit still for long minutes so the image would take. Daguerreotypes showed unsmiling people in neck braces to keep them stationary—no one could hold a smile for that long. I hadn't been in a neck brace in Wilmington—but I had been relatively motionless, in long elevator rides, coming and going. Why? Not to show me my hologram. To help *make* a hologram, to improve the hologram, of me.

Wilmington was likely a hologram production facility. My holographic appearance had been brief, not because its programmers were concerned about my comfort—although my anxiety had been real—but because they did not have enough of the right kind of imagery to keep my hologram in play. And they likely showed me my hologram, not so much to impress, but to get images of me with a variety of surprised expressions. . . .

So Frank had drawn me down to Wilmington mainly to help complete my hologram. Which made it more crucial than ever that I know if he was on the side of the angels. Because, if he wasn't . . .

I looked at my cell phone. I noticed a text message had quietly arrived, apparently when I was looking at the St. Bernard. For some reason, text messages sometimes took longer to register on this phone than voice mail. Maybe because written words were less palpable than sounds.

The message was from Jenna.

"Didn't want to interrupt you with a phone call, so I figured I'd tell you the good news this way: The doctors at Beth Israel say Mel is doing much better! They may even send him home in a few days."

Wonderful news! With all of this commotion, I had forgotten about Mel. I put a call in to Beth Israel.

"All right, I understand," I told the irritating resident I was finally able to reach. She had explained to me, in clipped, officious terms, that Mel could not be disturbed right now unless it was a police emergency. "No, it's not an emergency. Just tell him Phil D'Amato called, and please give him this number if he needs anything." I gave her my cell phone number and hoped she wrote it down.

I returned my attention to Frank and Jill. She was the best way, at this point, of finding out more about Frank. Better than confronting him head-on. Would she even be reachable at Cerebreeze now? Events had raced so quickly the past few days—I realized I had no idea what had become of Glick and his staff.

Well, no point in agonizing about whether it made sense to call the Cerebreeze number—I might as well call it and see what happened.

"Cerebreeze Laboratories," a voice answered. She sounded familiar.

"Jill . . . Cormier?" I asked.

No response.

Then, "Phil, is that you?"

Hey, sometimes I got a good break to balance the bad.

JILL CORMIER HAD told me squirrels were being outfitted with cerebral video transmitters, a development her apparent colleague Frank Catania had denied, or, at least, denied any knowledge of. Jill had pointed me in the direction of Gnarlingview, the pursuit of which had taught me nearly nothing, yet had nearly cost me my life. I had intended to track her down, and here she was, unexpectedly, on the phone.

"Good to hear your voice, Jill." No other way to play it, at this point.

"Same here," she said. "You heard what happened to us at the lab?"

"Yeah," I said. "But you're back in business now?" The impression I had had from Glick and the police in Cold Spring was that the damage was extensive—Frank had certainly implied that, too—but I hadn't actually seen Cerebreeze after the fire, or whatever exactly it was—

"Not quite. The calls are being routed to me, off site," Jill said.

"Ah, I see." I thought for a second. "Any chance I could drop by and we could chat?"

"I'm not supposed to reveal my location to anyone except folks with authorization codes," she demurred.

I wanted to say: You didn't seem too concerned about authorization codes when you hopped a southbound 4 train to tell me about squirrels in Cambridge. . . . But I had little to gain by being sarcastic or belligerent at this point. She could hang up on me in a heartbeat, and chances are I wouldn't be able to trace her location. I took a softer tack. "Things are moving too fast now for authorization codes. You seemed to trust me the other day—have I done anything to warrant changing your mind?"

Silence.

"Jill?"

"I can meet you on the south side of Central Park—Fifty-ninth Street, across from The Plaza—in about fifteen minutes. Best I can do."

"I'll take it."

FORTY-SECOND STREET TO Fifty-ninth Street was coincidentally about a fifteen-minute walk—more like ten minutes, actually, at the speed I moved. Good. Feet had always been more reliable than engines in the congestion of the city, and reconstruction, tunneling, and security were making the city more congested than ever. Too bad they didn't sell city-sized decongestants. Well, I guess that's what the tunnels were supposed to do.

Fifth Avenue was a busy tapestry today. Puffs of steam out of tunnel vents, glistening laser-cream drills like big dental equipment on wheels, bright red and blue construction hats, with Mr. Scruffs' "Get a Move On" playing from five different windows and a street band. I put two dollars in the bass player's case.

It felt Dickensian. I recalled a *New York Times* review of a Discovery Channel special I had narrated recently—"Digital Forensics." I had mentioned on the show that the logical pace and procedure of forensic science—much of it, anyway—still felt Victorian, step by step, even in the digital age. The review said, *D'Amato has the Victorian age on the brain.* Hey, I didn't write the script—I just consulted on it and spoke it. But the reviewer was probably right. That's the way I saw the world. Looking for history in every piece of plaster. And maybe it even had some relevance to the current investigation. Fechner and the psychophysicists had started, after all, in the middle of the nineteenth century.

I looked ahead at the oncoming traffic. I was walking against it—on the sidewalks, of course—but uptown on a downtown avenue. Looking at things from the wrong end, again? There was something else that was bothering me, that I wasn't seeing right. Not about the holograms, though they were no doubt connected to this, but about the spying animals, who was really behind them, and the dangers they really posed. I had a feeling there was more going on here than just illicit information. . . .

I could see Jill waiting for me north of Fifty-ninth Street, with the park behind her. For some reason, that mildly surprised me. I guess I quarter-expected her not to show. Or maybe I expected Frank Catania to be there in her stead. Or maybe a hologramic concoction of them both.

Jill looked good, tight mauve skirt, silhouetted against the bark of a tree near the sidewalk. She smiled at me as I approached. The smile was perhaps a bit more tentative than I remembered it. Or maybe it was just the sun making her face scrunch.

"So, here I am," she said.

I joined her by the tree, an oak devoid of leaves. "Thanks for meeting me."

"Sure," she said. "Should we walk in the park?"

I nodded. "Can we talk about squirrels?" I didn't see any point in small or even medium-sized talk at this juncture. I knew that getting any useful information out of her would be more than a walk in the park.

"Okay . . ." She looked around the asphalt path, as if some errant squirrel had prompted my question.

"Very few people other than you seem to believe in their telecommunicative capacities," I said. In fact, there was just one other that I knew—the grey Deborah Paton.

"Oh? Who'd you ask?" She didn't seem rattled.

I said nothing. The less I revealed of what I knew, the more I could believe her—or, at least, minimize her tailoring her response to fit what she thought I expected to hear.

"Why would I lie to you about that?" she pressed. "What would I hope to gain?"

"Throw me off track?"

"How? How would telling you that we can see what squirrels see throw you off track? You accept that transponders in the brains of hamsters can convey what they hear, so what's so different about a similar technology transmitting to us what squirrels see?"

"I don't know," I said, "Maybe because squirrels make far more appearances than hamsters in our everyday lives. Eavesdropping, video-recording squirrels would really change everything—at least, outdoors." Indoors, home behind closed doors, would be relatively secure from such squirrelistic incursions, as Temp had pointed out. All people at home would have to worry about—in addition to dogs on video leashes, if they existed—would be peeping squirrels on branches outside windows. McLuhan once pointed out that the telephone had sucked all privacy out of the home by making it vulnerable to public calls. The squirrel, for all its nimble footwork, would have a much harder time getting through the front door.

Jill was frowning.

A squirrel bounded up to us, looked at her, then me, as if to offer itself as evidence of some sort. I looked it in the eye. Could there really be a telecommunicating camera behind that beady eye, tucked somewhere in its brain? Likely all this squirrel was looking for here was a handout.

Jill apparently had the same idea. She reached in her pocket and pulled out a small bag of popcorn. She spilled some in front of the squirrel, who stuffed its cheeks, looked at us again, then turned and ran up a maple.

"Deborah told me she showed you a picture of you," Jill said, "conveyed by a squirrel. You didn't find that persuasive?"

"I'm no expert on digital photography," I replied, not entirely truthfully. "For all I know, some five-year-old whiz kid pulled it off the Web and souped it up on Photoshop." But at least I knew now that Jill and Deborah had been in contact.

We continued walking on the path. "What would it take to convince you that squirrelcams are real?" Jill asked.

"I suppose a demonstration like the one you gave me for hamsters in the Grace Building," I replied. Though of course I could not be sure of what I had heard in that lab, either. Conceivably, that whole setup could have been a fake. Ironically the evidence I was most sure was real was the hologram a mile below Wilmington Station.

I nearly lost my footing on a root which had broken through the asphalt. I recovered my balance and looked ahead on the path. About five or six squirrels, surrounded by an equal number of yammering pigeons, were darting around a green bench and feasting on what looked like breadcrumbs. I looked up at the hand that was feeding them.

"Maybe she'll be able to clarify a few things for you," Jill said.

The hand that was feeding the squirrels belonged to Deborah Paton.

"So, IS THIS part of the protocol?" I couldn't help saying to Paton, after she had risen and firmly shaken my hand.

She didn't smile. She was still dressed in grey—a different suit and shirt, but grey. "Dr. Cormier tells me you could use a little elucidation on a number of issues." She just stated this, plainly, not in a question.

I nodded. "And when did Jill tell you this?"

"Just before she left her office," Paton replied.

"Cerebreeze South?"

Now Paton smiled slightly. "Actually, not Cerebreeze at all."

"But Jill answered—"

"I know, Dr. D'Amato. She answered the phone 'Cerebreeze.' That's because we had all calls to Cerebreeze routed to her place here in Manhattan."

I reached for my cell phone, thinking maybe I should call that in—

"Don't waste your time," Paton advised icily. "Calls are now going back to Cerebreeze, and Dr. Cormier won't be returning to her apartment."

I took a look at Jill. She shifted, uncomfortably. She drifted a few steps sideways, backward. I couldn't tell for sure if she was still within earshot. This conversation, in any case, was now between just Paton and me.

I returned my gaze to Paton. "I assume you're now going to tell me why?"

Two squirrels scampered over a remaining bit of breadcrumb. Paton regarded them contemptuously. Something in her expression made me hope the breadcrumbs hadn't been laced with poison—à la Tom Lehrer—or some kind of anaesthetic—

"It's not much more than you've already guessed, Dr. D'Amato. You were right to look askance on me at Gnarlingview. I didn't really work for them. I'm no scientist. I was responsible for destroying that lab."

"Why?" I thought I knew, but I wanted to hear her explain.

"In part, because you were there, Dr. D'Amato—that's why I destroyed it then. But the place was already set to go. It would have happened in a few days, anyway."

Why was she telling me this now? Maybe to head off my investigating, and uncovering, more—not an unknown tactic. Throw the dog a piece of meat. But why did Jill send me up there? To see the facility before it blew? To get me out of the city?

"I belong to a group determined to stop the increasing invasion—and this new one, in particular—of American privacy," Paton continued. "We believe this to be far more destructive to our freedom, to our way of life, than terrorism."

"The American Civil Liberties Union?"

She scoffed. "They use the courts. We—as you've seen—take more direct measures. The ACLU is to our group as, well, maybe a flying grasshopper is to a jet plane."

"Jets can do a lot of damage," I said darkly.

"I assure you, we have the utmost respect for human lives," Paton said. "We've hurt no one."

"Except some animals," I said. "Like the ones that died in the labs."

Paton shrugged. "If that's what it takes. I guess we're chauvinists—human chauvinists."

"Then you're not much different from the researchers

you're opposing—they have no trouble using animals for their ends, either."

"Oh yes, we are, Dr. D'Amato. They would use animals, hurt animals, if necessary, to destroy human privacy and therefore freedom. We hurt animals only if necessary to prevent that."

I looked again at Jill. She had not said a word, and did not look as if she intended to. She just looked very uncomfortable.

"And you're telling me all of this because . . ."

"Because we think you're a fundamentally reasonable, freedom-loving man, Dr. D'Amato. Because Jill called me, right after you called her, and suggested I come here. Because we don't have the luxury, these days, of thinking things over for too long."

"So you're sure I'm not going to have you arrested, right now?" I asked.

"No, we're not really sure of anything, Dr. D'Amato. We took a chance with Dr. Cormier, not long ago, and she seems to be working out. Now we're taking a chance on you."

She turned around and caught up with Jill. They started to leave.

"Jill, I still haven't seen any proof or more evidence about the squirrels," I called out.

Paton turned back and regarded me. "They're mostly dead now. Doesn't matter—"

She was interrupted by at least half a dozen bicyclists, furiously pedaling, who came between me and the two women. The bicyclists seemed to slow down, almost stop, as they came past me. . . .

I could just make out Jill and Paton, dashing out of view, when the pedalers were gone. I started after the two women. But they were nearly on the street now, at Fifth Avenue, and the only way I could reach them was if no taxis were on hand to hail. . . . And they jumped in one and were out of range before I reached the street.

I thought of jumping in a cab myself, and pursuing. But what would I say, "Follow those cabs"? There were at least fifteen or more on the street, and I had no idea which one had Jill and Paton.

I could call the women in to the closest precinct. But they'd be long gone by the time any patrol car could get here, too, and besides, I wanted to think a bit about what they had told me before I brought in any law enforcement.

That left the goddamned enthusiastic bicyclists—did Paton put them up to this? I called the Park South Precinct. "How many cops do you have on patrol on the south end of the park? Good. There's a group of about six bicyclists, late teens to early twenties, I'd like you to stop and question. No, don't take them into custody unless they give you a reason. I just need IDs—names and addresses. No, they haven't done anything wrong. I just need the IDs to check something out. Be nice to them."

If Paton had put them up to it, she was as good at logistics as lying.

Could I believe what she said about the squirrels? *Mostly dead now . . .*

Jenna had mentioned two dead squirrels to me this morning. . . .

It was still no big deal. As long as the dead stayed squirrels, not people.

ELEVEN

In the past twenty-four hours, I'd been propositioned by a hologram working literally underground for the feds, and a make-believe scientist who said she really worked for some *uber* ACLU. All that was missing in this unholy mess was an offer from a talking dog—and the way things were shaking out, that didn't seem so out of the question now, either.

I walked slowly out of Central Park. As always, what I most needed to make more sense of this was evidence. Not to convict, but to learn. What was really going on inside those animal skulls? It was time for a visit with Rachel Saldana, the pathologist Ed Monti had put in charge of the squirrel autopsies.

"I never had the chance to ask you," I said to her when I had reached her on the phone, "how come you're so knowledgeable about squirrels. I mean, most pathologists specialize in human—"

"You're right," she responded, "they don't teach you about squirrels at Einstein."

"That's where you went to school?" I knew the place well. It was just a few blocks south of Columbus High School, in my old neck of the woods in the Bronx.

"Yes. But my father was a vet. I picked up a lot from him. I saw a squirrel only once in his office, but there were plenty of gerbils, guinea pigs, hamsters—they're not that different."

"Right . . . Look, I know this is last-minute, but do you have plans for lunch? I guess I should ask: Do you have *time* for lunch? I'd like to talk to you a little more about the dead squirrels, if that won't spoil your appetite."

She laughed. "No, yes, and no—I don't have plans, I'll make the time—I could use an hour out of here—and no, I'm used to corpses, so the topic won't spoil my appetite one bit."

"Great." I looked at my watch. "Should we say half an hour? How about something in the Village? I know an excellent Italian place, right across the street from an excellent Japanese place, on Twelfth Street. Does either appeal to you?"

"Can I counter with Korean? For some reason, I've had a craving for kim-chee all week."

"I know just the place—Seoul Soul, on University and Tenth."

"YEOW!" A TASTE of Rachel's kim-chee—cabbage peppered with little red hotspots—nearly burned out my mouth.

Rachel laughed, and offered some of her bibim bap—a rice, meat, and vegetable mix, with egg on top. "It's not quite as spicy as the kim-chee," she explained.

"Not quite? I think I'll pass, and stick with the bulgoki." It was thinly sliced beef, which I was cooking on the little hibachi grill at our table.

"Too bland for me," Rachel said.

I smiled and tended to the beef. "Okay, now that we've got our food preferences all worked out, let's talk squirrels."

"Well, my father once knew a girl who had a squirrel for a pet," Rachel said.

"Really? I thought they were too wild for that."

"Not when they're very young. The girl found this little squirming thing in her backyard—she thought it was a baby mouse because it didn't have a bushy tail yet—and brought it to my father. He of course knew it was a squirrel, and figured it had been blown out of its nest the night before. It gets pretty windy in that area."

"New York?"

"Red Hook—about a ninety-minute drive north of here."

"About half an hour above Cold Spring. Beautiful country."

"It is," Rachel agreed.

"So that was the squirrel you remember from your father's office."

"Yeah." Rachel bit into some kim-chee, and looked like she relished it. "It's an acquired taste."

I nodded.

"Anyway, my father started by giving the baby squirrel its nutrition by injection. And when it was strong enough, the girl took it home and fed it with a little bottle. She brought the squirrel into Dad's office once when I was hanging around. It was the most adorable thing—this little squirrel clutching a baby bottle with milk in its two little paws."

I turned over a slice of beef. "Maybe someone's injecting our squirrels with some kind of nanotech that's setting up telecommunications shop in their brains."

Rachel chuckled. "Not likely—at least, not in this decade. No, if squirrels are being outfitted with braincom, the equipment would have to get into their skulls via old-fashioned cut-and-paste—surgical operation. That's what the heavy sedatives would presumably be for."

"Of course, that assumes that there is such a thing as 'braincom'—a device that decodes squirrel perceptions and transmits them out to us as images we can recognize. You think that's less far-fetched than nanotech?"

Rachel shrugged. "I've seen evidence of neither. You've at least witnessed some kind of audio conversion for hamsters, right?" She sipped almond tea.

"Apparently. But I can't be completely sure."

"Audio conversion—visual conversion—they're all just questions of digital encoding and decoding, from what I understand," Rachel said. "I think that's a level of accomplishment less extraordinary than nanotech these days, yes."

"You're probably right. . . . But back to the squirrel surgery . . . You didn't find any evidence of that in your autopsies, did you?"

She shook her head no, sipped some more tea. "Just brains and skull. But the last two were crushed pretty good. Here." She reached below her seat and produced a folder with photos. She caught my expression. "Hey, that's the procedure—you take pictures of the dead, regardless of the species."

"I know," I said. "Don't mind me. Every once in a while these days I just flash back to thinking: What the hell am I doing investigating this case—the death of squirrels. . . . But tell me what I'm looking at here—is there something unusual about these . . . victims?"

"I'm not sure," Rachel replied. She sipped the last of her tea.

I refilled her cup. I hadn't even touched my own food as yet. I took a tentative bite of my bulgoki—it was tasty.

"I was thinking as I gave you those pictures that the skull damage is pretty extensive," Rachel said.

"Extensive in what context?" I asked. "Too much damage for a fall from a tree?"

"Yeah," Rachel said. "I don't know. Maybe."

"You think maybe these two squirrels were killed by surgery that for some reason went wrong? Why would the inept surgeons dump the bodies in the park? Easy enough to toss them in an incinerator or with a bag of rocks in the Hudson."

"I don't know," Rachel repeated.

"Well, could be the surgeons thought the operation was a success," I took a shot at an answer. "So they put the squirrels back in the park—but too soon, it turns out. The squirrels aren't fully recuperated. So they fall out of their tree, and the damage we see is from the surgery plus the fall."

Rachel nodded, and emptied her second cup of tea. She didn't look convinced.

I refilled her cup again, then called for the waiter to bring more. I ate more bulgoki. It was actually delicious.

"You know, I hate to say this," Rachel said, "but we should really get one of those microphonic hamsters down to my lab so we can get a better handle on the device inside *its* head. My father always used to say we learn more from living specimens than corpses. Much as I hate to admit it, in my line of work, I think he was right."

"Your boss would agree with you. So would I."

Rachel smiled. "Ed's a good man."

"So if I'm able to get my hands on a disco-hamster, you'll examine it by MRI, CATscan?"

"As a start. But we'd probably learn more if we could somehow get it hooked up to a computer down here so we could see exactly how its braincom processes sounds. . . . I know some people in tech who are good at that. You think you can get one?"

I SAID YES, but as lunch ended, I realized that procuring a microphonic hamster would not be simple. I said good-bye and touched her hand for luck—not to rule out the ridiculous possibility that she was a hologram, but truly for luck, because, after all, I had just seen her put away a portion of beep-bop-a-loo or whatever they call it and that fiery kim-chee, too. So why was I still thinking about holograms?

I walked up to Fourteenth Street, and thought instead about how to kidnap a hamster.

Mel would be no help in this, even if he were one hundred percent recuperated. That reminded me, however, to call Beth

Israel. This time the resident was sweet as could be—a sure confirmation that there was good news.

"That's really wonderful, I'm so glad," I said. "Well, yeah, I guess that's what fifty-fifty means. . . . Thank God the glass was half full this time. . . . Can I talk to him? . . . Sure, okay, I'll call back later."

So Jenna's information had indeed been correct. Mel was well on the mend. He was undergoing some tests now, but he would really be home by the end of the week.

That prompted another call.

"McQuail? Just checking to see if you've got anything more on the Melvin Kaplan case. . . ." McQuail—no one ever used his first name, I doubted if anyone other than his mother *ever* did—had been assigned to investigate the beating. He'd been a detective at least twenty years, and I was always glad when our paths crossed.

Today his news was both reassuring and disturbing. "All right," I said. "Let me know if you find anything more. . . . Hey, the Yanks are due for a turnaround, don't worry. We'll get 'em next year."

McQuail had discovered that Mel had lost a pile of money on the Yankees a few months ago. I wasn't really surprised. Mel had said that his finances were fine, but losing a big bet on the Yankees is not the first thing you'd tell an old friend you wanted to impress and were seeing for the first time in five years. Especially if you'd lost the bet to bookies.

This was a relief, insofar as it meant that Mel's attack apparently had nothing to do with hamsters or squirrels or bombs. But it was still worse than the attack being random, since it meant that Mel was likely still in danger. Until he paid his bet.

Well, short of being in protective custody, Mel's safest place now was right where he was, in the hospital. That gave me a few days, at least, to figure out how to keep his creditors at bay . . .

Okay, back to getting my hands on a hamster with Intel or whatever the hell they put in its head . . .

I didn't need any more authority than my NYPD ID to go back up to the Grace Building on Forty-second Street and just request a hamster from that lab. If I was told no, then, okay, I'd come up with a next step. But a forensic ID still had to count for something in this town, even at a federal facility. I was conducting an investigation, for crissakes.

In other circumstances, calling Frank would have been the logical step. But he was still under some suspicion—mine, at least—in this case.

I caught the Lexington line up to Forty-second Street; the train stalled a few minutes out of the station. But my cell phone was in service, no one was seated next to me, so I decided to use what time I had to brief Dugan. Wouldn't hurt to have him on board if something went sour in the Grace Building. And if he said I should desist from grabbing a hamster, I'd go ahead and try to get one anyway.

He was supportive. "Good idea to get the hamster. More important than the hologram. You and Saldana are on the right track with this, Phil. Keep it basic, tangible. Get that chipmunk under a microscope, an X-ray machine, so you can see what's actually going on there. Too many wild ideas flying around. Too much digital . . . Keep it tangible. Keep it—what's the opposite of digital?"

"Analog?"

"Yeah, analog—keep it analog. Same for the squirrels. Forget about the Web, and that blurry picture of you. Get a videotape of what those squirrels see, if that's what's going on—something that won't rinse away in the rain."

The train started moving.

I WAS IN front of the Grace Building in ten minutes. There was no sign of yesterday's explosion, no sign of today's almost-explosion across the street. And that was not only because everything was cleaned up. And it wasn't because there were no cops around. In fact, it was just because of the opposite—there were lots of cops around, and that was entirely normal. Standard procedure in an ongoing age of terrorism. New York was like Tel Aviv. Rapid cleanup after bombings, armed presence on major street corners.

The first guard from yesterday—the one who been at his station as I snuck by—was there again now. I was glad to see him. I had been concerned that he hadn't been there on the way out. I had assumed that he'd been off looking into the false alarm. But the subsequent explosion out in the street had made me think that maybe he'd been away from his post, planting the bomb. . . . Well, not likely, if he was here back at work today.

This time I just strode up to him, announced who I was, and displayed my ID. If he called upstairs and that brought down Frank Catania, that would be no worse than my running into Frank upstairs if I went up there unannounced.

"Didn't I see you hanging around here yesterday, checkin' out that booty, Dr. . . . D'Amato?"

"Very good chance it was me, yes."

He smiled through his moustache. "Should I say this is police business?" He gestured to a scanning device on his table.

"Yes," I said, and handed him my ID card.

He ran it through the scanner. He nodded and returned it.

"You're all set, Doctor."

"Thanks. I'll let you know if I see anything appealing up there."

His smile widened.

I walked to the elevators, entered an open one, and pressed forty.

When I had been here on the fortieth floor yesterday, Frank had whisked me through the maze. I thought about seeping anonymously through the corridors within corridors now, slipping past secretaries if I could, but decided instead to just present myself and my credentials to the first person I saw behind a desk.

She was about halfway along the corridor between the glass and the wooden doors. Everything about her was red—red hair, red glasses, red lipstick. Well, better than grey, but this seemed to be my week for seeing monochromatic people. She looked like she should have been chewing Bazooka bubble gum, but wasn't. Maybe that was because bubble gum was actually pink, not red.

"Phil D'Amato," I announced, and showed her my ID. "I need access to the lab." I pointed to the door beyond.

"Certainly. And what shall I say this is in reference to?" She had a nasal Queens accent. She picked up her phone.

"I'd prefer you didn't say anything, to anyone," I replied. Technically, I had no right to order her silence—this visit was not formal enough—but my expressions of preference on these matters usually did the job.

It did this time, too. "Certainly." She put down the phone, then pressed something on her computer, which caused the door to click open.

Apparently, Frank's, or some other authorized palm print, was not the only way to open these doors.

I walked down the corridor, which had a medicinal odor. Unfortunately, I saw no one behind any desk—there hadn't been any desks in this corridor on either of my previous visits. So how was I to get in?

I put my palm on the palm-niche.

Nothing happened.

I banged, lightly, on the door.

I banged harder.

Nothing.

I groped around on the walls, hoping to somehow engage the virtual-wall operation.

No change. No click. The same unresponsive walls.

I sighed. I guess I'd have to go back to the secretary who should have been chewing Big Red gum and ask her how—

"Phil—"

The voice was familiar. I turned around.

"You can come in here."

A door appeared, which I opened.

"Have a seat, Phil. Take a load off."

It was Temp, behind a desk.

"DON'T LOOK SO surprised," he said to me, as I continued to stand. "You know as well as I that electricity travels at the speed of light."

I glanced at the ceiling and around the room for the cameras that conveyed to Temp how I looked, but there was nothing but acoustic tile on the ceiling and paper on the walls. At least, nothing else that I could see. What was behind those tiles? There had to be an optical device somewhere in the vicinity, however small and effectively invisible it was.

"I was actually programmed up here about forty seconds ago," Temp continued, "but there was some kind of congestion in the system—you know how that is, traffic jam of electrons. Sorry to keep you waiting out there."

I nodded. "And you knew I was coming as soon as the guard downstairs scanned my ID."

"That's right," Temp said. "So, if you won't have a seat, will you at least tell me what I can do for you here?"

"I'd like to borrow one of the hamsters next door," I replied.

"Hamsters?"

"That's right."

"I couldn't possibly hand you a hamster," Temp said. "I can't hand anyone anything. I'm just a projection, after all."

"I wasn't asking you to hand me a hamster," I said. "How about you just cause the door across the hall to open, and I'll take it from there."

Temp scrunched his face, and considered. Amazing imagery—better than hi-res TV—and off the screen, behind a damn desk, in three dimensions. "I suppose I could do that," he finally said. "But wouldn't you like some information, first, as long as I'm here?"

"We back to that again?"

He just smiled slightly.

I resisted the impulse to stare him down, because, once again, I had to remind myself that this image of a face, those eyes, could not see—any more than a painting of a face or eyes on a TV screen could see me. The source of Temp's vision—of what he could see of me—came from elsewhere in this room, in unseen but seeing lenses of cameras.

"I thought you told me in Wilmington that you were a one-night stand," I said.

Temp shrugged. "I guess they changed my mind." Then he laughed. "Or you changed their mind, and they changed mine. My mind."

"There's no point in calling you Temp anymore, then, is there?"

"So call me Perm. Call me Ishmael, call me e-mail, call me maelstrom, into the maelstrom, like Poe. Call me whatever you please."

"Let me into the hamster room."

Temp exhaled, tiredly. "Okay, since you're not going to ask, let me give you a little more information."

"I'm listening."

"You're still struggling with whether to throw in with us—your own government—or stick with your narrow New York agenda."

"I'm a New Yorker. The city I work for is my government, too."

"Hey, I'm a New Yorker, too—"

I scoffed. "Why? 'Cause they got you programmed to talk with a New York accent? I don't think so."

"No, it so happens that most of my real-life sources, just about all of them, in fact, are also from this town—after all, they're all your friends," Temp replied. "But regardless, even if I were alive, and had lived my entire life here, I don't think I would let the place of my residence get in the way of our national defense."

I shook my head. No point in debating loyalties of flesh and street with a hologram. "What makes you so sure I've decided not to work with you?" I confined myself to asking.

"You certainly haven't joined our side as yet, that's clear. Otherwise, you would have just called Frank and asked *him* for your hamster."

"Is he outside now, waiting for me?"

"For God's sake, Phil. You act as if Frank were a federal marshal, waiting to put you away."

"So, is he? Outside in the hall, I mean?"

Temp shook his head. "I honestly don't know. I suspect that, one way or another, you'll leave here with your hamster. But let me also give you a few last words of advice, for now, that you can also take with you."

"All right."

"Video meliora proboque deteriora sequor," Temp said.

"Come again? My Latin's a little rusty." I understood enough to know he wasn't telling me that videotape was better than DVD.

" 'I see and approve of the better things, yet I follow the worse.' That's Ovid. Think about it, Phil."

And Temp vanished.

I PUT MY hand on his desk. It was cold, slightly sticky, definitely real. I walked around it, and sat in Temp's chair. It was stiff, lumpy, also real. I looked in vain for an orifice from which Temp might have been projected. Nothing on the ceiling or walls or floor. No orifices in this office. Just me.

I considered staying in the room. If I sat here long enough, if I walked around, perhaps something would reveal itself. What? A glint of light off a lens that had been invisible to me from other angles? I doubted that.

I walked to the doorway. If I walked out, would the room disappear, and along with it, any chance to find out more about what was really going on here? I had had that same feeling in Wilmington, but had buried it, lest I get buried down there myself, and never get out—

Dammit, that Temp and his Latin had me thinking in archaic English now. . . .

I needed to get my paws on a hamster and deliver it to Rachel Saldana. Staying in this room was not likely to help with that. This was one of the problems that had been plaguing my every move in this investigation: Every time I went off looking into one thing, I got sidetracked into something else, also relevant, and then sidetracked again. That was not a good way to proceed, unless the tracks all led to the same place. . . .

I opened the door to the hallway and patted my pants pocket to make sure my cell phone was still there. I did that pretty much instinctively now—my phone had once slipped out of my pocket, about a year ago, at a meeting. But that gave me an idea about something I could do right now. Maybe I could have my cake and eat it, about not leaving this room. . . .

My cell phone was real. If this room was not—if it was

some sort of illusion—then I could leave my cell phone here and it would be interesting to see where it ended up after I left the room. I could call it, and then I or someone might be able to track down its ring.

I walked back into the office and took out my phone.

It was set to my favorite ring—the first fifteen notes of the Lovin' Spoonful's "You Didn't Have to Be So Nice." Had no connection to this case, but I liked it.

I made the ring as loud as possible. If the phone got acquired by someone I didn't like, that would pose no real problem. The tiny keys were programmed to respond only to my thumb and its print. And if I never saw it again, that would be okay, too. All of the names, phone numbers, and codes were backed up on computers in my office and home. I could get a new phone from the Department in under twenty-four hours—they were coming out with new models just about every month now, anyway.

I placed the phone on the sticky desk and left the room.

The door vanished, from the outside, a second later, just as I had expected. But at least my phone was inside. I'd call it as soon as I finished with the hamsters and was able to get my hands on another phone. Maybe the secretary's, down the hall.

I turned to the door across the way.

THE PALM-NICHE WAS still there—no real reason to think that *it* would vanish. But it was as unyielding to me now as it had been earlier. This time I refrained from pounding on the door.

What to do?

That matte hologram has said that it would open this door for me—no, actually, it hadn't, it had merely indicated its expectation that I would leave with a hamster. Great—I was going to the bank on a supposition from a light beam. . . .

I clenched my fist and raised it. I might as well pound on

the door anyway; at least it would make me feel a little better, and it might attract someone who could help—

I heard a door open—not the one in front of me.

I turned. It was the door at the end of the corridor, the one connecting to the outside corridors, through which I had entered in the first place.

The triple-red secretary walked through, and this time she was chewing gum. She was also carrying something.

It looked like a small box.

"Dr. D'Amato?" she asked, though she clearly knew who I was.

I nodded. "Yes—that for me?"

"Yes," she smiled and cracked her gum. It looked green. So much for color consistency.

"And this, too." She reached into her pocket and produced . . . a cell phone. It looked like mine.

"Where'd you get that?" I demanded.

"The box?"

"Yeah, that, too. But I was asking about the phone."

"Well, you don't have to get all huffy about it, Doctor. I'm just a salaried employee."

"I know," I said, more calmly, apologetically. "It's just—"

"This is your phone?" Now she had the demanding tone.

"Yes, I—"

"So, I think you'd be *happy* to have it returned," she said, "after you lost it."

"I am, really I am," I said, doing my best to apply the balm. "So, whom should I thank for returning my phone?" I asked, as sincerely as possible—and I was sincere about wanting to know. "Was it the same person who gave you this box for me?"

The box had slits, and I could see a little hamster, with what looked like little wires protruding from its head, crouching in a corner, inside. I took the box carefully. I also had the presence of mind to take a clean napkin out of my pocket—fortunately, I had one there—and use it to claim my phone. I carefully put it in my pocket.

"I assume so, Doctor. I received an e-mail asking me to retrieve them and bring them to you—would you like to see the printout?"

I nodded.

She showed me a piece of paper on which was printed, in common computer font: *Please retrieve two items in the mailroom for Dr. D'Amato and return to him. He's in the corridor beyond.*

"I don't see a name or address for the sender," I said.

"Our e-mail addresses are strictly confidential, Doctor—you'd need a warrant."

I assumed that applied to the name, as well. "I don't suppose I could see the mailroom."

Red shook her head no. "You'd need a warrant for that, too."

I thought quickly. I had what I'd come for. If I got belligerent with my badge or called in Dugan, I might well attract some federal agents and lose the hamster.

"Can I keep this paper?"

"Suit yourself."

"Thanks," I said. "Look, I'm really sorry about the attitude. It's been a long couple of days."

She softened. "I know. My friend just got out of the hospital from that bombing."

"I'm trying to help stop some of those things—that's why I was so pushy," I said quietly.

She nodded her understanding. "So, I better be getting back to my desk."

I decided to hazard one more question. "Do you get back here often—to this part of the corridor?"

A cell phone started ringing—hers, not mine, no Lovin'

Spoonful. "Hold on a second, Mom," she spoke into the phone. She looked at me. "It's my mother—" she started to mouth.

"Okay, thanks for your help." I shut up and walked with her toward her desk, through the various doors, all of which opened easily from our direction. There was no point in staying back near the hamster lab, now that I had a hamster—and I couldn't get in anyway.

". . . Yes, Mom, I promise. Yes, Mom, that's what I said . . ." I noticed her ears were turning red—an embarrassing conversation. But the color fit . . . She was still talking when we reached her desk. I left her with a card and a smile.

I walked to the elevator.

Well, so much for my brilliant cell phone idea.

But I did have a hamster.

Who was my benefactor? Certainly Temp had no physical way of delivering anything to me. . . . And who had done me the favor of retrieving my cell phone from the room with the vanished door?

Well, maybe the reunion with my cell phone could have a useful result—perhaps a suggestive print, or who knew, maybe even a pot of DNA gold.

TWELVE

I waved at my friend at the guard station as I hurried out into Forty-second Street and its sunshine. I liked it better this way—sunlight as a chaser to a hologram—than the night in Wilmington.

I reached for my cell phone to call Rachel and let her know a hamster was en route, but stopped myself in time. No need to further muddy whatever DNA or prints might be there. I looked around for a pay phone. (POORMAN'S CELL PHONE, the pay phone had been labeled in the early days of the cell phone boom.) I thought again about the woman in Henry's.

There were no pay phones—either in booths or on stalks—on bawdy-gaudy Forty-second Street today. I crossed the street, sat on a chair on the lawn in Bryant Park, and regarded my hamster. I could see the little wires sticking up above its ears, quite clearly. They almost looked like toy antlers. They were very thin, and must have been fashioned from one of those new superconductive composites.

How would these wires convey the sound within—the words, the music, the environment overheard by this hamster? Surely the wires would require connection to something more than just a standard computer. Likely the receiving device would need some kind of special program that could take what the wires delivered and convert it back into sound. . . . Though, for all I knew, maybe the crux of the work was accomplished in the module inside the hamster's head, and its output was a straightforward digital stream readable by any computer. . . . Hard to believe anything that could fit inside so small an area could telecommunicate. . . . But we'd been in the age of miniaturization for nearly a century. . . . Vacuum tubes to transistors to microchips, and now even smaller things. Hell, Gabe Nebuch had even talked about bombs in dog skulls. . . .

I looked carefully at the hamster. No way could I tell anything just by looking at it, of course. It did look sort of happy, though. Nothing like fear in its eyes. Well, it was probably lucky to understand nothing that it heard.

I recalled what I'd read on the Web about Alexander Graham Bell, when I'd arrived home after my first briefing on this by Frank—and Jill—at the Grace Building last week. Bell had invented the telephone in pursuit of a hearing aid for the deaf. He had understood that sound could be converted into electricity which in turn could be transmitted through wires, and had envisioned, what, wires going through the ears into the brain? Well, no way that could have worked, back in the 1870s, but here it was, in a reverse way, in this very hamster. Wires in its brain not to help it hear, but to let it speak—to tell us what it was hearing.

The little hamster looked up at me, cheeks slightly puffed, chewing on something. Ah, yes, I could see what looked like food in a corner of the box. Damn, if only I had a useable phone, I could call Mel right now, find out how he was feeling, see if there was anything special I needed to know to take good care of this hamster.

I arose, instead, and glanced back at the Grace Building across the street. From this angle, it looked like an asymptotic curve rising against an invisible vertical axis to the sky. Asymptotic curves, getting closer and closer to their destination, but never reaching it. There was a destination, a terrible danger to avert, that had been eluding me in this case. I was determined to reach and confront it. Getting a look at just what was going on inside this hamster's brain seemed a good way to proceed.

I DECIDED TO stop by my office and get my cell phone into forensics for fingerprints and DNA. I was glad no one had tried to call me on the cell phone since I had left the Grace—the urge to answer would have been hard to resist.

I held on to the hamster and its cardboard box, however. Although I wanted the outside of the box swept for prints and nucleotides, too, I had no other place to put the hamster where I could be sure it would stay comfortable—and, for that matter, alive, for all that I knew about hamsters and their tolerance for sudden environmental change. (I had killed a goldfish once, years ago, when I attempted to move it to a bigger tank. I guessed that had to do with living in water, something the hamster didn't have to worry about. Nevertheless . . .)

I'd get the box back to forensics after I delivered the hamster to Rachel. I put the box on my desk and called her on my desk phone. "Back in fifteen minutes," her outgoing message told me, and I hoped she had one of the newer devices that actually kept track of time and changed the announcement accordingly. Well, I'd try again in five minutes and see if the message told me she would be back in ten.

I tried Mel on the phone. His hospital extension was busy, and it was apparently the one line in New York without voice mail—the other end of the telecom gamut from Rachel. I'd have to call him again later, too.

I rubbed my eyes, turned to my screen, and requested my e-mail. A message was waiting, about halfway down the queue, from Temp. It carried a binary attachment.

I opened the text part. *Hope you received Walter, and he's safe and sound in your possession,* the message read. *Attached is a program you'll need to hear what he's hearing. It's self-extracting in any computer Delft-status or above*—Okay, those blue-and-whites had been common in the Department for a couple of months now—*and the wires hook into their input ports with standard jacks. . . .*

I considered forwarding the message to one of our cyberensics people, who might well be able trace its origin. But did I want knowledge of Walter and his implanted powers disseminated that far? There was no reason to think I was the only one in the Department under intensive federal recruitment. Best to keep knowledge of Walter's vacation as limited as possible for now, no matter who was programming Temp.

I put in another call to Rachel. "Back in fifteen minutes," her outgoing message told me again. So much for replacement of dumb voice mail with intelligent systems—hers was still traditional imbecile level. Not as far from Mel's hospital phone as I had supposed.

I drummed my fingers on the desk and squinted at Walter.

I might as well try Mel again—

The phone rang.

Walter and I jumped.

I answered it.

"What do you think you're doing?" It was Frank. Clearly, Temp was not doing Frank's bidding. Frank was not happy.

In less tense times, I might have replied, "I don't know—I often act without thinking." But I had a feeling that wouldn't fly too far right now. "You're concerned that . . ." I parried.

"You know exactly what I'm concerned about, Phil—you had no business grabbing the hamster. If it winds up running up the wrong person's leg—"

"I thought you think you and I are on the same side in this," I interrupted. "What's the problem?"

"You still have the hamster?" Frank asked.

I thought about lying. Didn't make sense, given that Walter's telecom module might well be traceable. "Yeah."

"All right, good at least for that. I'll be right over."

"Look, Frank—"

He hung up. His dial tone rang in my head.

I looked at Walter.

"Let's go, buddy." I grabbed the box and dashed out the door.

"Phil—" one of the secretaries started.

I brushed her off and scooted into the hall.

I had no idea where Frank was, where he was coming from. He certainly had the wherewithal to call in a team to intercept me. I pressed the elevator button, agonized for a second, then went for the stairs.

I got to the ground floor, huffing and puffing. The lobby was crawling with cops and people in everyday clothes who were most likely one cop for every civilian, too. Exactly as it should be for a police facility. Except it made me look nervously around like a damn perp.

I hated feeling like this. If Frank was the bad guy, then why the hell should I feel like the goddamn criminal? Well, probably Frank was just another version of good guy, was all. . . . Didn't matter, though, in these circumstances. Good guy, bad guy, anything in between—I still couldn't let him get Walter.

I made it out into the street. The sunlight hit my eyes and momentarily blinded me. The colors of the day slowly seeped back into focus. But I realized how vulnerable I was out here, carrying this box with Walter. All the vision in the world wouldn't make me invisible to Frank or anyone else who knew my face.

I looked up and down the street. I could see the subway entrance that could take me to Rachel's lab. There were vault lights on the sidewalk in front of me, thick insets of translucent glass, that stretched all the way to the subway entrance at the end of the block. Architects and city planners loved them. The glass blocks had been tried, on and off, for over a hundred years. But they were especially prized these days. They let daylight into the tunnels. They humanized the profusion of shops and passageways below. Sometimes, if the lighting and angle of scrutiny were right, they would give off a soft, golden glow to people above, on the sidewalk. I clutched Walter's box tightly to my chest, scanned the passersby for anyone suspicious, and hurried along my yellow glass road to the subway.

I ARRIVED AT Rachel's stop without incident. I walked up the stairs, and half-consciously reached for my cell phone—I still reached for my cell phone whenever I climbed out of the subway, a habit from years of no service down there. I wanted to let Rachel know I was coming. But all I had in my pocket were keys and quarters.

When was the last time I had been without a cell phone so long? I couldn't remember. I felt deaf and dumb.

Rachel's lab was in one of several medical examiner "satellite" facilities that had sprung up around the city in the past few years. This one was in a reddish sandstone building that New York University had vacated and sold to the city just six months ago. I had always liked this area around Washington Square Park, but I could have done with just one or two fewer weirdos walking around here today.

NYPD security was outside the building. Good. I nodded. They knew me. I slipped my ID through the sidewalk scanner anyway. I wanted my visit here on record, in case anything happened to me. (Though I realized, as my card came out of the scanning slot, that digital records could be expunged almost as easily as people.)

The sergeant in charge—Del Rios was his name—peered into my box. "Adorable, aren't they? My nephew's been begging for one."

"Yeah." I smiled.

"What are those wires coming out of its head?"

"We're making it look like it came from another planet," I replied. "You know, receiving signals from the mother ship. This guy's gonna wind up at *my* nephew's birthday party tonight."

Del Rios took another look. "Cool."

"By the way, have any FBI or federal people been around here today?" I asked.

Del Rios shook his head. "Not since I got on here, about three hours ago, Dr. D'Amato. You want me to check further?" He gestured to the scanner.

"Nah, not necessary." I said "So long" to Del Rios and entered the building. No sign of Frank or anyone significant. There were a couple of cops chatting by the elevators.

I approached and nodded.

They returned the nods.

An elevator arrived from an upper floor. It was empty.

Two of the cops entered, as did I. "Three, please," I said.

The cop nearest to the buttons complied with my request.

The doors closed, the elevator moved up, and stopped on the third floor. I walked out slowly, looked around, and proceeded to the receptionist.

I announced myself and he pointed down the hall. There was something about his expression that made me uneasy. Maybe it was the box I was carefully carrying. Maybe it was just me.

The door to Rachel's lab was half-closed. I knocked and opened it.

"Hello, Phil."

Frank greeted me with a phony smile.

Two other guys, obviously agents, in dark blue blazers, stood next to Frank. One walked between me and the door. The other patted a bulge in his vest, which I assumed was a weapon. Rachel was seated next to a computer, on the far side of the little lab. She didn't look happy.

"We'll take this off your hands, if you don't mind." Frank took the box, looked inside, and then back at me. "And we'll leave you two to your business. We don't like to intrude on local law-enforcement, you know, except when absolutely necessary."

He and the other two left with a flourish.

"I'm sorry," Rachel spoke up, very upset. "They just barged in here a few minutes ago. I tried to call you on your cell phone, through my computer, and send a text message before those agents realized what I was doing, and I managed to do it, but there was no response from you." She was near tears.

"It's okay," I said.

"But—you had one of those hamsters in that box, right? Agent Catania told me you'd be bringing it, and that you had no authorization. I couldn't care less about authorization, but—you must have gone through unbelievable hoops to get it, and now it's right back in their hands."

"It's okay. Really."

She looked at me.

I reached inside my left jacket pocket and pulled out a small pouch. It was made of unchewable plastic and had holes for air. It contained Walter.

"How—?" Rachel asked, peering through the air holes.

"I passed by a pet shop in the tunnel by my subway stop and realized we could use a little failsafe. So I got Walter—that's his name—all set up in this pouch. I bought another hamster, and talked the owner into making it look like it came from Pluto—told him it was a present for my nephew."

Rachel laughed with relief. "Good job."

I gave her Walter. "I don't know how much time we have before Frank—Agent Catania—catches on. Is there somewhere you can take Walter, relatively safe from fed reach?" No place was totally secure from national intervention, but some were better than others.

Rachel nodded. "This way." She walked to the back of the lab, and a closed door. This one was carded—less sophisticated than the palm-niche; cards were all that the city could afford—but it worked the same. She slid her card through the scanner and opened the door. A flight of narrow stairs spiralled downward behind it.

"We've got a new lab tucked away on the second floor," she explained over her shoulder as we walked carefully down. "There's no entrance from the second floor. I don't think many folks in the building know about it—it just became operational last month."

"Good."

Lights flickered on automatically as we stepped off the stairs. "I made a bunch of calls—did a little research—don't worry, no one I talked to knows what's going on," Rachel continued.

I nodded.

"And I picked up some good acoustic resolution programs on the Web—should help us see what's really going on in Walter's head." She looked at the pouch. "And a nice, comfy cage for him, too. I assume those wires in his head—"

"Yeah, I was told they should hook up and work with any computer. Oh—that reminds me. I've got a program I need to e-mail to you. It's back in a computer in my office. I had to rush out of there so quickly, I forgot . . ."

"Hey, you made it here with Walter, that's what counts," Rachel said.

I smiled. She put Walter and his pouch in a cage and removed the pouch. Walter took in the new scene. He did look comfortable.

I MADE MY way back up the stairs to Rachel's lab on the third floor. The place was quiet. I looked at my watch. It had been nine minutes since Frank had left with the dummy-com hamster. I might have a few minutes before he came back here, angry. Or maybe just a few seconds. I walked out the door.

The hall was empty. A pink exit light glowed at the end of the hall, to the right. I thought it made more sense to walk down the stairs than stand like a sitting duck by the elevator.

The stairs and the lobby to the street were clear. I walked out, once again, into bright sunlight, and was glad to feel it on my face.

I had to get back to my office as fast as possible. The sooner I could get the program to Rachel, the sooner she might have some results. The general stuff she had scored on the Web likely wouldn't be as good, if it worked with Walter at all.

There were other reasons I needed to get back to my desk. I needed to learn what the lab folks had found on my cell phone. For that matter, I needed to be in touch. Deprived of my cell, I once again looked at my office as a source of crucial information. Just like the good old days.

The subway ride was quick. A woman got on with two little boys at the stop before mine. They were all excited about some white mice they had in a colorful cage. I smiled at them. But it bothered me. . . .

My desk phone was pulsing with waiting messages when I arrived at my office. The first was from my lab. "One set of useable fingerprints, three good samples of DNA," the voice mail said. This difference was not surprising. A useful bit of DNA—one capable of generating a good ID—was far easier to obtain from most handled objects than a complete or unblurred fingerprint. "The fingerprint and one of the DNAs was yours," the message concluded. "We're running full-bore searches on the rest."

Hmm . . . that meant that most likely Frank had not touched my phone—there had to be lots of records of his DNA and fingerprints in federal files. On the other hand, Frank and his people might well have access to those files—maybe they inserted bogus DNA profiles and fingerprints. Other hands, other hands. They went hand in hand these days with fingerprint and DNA IDs that were only as good as the digital, crackable records the IDs relied upon.

The next message on my voice mail, and the one that followed, were less amenable to alternate interpretations. Dugan, annoyed, wanted me in his office right away. So much so, he left two messages about it.

Then my phone rang.

"Phil," Dugan said, not livid but even more irritated live than on the voice mail, "nice of you to finally pick up a phone."

I started to explain why I had been away from my cell phone—

"Save it for later," he interrupted. "Frank Catania wants to see us—in my office."

Dugan hadn't said that in his messages, but I wasn't surprised. And better that than having Frank go after Rachel. "What time?"

"Ten minutes ago," Dugan replied. "I doubt he'll stay around much longer, and I'd rather we all came to some sort of accommodation in my office."

I reminded Dugan that I had some concerns about Frank—

"I'm not aggravated that Frank's fuming about you," Dugan broke in. "I'm used to people fuming about you. I just can't believe that you'd allow yourself to be out of phone contact for so long."

"All right, I'm on my way."

I TOOK THE additional minutes, anyway, to e-mail Temp's program to Rachel and retrieve my cell phone.

"You identify any more of the prints or DNA?" I asked the technician, Manny Motolo.

"Not yet, but I've seen some of these searches take days, weeks even. Some DNA samples in some places, even here in the States, are still off-line. Some DNA is still just in the people, and stored nowhere. That's why we need a national DNA card."

I nodded—a succinct presentation of one side of a nasty debate—one of several debates with a side I still had not fully chosen. Everyone's DNA in some national archive, matchable to DNA embedded and scannable on a card? Government access to everyone's potential for whatever genetic tic? Would that be worth the chance to stop the ticking bomb of a terrorist? "*Video meliora proboque deteriora sequor,*" Temp had said. I see the good things, but I do the bad things. Maybe my problem was that I saw too many bad things—too many bad things in the government's attempt to do a good thing. "Well, you know where to reach me as soon as you find anything else," I told Manny. "Either here"—I pointed to my cell phone—"or my office."

"Sure thing, Doc."

I ran down the stairs and put up the "Missed Calls and Messages" menu on my cell phone screen.

Well, Dugan had certainly been telling the truth about trying to reach me. The screen showed five calls from his office, interspersed with one from Jenna, one from Mel, and—

I scrolled back to the Dugan screen. His last call, I realized, had just come in four minutes ago. He'd tried to reach me on the cell after our conversation in my office? Yeah, that would make sense—I hadn't been able to finish telling him that I'd been separated from my cell phone.

I stepped into the light and the street and returned Dugan's call. Dammit—circuits busy. No matter how many new satellites they put up, the circuits were still busy way too often down here, usually at times you needed them most. Murphy's Law, Cell Phone Version: the more urgent the call, the more likely it won't go through.

I looked at my watch and hailed a cab. "The New Muni Building," I told the cabbie. She had a great head of thick blond hair.

I tried Dugan two more times. The circuits were still busy.

The cab pulled up to the stout building, about half a block from City Hall. "Keep the change," I told golden mane. I got rewarded with a hair flip and a smile.

The first thing I noticed when I stepped out of the cab was a squirrel. This one just looked right at me, with a noncommittal air, and stood its ground. I still knew next to nothing about how squirrels figured into this—other than that some had died, and most of the people in this case professed no knowledge of squirrel telecom—

My cell phone rang.

Ah, Dugan. "Jack, sorry I've been so hard to reach. I'll be right up—I'm downstairs."

"Phil—"

Now my incoming beeped. I looked at the screen. Rachel.

"Hold on, Jack." I put him on hold and switched to Rachel.

"Phil—"

I heard her voice—then an explosion.

"Are you okay?" I started to say, but then I realized the cell phone was no longer in my hand, and I was no longer standing, and the explosion was not there but right here. . . .

I hit the ground, painfully . . . and as the lights started dimming and the cell phone skittered away from me on the sidewalk, I thought, damn, this has been one hard day for phone calls. . . .

THIRTEEN

I don't believe I ever fully lost consciousness. Not completely . . .

Rather, my connection to the world, my view of it, tore into at least half a dozen pieces, each of which slowly drifted apart, leaving . . . gaping holes of blueness in between. . . .

The content of the slices themselves changed . . . smoke, people, noise. They were difficult to follow, though, because there was so much empty space around them.

They finally began reassembling in the ambulance. Out of the noise, I heard "mild concussion . . . minor lacerations . . . you'll be fine, Dr. D'Amato."

Jenna was waiting for me at the hospital, St. Vincent's, in the Village.

"What happened? How is Dugan?" I asked her.

"I don't know about Jack. Several people were killed in the street. That's where the bomb went off." She started to cry.

I reached out to comfort her—

"You'll have to step aside, ma'am, and give us some room," an orderly's voice boomed out.

"I'm okay," I replied, and tried to get off the cart. I had to admit that my head did hurt.

"Just let the docs here have a look at you," a softer voice

said, a woman's, maybe the voice from the ambulance. "They'll be here soon."

I nodded. I turned to Jenna and took her hand. No one said anything more about her stepping aside, so I left it at that.

THE MDs EXAMINED me and concurred that my concussion was not serious. But they wanted me admitted for overnight observation anyway, just to be safe. I reluctantly agreed, after wringing out their assurance that Jenna could stay with me.

An orderly gave me an update on the damage in front of the New Municipal Building as he wheeled me to my room.

Forty-two people, including me, had been hurt. Three had indeed died. The orderly thought he heard that one had been a cop. Jenna gasped.

She tried Jack on her cell phone, but there was no answer at any of his numbers.

I closed my eyes, and she went down the hall to get me a ginger ale or a reasonable facsimile.

The door opened.

"I'm glad you're all right, Phil."

I opened my eyes. "You, too!"

Jack Dugan smiled, but he looked awful.

Jenna walked in, carrying a can of ginger ale. "Jack!" she said, delightedly. She put down the can and flung her arms around him.

He managed to hug her, but he looked so tired.

"Have a seat," I said, and propped myself up.

He plopped down like a limb sawed off a tree.

"How about some ginger ale?" I asked him.

"No, thanks," he said.

Jenna opened the can and poured some in a cup.

"So, what the hell happened back there?" I asked.

He breathed out slowly, then shook his head. "They got Frank," he finally said. "They got Frank."

"What?"

"The damn bomb practically blew up in his face. He was killed instantly. I just ID'd his body."

A KILLING CAN be cleansing, clarifying, in a situation with too many suspects and halftones. Unless the attack had nothing to do with this case, which I didn't believe for an instant, Frank's death likely meant he was not one of the bad guys. Through the pain and the emptiness of losing someone I had known—I wasn't sure exactly how, somewhere between a colleague and a friend, with a little antagonist thrown in—a part of me was strangely grateful for that subtraction. It felt good to know that law enforcement, or at least Frank's, had likely been on the side of the angels, after all, in this one. It was good to know that about Frank, even though it made me feel worse about his murder, lousy that I ever doubted him, though he had given me ample reason. . . . I ran through some of our conversations. . . . There was something he had told me on the train to Wilmington, something that had relevance—no, not exactly to what had happened tonight, but to something much worse . . . Something else that Deborah Paton had told me, too . . . I had some of the pieces, but there was still too much blue, blackness, between them. . . .

I opened my eyes. Jack had left—depleted, exhausted—a while ago. Jenna was now in a chair, dozing. Her face was creased with concern, even in sleep. I wanted to go over to her, cradle her head in my arms. I carefully stepped out of bed—

"Hi." Jenna looked at me and smiled. I guess she hadn't been sleeping deeply. She rose, came over to me, and we held each other.

I sat back down on my bed. She joined me.

"How long was I napping?" I asked her.

She looked at her watch. "About forty-five minutes."

"What time is it?"

"About a quarter past midnight."

"Hell of a day," I said.

She didn't answer. She just looked at me. "I'm glad you're alive."

I squeezed her hand. In times past, her reaction would have meant: You've got to get out of this business. How can we build a life together when you're constantly in danger?

But now her reaction meant something else. She fully understood that everyone was in this business nowadays—that just to be here on this Earth, certainly here in this city, meant your life was in danger.

I sighed. "I haven't spoken with Rachel Saldana since before . . . the explosion," I said. "Maybe she tried me on my cell phone, but God knows what happened to that."

"Try your office," Jenna said, and handed me her cell phone.

I did. And Rachel had indeed left a brief message for me there. "I left a longer message on your cell phone," she said, "so I'm leaving this, as a pointer. So far, so good, about Frank Catania—no one has interrupted my work here. And Walter seems to be the real thing. I hooked him up, installed the program you e-mailed, and I'm hearing some very interesting things—more than just overheard conversation. Give me a call here"—she gave what I assumed was a number in the private lab—"as soon as you get this. I should be around until at least ten this evening—I had a big lunch."

I listened to the date stamp on my voice mail. She had left the message shortly after we had been disconnected in front of Dugan's building—by the explosion. She had had no knowledge of the explosion then, and what it did to Frank.

I tried the number she had left, even though it was way past ten. No answer, not even voice mail. I guess that made sense, as a precaution against hackers.

I looked at Jenna and smiled weakly.

"No luck?" she asked.

I shook my head no.

She put her head on my shoulder. I leaned over and kissed her.

"Why don't we get out of here," I said. "We can get a better night's sleep at home."

"I guess this is the time for me to say the obligatory, 'Doesn't it make more sense for you to stay here, as the doctors asked, so they can check you out in the morning, just to be sure?' "

"Consider it said," I replied. "But you didn't really seem to have your heart in it, anyway."

She snorted, shook her head, smiled crookedly. "I don't like hospitals—what can I say?"

"I hate 'em," I said.

"You sure you're okay?" she asked.

"Yeah."

She helped me dress. I was able to walk to the elevator with no problem. I didn't feel great, but my head was clear.

I filled out the necessary forms—including the one that said the hospital had no liability if I dropped dead—and left, over the resident doctor's strenuous objection.

"I understand," I said for the tenth time. "But there's an extremely important, ongoing case that needs my attention." And we left. One advantage, at least, of being in my line of work.

We got back home, took off our clothes, quickly showered, and got into bed. We were so tired that all we did was fall promptly asleep in each other's arms.

I DREAMED I was back in the hospital. Actually, it was not the hospital I had just been in, some other part of my brain reasoned/realized, because usually experiences are not incorporated that quickly into dreams, right? I could overhear some people talking. One of them sounded like Frank, or Jack, or Temp, I couldn't be sure. He was saying, *Let's put both the hamster* and *the squirrel module into his brain. It's big enough to accommodate both—big in size, not necessarily intelligence.* . . . Someone objected. Good—at least someone was on my side! *Forget about the telecom module,* the new voice said, a voice I could not identify. *Just put a bomb into that muddled head of his, that'll clear things out—*

The phone rang.

It was morning.

Jenna was sleeping, face against my chest.

I reached gently over her for the phone.

"Hello," I said very softly. Jenna stirred a bit anyway.

"Phil, that you?"

"Yeah . . ."

"It's Rachel. I saw on Caller ID that you tried to reach me last night from the hospital, and I tried to get you there now, but they said you left last night—against doctor's orders—and so I used my best departmental bravura to pry your home number from them. . . . Are you okay?"

"Sure—"

"Is it okay that I called you at home? It's important."

It did feel a little . . . unusual . . . having a conversation with a colleague—an attractive woman, at that, with a warm contralto voice—with me stretched out naked, and Jenna the same, her head on my chest, and now she was waking up, and beginning to stroke my abdomen. . . .

But I needed to talk to Rachel. "Sure," I told her. "It's okay. Go ahead." I put my hand over Jenna's, much as I hated to halt what she was doing. She looked at me, surprised, and saw

I was on the phone. She flicked her tongue across my chest, patted it, and pulled away.

"—two kinds of data," Rachel was saying. "Most is like streaming audio—a live rendition of what Walter is hearing—like in the demo they gave you in the Grace Building. But there's something else. Part of it is garbled, so I can't be sure, but it sounds like some other voices. . . ."

"You mean, voices not in the room with you and Walter?" I asked, just managing to get my concentration back.

"Right, I did this alone. I set most of it up—the wires and the computer program you e-mailed to me—yesterday. I thought I heard the voices then. But I was really exhausted—at that point, with all the excitement, then all the adrenaline ebbing, I wasn't sure what I was hearing. But I checked and rechecked everything this morning. There are definitely some voices there."

"You sure they're not some . . . concoction of the computer program?" I still had little trust in Temp, or whoever it really was who sent me the program.

"I'm not sure of anything." Rachel still sounded exhausted.

"Whose voices are they?" I asked.

"I don't know that, either. One sounds a little familiar. I thought maybe you might have some idea."

"I'll be right down. You in your second-floor office?"

"Yeah."

I hung up the phone.

I looked over at Jenna. She was on her tummy and seemed to have drifted back to sleep.

I ran my fingers down her back.

She turned over, put her hands around my neck, and kissed me.

"Sounds like you have to go," she murmured.

Most of the time—almost all of the time—when she said

this, we both knew I would say "Yeah," and then scoop her even closer, and then—

But this time, today, we both knew I couldn't contest what she had said.

Jenna turned back on her side.

I settled for a small pat and got out of bed.

"How's your head, from yesterday?" Jenna asked as I quickly dressed.

"So far, so good. I'll call you later."

I GOT INTO Rachel's secret place with no problem.

"You hear the Secretary of Homeland Security and his address to the Press Club last week?" she asked me.

"Machem's? No." I didn't particularly like Julius Machem—not the policies, not the man. I had met him at a forensic convention in Washington about six months ago, and he seemed more interested in his image—how he was regarded by police departments around the country—than what was actually being accomplished. On the other hand, I hated to be too critical of him, even to myself. His job was thankless. Short of eliminating all terrorism—not likely to happen anytime soon—there was nothing he or anyone could do to make everyone safe, all of the time. . . .

"He said we need to strike a balance between protecting lives and protecting freedoms. Wait until you hear this stuff." Rachel pointed to the computers; Walter was hooked up to one of them. "This is gonna move the balance *way* away from freedoms."

She explained, again, about the two types of readings. "Here's what they demo'ed for you at the Grace Building, right?" She worked the keyboard.

"Here's what they demo'ed for you at the Grace Building, right?" the computer spoke out, in what I now recognized as hamster-speak.

"Yes, that's it," I said.

"Okay, now listen to this."

I looked at what she was doing on the computer—she seemed to be accessing a different part of the program.

"You hear the Secretary of Homeland Security and his address to the Press Club last week?" the computer asked, in hamster-voice.

"Interesting," I said. "So the module has a bit of memory."

Rachel nodded. "More than a little." She did something else to the computer.

I looked at Walter. He seemed, as always, as happy as a clam—or hamster.

"The goddamn Secretary may be wimping out on us," Walter's voice spoke up. Except, of course, it was a recording, a hamster replay, of someone else's. Not Rachel's. Not mine.

"Jeez, that's Frank," I said.

She stopped the recording. "I thought it might be."

"So the hamster telecom gets not only what it just heard, but what's been stored in its brain," I mused.

"Yes."

"When was that—Frank's voice—heard by Walter?" I asked.

"I can't tell yet," Rachel replied. "There may be some way to sort Walter's acoustic memories by date—by time first experienced—but I haven't been able to find it on the levels of the program I've been using. But I can see there's much more to the program."

"Well, we know for sure that Frank didn't say this today, or anytime after yesterday afternoon—" I suddenly realized that Rachel might not have heard about Frank.

I asked her; she had not; I told her.

The color abandoned her face, stranding the slight bit of rouge she had on.

"What the hell's going on here, Phil?" She pointed to a

copy of *The New York Times.* The explosion was all over the front page, but with apparently no mention of Frank.

I shook my head. “That’s what we’re trying to find out.”

Rachel breathed slowly and composed herself. “There’s more on the recording,” she said.

“Let’s hear it.”

“The goddamn Secretary may be wimping out on us,” Frank/Walter said again.

Then, “What should we do about that?” another voice asked. It was a woman’s.

“Can I hear that again?”

Rachel obliged.

The voice was Jill Cormier’s.

I DECIDED TO tell Rachel everything about this case that I hadn’t already told her. For all I knew (as always), she could be part of the problem—in league with Jill or Frank’s people or who-knew-whose people who were behind the worst of this. But also (as always), I had to trust someone. I needed another set of eyes and ears and brains—yeah, I’d take someone with two brains, or certainly two Rachels, if I could, at this point.

And if it turned out I was mistaken about Rachel . . . well, I’d know where to look if the bad guys, the bombers, whoever was behind this started acting on knowledge that only Rachel had, via me . . . assuming those actions hadn’t killed me.

“So the evidence is mixed about Jill’s connection to Frank,” Rachel remarked.

“Well, up until this recording, the gist was going against the two being on the same side, which is the way they seemed at the beginning,” I responded.

“But we can’t date the conversation yet. So, conceivably, it could have been heard by Walter—in the Grace Building, I’d assume—at a time when Frank and Jill were still partners, or at least pretending to be.”

"Yeah," I agreed.

"You want to hear more of the recording? There's not much more. Should we tell Ed on First Avenue? Are you going to tell Dugan?"

Lots of questions—I was immediately prepared to say yes to just the opener. But I didn't blame Rachel for feeling overwhelmed. "I'd say there's no rush to tell either Ed"—the chief medical examiner's office was at Thirtieth and First—"or Jack, until we learn a little more. You comfortable with that?"

She looked at me. "You don't think either of them is involved in this?"

"No. I don't. Certainly not Jack, and I've never seen anything untoward out of Ed. It's just really normal procedure, for me, whenever someone on our side—in law enforcement—gets killed, and there's any chance at all that the bullets or bomb or whatever came from someone on our side."

"Okay."

"But let's hear the rest of Walter's brain."

"I'll play it from the beginning." Rachel touched the keys.

"The goddamn Secretary may be wimping out on us," Frank/Walter said, once again.

"What should we do about that?" Jill/hamster repeated.

"Nothing, yet," Frank/Walter replied.

"How far along is the hologram?" Jill/hamster inquired.

"Not far enough. The impersonation holograms take a lot of work—it's easier to do composites."

Jill/hamster sighed.

The thin sound of her "voice" gave me the chills.

"What are our other options?" Jill/hamster finally said.

"Other than—"

Frank's voice via Walter the hamster was interrupted by a ringing sound, more like an old-fashioned phone than a cell phone, but who knew how that sound played through a hamster?

Rachel cut in. "That's it. I haven't been able to access any more."

I pondered.

Rachel asked: "That stuff about the composite hologram—that was alluding to a hologram like Temp, the one you told me about?"

"Yeah, probably."

"And the impersonation hologram was like the one you saw of yourself—which you thought they were still working on. So the question is, has that level of hologram been perfected?

"Yes, that's the question. It would be very good to know when that little conversation took place."

FOURTEEN

Rachel and I caught a late breakfast in the Scrambled Book down the street—a small bookstore which sold made-to-order, print-on-demand compilations of stories and articles, and featured a little cafe that served only breakfast all day.

"I didn't realize how famished I was," Rachel said, and lit into her eggs-over-easy. "I was so in a rush to get to the lab that I barely had time for coffee."

"Me, too," I said. "Except for me, it was tea."

The waiter put down my toasted bagel with cream cheese. Then Rachel's mocha. Then my vanilla-almond tea.

"Thanks," I told him.

Rachel looked very content with her eggs and coffee. She had a bit of egg on her upper lip. But I didn't say anything, because it sort of looked nice.

"I don't know much about you personally," I said.

She smiled. "Not married. Not yet. Long-term boyfriend."

I munched on my bagel. "Well, that's good."

"Who knows?" Rachel said. "He's not too thrilled about my work. He likes my ass in bed with him in the morning, rather than my rushing it down here."

"You don't usually get up so early, do you?"

"No, but he tends to sleep late."

"And he's . . ."

"A writer," Rachel said.

"Ah."

"He has a lot of talent, but . . ."

I nodded understandingly.

"I met your wife once, at a Department party, right?" Rachel asked.

"I'm not sure," I replied honestly.

"Jennifer?"

"Jenna, right."

"Yeah."

"So let's get back to what we were saying about the case," I said.

"Okay."

"I guess the main thing we need to figure out is who the hell gave me Walter—who was acting through Temp," I said.

"Well, we know it wasn't Frank. Because, first of all, he tried to snatch the hamster back, and, second, now we know why—Walter overheard him and Cormier."

"Right."

"So the real question is, who's directing Temp? And your hologram in Wilmington, too, for that matter. That's been your question all along, right?"

I put my nose in my almost-empty teacup. The aroma was great. "Frank set up that whole subterranean meeting in the first place. He must have had something in mind."

"What? To introduce you to a hologram who eventually would give you a hamster who would reveal Frank's conspiring against the Secretary of his own damn agency?"

"No," I said. "The only way this makes any sense is Temp in Wilmington is not the same as Temp in Grace."

"You said they looked and sounded the same."

"Yes," I acknowledged, "but that's just superficial—external sensory impression. Says nothing about who programmed Temp the second time—who talked to me in that little room on the fortieth floor of the Grace Building—who sent me that e-mail with the marvelous program attachment that lets you access Walter's history."

"Who could that be?" Rachel asked. "Jill Cormier? She was up there in Grace with you and Frank when you first heard the magic hamsters, but she sure didn't come out sounding any sweeter than Frank on this recording."

"No," I agreed, "she didn't. I don't know . . . Who's left? That Paton woman?"

"The tightass?"

"Yeah. And Marty Glick," I added.

"You never got a chance to verify that he wasn't a hologram," Rachel considered.

"I don't think he really is," I said. "Too much work on too short notice—actually, no notice—would have been required at Henry's, the restaurant."

"But if by some crazy chance he is, then that would show that the impersonation holograms have been perfected, at least to your satisfaction in the lab and then the restaurant. And the other people at Glick's table—either they were holograms, too, or flesh-and-blood people who were going along with the Glick impersonation."

"Yes—though I didn't know Glick beforehand, so, conceivably, he could be a hologramic composite—and not an impersonation—himself."

Rachel finished her eggs and the last of her coffee. She wiped her lips with a napkin and erased the little egg smudge. She looked less happy than when she had started her breakfast.

I squeezed her hand and let go. "There, at least we know that we're both real, right?" I said. "Let's get back to hamster angle. I was wondering, coming down on the subway today, do you think hamsters could live on their own down there? You know, like what you sometimes hear about alligators . . . I know you're not a veterinarian, but . . ."

"I doubt it," she said. "My father once told me about a vole that made a nest under the hood of a Chevy station wagon that was parked in the driveway all winter, but as far as the subways go, I'd guess it was all rats and mice." She made a slight face.

"You don't like rats and mice?"

"They're boring . . . Anyway, what good would hamsters like Walter be in the subway? All they'd be likely to pick up was noise."

"Yeah . . . All right, why don't you go back to your lab and see what more you can pry out of Walter's brain. Maybe I'll track down Glick and shake his hand."

Rachel smiled. "Okay."

"And about Ed," I said. "You might as well write him a little e-mail about all of this, with a delayed send date of tomorrow at this time, and we can reevaluate the situation then. I'm going to do the same with Dugan." I tried to say this as nonchalantly as possible.

But Rachel understood its thrust just perfectly. "In case we don't make it to tomorrow, huh?"

I shook my head slowly. "I guess you're sorry I ever drew you into this."

"No, I'm not." She shook her head, too. "Getting into this is what the City of New York pays me for."

I STOPPED BY the Highrizon shop down the street to get a new cell phone. I had decided, just to be on the safe side, to get the new phone on my own and bill the Department, just in case someone had an idea—NYPD or fed—to put a bug in whatever phone I might request through NYPD channels.

I explained to the sales help—pert blonde who seemed pretty sharp—that I needed my old number automatically converted to the new number so that no one who called the old number would notice the difference, and any calls that I had received but not answered on my old number in the past day would be stacked up and waiting for me on my new phone.

"No problem," she assured me. "Just fill out this form and we'll have your new phone all set to go, just the way you want it, in five minutes."

"Thank you." I took the form she gave me. It was a paper-thin computer screen. I filled in all the relevant details, including my crucial authorization code, that only I and Jenna knew. It was an anagram of my grandmother's maiden name, with a few arbitrary numbers thrown in.

Blondie was as good as her word. I had my new phone in hand in five minutes. I thanked her and left. My authorization code would also automatically deduct the cost from my account.

I stopped outside, leaned against a brick building, and looked at my new phone for waiting messages and missed calls. These would have been the ones which came in after the explosion yesterday.

I didn't know exactly what I was expecting. Nothing from Dugan, because he probably still thought I was in the hospital. There was just one missed call and one message, from the same person: Mel. Come to think of it, he had tried to contact me yesterday—maybe my attempt to call him at Beth Israel had registered on some kind of voice mail, after all, and he was returning the call.

I listened to the message. Excellent news—he was doing so well, the hospital had sent him home this morning. He left me his number.

I reached him on one ring. "Mel. How are you feeling?"

"Phil! I'm fine. I've been trying to reach you."

"I know," I said. "Sorry I've taken so long to get back to you—we had a little explosion yesterday—"

"You okay?"

"Sure."

"Good . . . anyway, I wanted to talk to you about something. . . ."

"Absolutely," I said.

"Well, I've been feeling bad about something I left out of our conversation, and especially after the beating I got, and then decked out in the hospital . . ."

"Mel, you know, while you were in the hospital, I was thinking . . . Your club is really nice, and I was wondering if you might like a little investment—you know, a little influx of capital, to help with The Grace Note. We wouldn't be partners or anything. We could work out repayment later—"

"Wow, that's really out of left field, Phil."

"I know, but—"

"I'm fine, Phil, really. Like I told you, I'm doing all right, financially."

I told him what McQuail had told me.

Mel didn't reply.

"How much do you owe them?" I finally asked.

"Fifty thousand."

"All right, look, we need to think of both immediate and long-term strategies on this," I said. "As an immediate strategy, I'm going to give you a couple of thousand—that way you can make your payment. And we'll figure out something long term." This was the safest course for Mel. If McQuail brought in Mel's bookies, there would still be people above them who would come after Mel. The Russian mob had a deep grip on parts of this city.

"I hate to have you do this, Phil."

"I know. But, hey, how many friends do I still have from way back in Junior High School, and how many can tell me what I need to know about hamsters? I'll have Jenna call you right after we get off—you just give her your bank account number, and we'll transfer the money to you right away. I wish it could be more."

"I really appreciate this, Phil."

"It's okay."

"Look, about the hamsters . . . that's why I was calling . . . I guess I should have told you when you came down to The Grace Note—but I didn't want you to think I was some sort of nutcase. Anyway, there's been a long-standing, I don't know, rumor about hamsters, that there's something strange about some of them."

"Long-standing?" If the rumor had been around long, it likely had nothing to do with what I was investigating.

"Yeah—I first heard it, if I recall, when I first was getting into hamsters—when you and I were friends in school, way back when." Mel chuckled a little.

"Okay, and what was the rumor?" I asked.

"Well, it's just a rumor," Mel replied, "but I wanted to let you know about it. It's that hamsters have something to do with outer space."

"What?"

"I know. It's nuts. I've never seen any evidence of this myself, but I wanted you to know," Mel said sincerely.

"You mean, like, they took hamsters aboard some of the early space satellites?" I tried to recall if I'd ever come across anything like that. What the hell did the Russians have in Sputnik 2? Dogs—or one dog, Laika, I couldn't recall—but I didn't think hamsters . . .

"No," Mel said. "The rumors have been around longer than that. I don't know. I can look into it some more, if you like."

I didn't know what to say.

"Phil?"

"Sure, that would be great, if you could look into that for me, Mel. But most of all, I want you to try to get more rest now, okay?"

"You think I'm crazy, right? That's why I didn't mention this in the first place. It's just that, in the hospital, facing my own mortality, I felt I didn't want to keep anything from you—"

"No, no. You were absolutely right to tell me, and I don't think you're crazy," I lied, I hoped convincingly. "So let me know what you find out. But first, I'll have Jenna call you about the fund transfer."

"Yeah, thanks, that would be good, thanks," Mel said.

I pressed "End" on my cell phone and pulled it away from my face. I felt like crying. Either Mel had been crazier than I'd realized all along, or the trauma of his beating had unhinged him. . . .

I called Jenna and told her about Mel. She didn't object to the "investment" in The Grace Note, though I knew she couldn't have been happy about it, given everyone's financial uncertainties these days, including the NYPD's. But she had a generous soul.

I put the phone in my pocket, shook my head about Mel and outer space, and headed for the subway.

HEARING A BIT of the really insane could make the merely insane, the mundane everyday insane I was struggling with, seem a bit less insane, and thus more amenable to solution or remedy. At least, that's what I told myself.

I walked toward the Lexington Avenue line. . . .

There had been one thing I had been wrong about, too categorical about, in my conversation with Mel, I realized. Not what I had actually said to him, but what I had thought. About long-standing rumors and information. It could have relevance. It was stupid to ignore a development just because it wasn't recent, wasn't staring me in the face. I recalled what I had been thinking about in the hospital last night. Frank had told me, on the train north of Philadelphia, that mice had been the first animals to undergo telecom enhancement. Paton had told me, in Gnarlingview, that rats had been the first rodents to be remotely controlled. Mice and rats . . .

I walked down the old stone stairs to the station and the tracks. I didn't see anything but rails, dirty and gleaming, here, but I knew that mice and rats were all over the subway tunnels, in the stations, too. I'd read just a few months ago about an outraged Port Authority official who had her lunch disrupted by a mouse on the floor on a posh new restaurant in Penn Station—but I hadn't seen a hair of them in either Cerebreeze or the Grace facilities. Hard to believe that the government would phase them out completely—hell, I'd seen manual typewriters in government offices as late as the mid-1980s. . . .

I thought about calling Dugan. No, as reasonable as he was being about all of this, he'd balk if I asked him to start rounding up mice and rats in the subways for CATscans. He'd want evidence first. Evidence to get evidence . . .

Grace was the only place I could think of that might have it now. I hopped on a train.

I SPRINTED UP stairs from the subway, through bustling corridors, into the luminous center of Grand Central Terminal. I paused twice, this time, and looked up at its ceiling sky. It reminded me today of a robin's egg. I shuddered. It could crack as easily. For all that Jacqueline Kennedy had worked to save it from the bulldozers those decades ago, it could shatter, just like that, from a terrorist's bomb. I had confidence that our cops would be on any unattended package. I believed we even had a fair chance of stopping a suicide bomber. But those might not be the conduits of the deepest threats. . . .

I walked out into the street, toward the Grace. Maybe I'd get lucky in that cutaway tower. Twining diamonds of daylight played off its face—in what code were they talking?

I entered the lobby for the third time in as many days. My

mustachioed friend was not at the security post. In his place were a bank of computer screens and a recorded announcement.

"Step right up to a screen and state your business," the announcement requested blandly. "We'll advise you how to proceed."

This was an odd security arrangement. I didn't see any gate or other obstacle to people proceeding as they pleased, without announcing their business.

A harried woman dressed in a business suit apparently had the same idea. She rushed past me and the screens and the announcement—

Whoosh! Four sides of Plexiglas shot up from the floor and encased her.

"Goddamn it!" she shouted. "I'm late for an appointment. My client is waiting to see me!"

"Ms. Tredwell. Cynthia P. Tredwell, attorney-at-law," the announcement-voice stated.

I noticed that her image was now on every computer screen.

"Yes, yes," she said. "Now let me out of here or I'll sue the shit out of you!"

"You may proceed with your business," the voice said, still blandly. "Next time, please follow our instructions."

The Plexiglas plates retracted.

Ms. Tredwell continued cursing under her breath, then turned and elegantly lifted her slender middle finger to no one and everyone, including me.

I smiled. Well, I was not a completely inappropriate recipient. I was, after all, part of law enforcement, and from Ms. Tredwell's perspective, part of the problem.

She caught my gaze and shook her head. "I'm out of here, out of here, after the spring," she said to me, everyone, no one. "I can't take this anymore. I'll start a practice in northern

Maine if I have to. I'd rather have moose for clients than go through this." She turned around again and proceeded to the elevators, heels clacking loudly on the lobby's marble floor.

But there was obviously more in the floor today than just marble.

What had they done? Rigged the floors with instantly emerging and retracting "smart" cages overnight? I had heard that such security features were in the works, but this was the first I had ever seen one in action.

I looked at the screens ahead and considered. No reason I should fare any better than the harried Tredwell if I tried to run the gauntlet.

I approached a computer and said, "Dr. Phil D'Amato, forensic investigator, NYPD," and displayed my ID.

I assumed there was a camera and microphone picking up and relaying all of this. I looked for a slot to insert my ID for proper scanning. I saw none.

It wasn't required.

"Thank you, Dr. D'Amato," the bland voice spoke. "Identification authenticated. Please state your business."

"I need to interview someone on the fortieth floor," I said.

"Whom?"

I detested playing chess with computers, but I had no choice here. "I don't know her name." Dammit, what was the name of that nearly all-red secretary? I couldn't recall—I wasn't sure I had ever seen or been told it.

The computer hadn't replied. I took advantage of the silence. "She'll know who I am," I offered. "I was here yesterday. I didn't get her name."

"Just a second, Dr. D'Amato. We'll have a response to your request."

"Okay."

I glanced at the screens. They were blank.

"Authorization to proceed denied," the voice said. "We

suggest you seek such authorization from your superior."

"May I ask why . . . why authorization to proceed is denied?"

"We have no record of any appointment by you with anyone in this building."

"Of course not," I said. "I'm conducting an investigation. You expect me to make appointments with possible suspects?" I didn't think the secretary was a suspect, but I thought it was a good point.

The bland voice was not persuaded. "We have no record of any investigation in, with, by, or otherwise relating to your name as an investigator, Dr. D'Amato. We suggest you consult with your superior."

I mulled over what to say next.

"Dr. D'Amato, we are now requesting that you leave this building. People without authorization to enter are requested to leave within sixty seconds of denial of their request to enter."

I glared stupidly at the screen and turned to leave. I didn't need a scene. I needed to get to the fortieth floor.

I WALKED OUT of the Grace.

Jack was my best chance of getting there. I walked and thought for a bit. Maybe I should go see him in his office. I had lots I needed to tell him about—not only my concerns about mice and rats, but what Rachel and I had heard in Walter. . . . I looked back at the Grace. It almost looked like mother of pearl from this angle. . . . I took out my cell phone—

I got a "circuits busy." Of course. I tried again. And—

In the corner of my eye, in the periphery of my vision, was an irritant, a grain of sand. Actually, two grains of sand, two heads of hair, moving quickly toward me on the other side of Fifth Avenue.

Marty Glick and . . . jeez, that was Jill beside him.

Were holograms capable of precise projection across the

expanse of Forty-second Street? Highly unlikely. It would take a huge, hidden projection device on top of the Grace Building to do it—a glowing Masonic eye, like the one on the back of the dollar bill. Not much would surprise me anymore about that building, but for whose benefit would a hologram of Glick now be projected?

Glick was real.

I became aware of the "circuits-busy buzzing" like a monotonous bee in my phone. I ended the attempted call.

Glick and Jill were now beginning to cross Fifth Avenue. Maybe there was a way I could parlay this into a ticket to the fortieth floor.

FIFTEEN

I figured Glick and Jill would be heading to the Grace Building.

I was wrong.

As soon as they got to the west side of Fifth Avenue, the light changed, they turned—and walked across Forty-second Street . . . up the stairs, past the two stoic lions, into the New York Public Library.

I followed; I hurried up the library stairs.

What were Glick and Jill doing here? Not fetching a pail of water.

Maybe something to do with the canine bomb scare the day before?

Or maybe they were taking an underground passageway from here to the Grace Building?

Glick and Jill approached the first security station. Dugan and I had breezed through here on the strength of his face. I couldn't see, from my vantage point, what Glick and Jill were showing or saying to the guard. They had no law-enforcement ID, as far as I knew. But whatever they said, worked. The guard waved them through.

Well, I was glad, at least, to negotiate with human security rather than what they had now at the Grace. But should I question the guard about why he had let them through, and where they were going?

I decided to err on the side of caution. No telling whom the guard might contact in response to my questions after I left. I walked up and showed him my ID. He nodded perfunctorily and let me through.

This was the problem with human security. He probably should have been tougher, at least with me—who knew what connections and authority Glick and Jill really had?—certainly so soon after the dog-bomb scare. But there were only so many sharp security people to go around, and the NYPD was already stretched razor-thin. So the alternative was that damned cybergestapo over at Grace. I shivered, and kept pace with Glick and Jill.

They, and then I, went through one more of the security posts Dugan and I had gone through, and then Glick and Jill took another unexpected turn. I followed. They had entered a room marked RARE BOOKS, NINETEENTH-CENTURY NEW YORK on the door.

I opened the door very slowly. This was dangerous—Glick and Jill could have been standing right inside. But I had no other option.

The room was musty and deserted—just what you would expect of a rare books room—with the exception of two old gents, poring over books, writing, sitting at two separate desks. Neither so much as lifted an eyebrow in response to my presence. This meant they either (a) hadn't seen or heard Glick and Jill, or (b) were working very hard to give that impression.

I looked at one, then the other, very carefully. I honestly couldn't tell whether they were insensate or faking. They were dressed in Paton/Temp grey. For all I could tell, they, this whole scene, were another hologram.

I walked around the sides of the room, and peered around stacks of books. I finally noticed a door in a corner—

"May I help you?" One of the pen-and-ink gents, suddenly

come to life, surprised me with the question. He was standing right behind me.

"Well, I was wondering what was beyond that door," I said, and pointed.

"Do you have authorization?" The gent's partner now also sprang to action, looked at me questioningly.

"Don't be deluded by our looks, sir," the first gent advised. "We have a lot more strength at our command than you might think."

Jeez—this was happening to me again? Twice in one morning, this time with codgers instead of computers?

"I'm Dr. Phil D'Amato, NYPD, and here's my ID," I said, and handed over my card to gent number one. "Did you give the couple who were just here the same treatment?" To hell with being careful about what I revealed—those fish were too big to let slip away.

He put my card into some sort of small portable scanning device. He regarded the screen, nodded, then looked up at me. "We're not authorized to tell you that, Dr. D'Amato, as you probably know. However, you are authorized to proceed."

He pressed something on the scanning device, and the door clicked open. The sound reminded me of doors clicking open on the fortieth floor of Grace.

"Are you authorized to tell me where that leads?"

"The passage leads to the Grace Building. And there's no need for the abrasive attitude, Dr. D'Amato—we're all of us working for the same goal."

"You're right, of course." I extended my hand. The gents regarded it, nodded, and returned to their seats. Well, one of them had, at least, physically handled my card.

I WAS JUST interested enough in these gents to question them further, but getting after Glick and Jill was more important.

The two had a good few minutes on me. I walked quickly, on a downward incline. Whatever the passage was made of—it looked new—seemed to muffle footsteps. I wouldn't be heard. That was good. But neither could I hear anything ahead.

I had no idea exactly where in Grace this passage would take me. No doubt via a tunnel under Forty-second Street, but where in that computer-fortified fortress? Was there another gauntlet of cybersecurity on some other floor? The oldster security in the rare book room was pretty sharp, even though it was older not only in "equipment"—the gents had at least seventy, even eighty, years on the computer setup at Grace—but procedure, since the library passage still required a physical scanning of my card. But the geezers were good. It seemed unlikely that, after passing through their level of security, an applicant to Grace would have to face the additional bells and whistles that had stymied me in the lobby. Or, at least, that's what I hoped. . . .

Well, hopes and logic could take me only so far in this. The answer would be rendered by my feet.

They felt as if I had walked a distance under and across Forty-second Street, and then some, when I spotted an elevator. There was no indication that Glick and Jill had taken it, but I decided to see what it looked like on the inside, and make a decision. I pressed the button—there was only one, pointing up.

The elevator arrived and opened. It had the look of a freight elevator, but that was likely because it was bare bones—no gold leaf, no art nouveau or deco, no standard midtown elevator decorations.

Most interesting was the control panel, which listed only three floors: one, four, forty.

That convinced me. I pressed forty. The doors closed.

THE DOORS OPENED on the same fortieth floor where I had seen Temp, Red, Jill, and Frank. And right in front of me was the lab in which I had been treated to my first hamster demo, I was sure of it. I was also sure that I had not seen an elevator right across from the lab here previously. I looked back at the elevator and saw why: the wall "healed," leaving no indication that an elevator had just been there. The Wilmington-style decor was apparently more in vogue than I had realized—it was all over this floor.

I returned my attention to the lab. Its door was closed. When I had been here the day before yesterday, I had pounded on that door, hoping to attract someone, and Temp had appeared, replete with another door and office. Both had vanished after I had exited the office, and, unsurprisingly, were still gone.

So how was I to get into the lab now? I put my hand on the palm-niche. No result. Of course not: my palm hadn't done the trick last time, either, which was why I had pounded. But banging on the door now could alert Glick and Jill, if they were inside, and they might leave through some other exit. It could also alert security. I supposed I could camp outside here, in the hope that Glick and Jill would eventually leave through the door in front of me, but that was risky, too, for the same reasons. I didn't know enough about the layout of this lab, how many doors it had, and where. Not to mention the habit the doors on this floor had of appearing and disappearing.

Other options: I could see if I could find Red, and enlist her help. I didn't know for sure if she was at her desk now. I looked at my watch: 1:45. She could be out to lunch. I could walk down the hall, through doors that locked behind me, only to find either no one behind her desk or someone in no particular mood to help me.

I took out my cell phone. Time to try Jack again.

I GOT RIGHT through to him. "Glad you're okay, Phil. I was just beginning to wonder why you hadn't called today."

"There are some important things I need to talk over with you," I said, "but I could use your help with something first."

"We should be getting a full report from the bomb squad about yesterday's explosion—the one that got Frank. I thought you might want to come over to my office and we can look it over—"

"Yes, I would—"

"Good. So, what did you want my help with now?" Dugan asked.

"Actually, it's about Frank." I explained my need to get into the lab where the door had responded to Frank's palm.

Dugan saw right where I was going. "You want me to see if I can get the equivalent numerical code for Frank's palm from the feds, so you can use that?"

"Yes." The latest palm devices also responded to numerical equivalents, which the feds claimed to have records of—not just for agents, for lots of people. But they were very careful about giving them out, even to local police. The NYPD and other city officials had been briefed about this, just last month.

"I don't know if I have the juice, or if Frank's number is still valid," Dugan said. "They don't give them out at all, when the person's alive, without the person's permission. But for someone dead . . . I don't know, but I'll try."

"Thanks." I took a load off my feet and sat down against a convenient wall. It held firm.

DUGAN CALLED BACK six minutes later.

"I was able to plead local investigation into Frank's death," Dugan said, and rattled off a string of numbers. I wrote them down and read them back to Jack for confirmation.

"That's it," he said. "My source said she's pretty sure it's still working—updating computer files for deaths is still one of the slowest things going. . . . So, I'll see you here in about an hour."

"Yeah." I pressed "End."

It occurred to me that, just possibly, Frank had not been killed yesterday. No mention of his death in *The New York Times* . . . his numerical ID still apparently valid . . . Well, I'd see about that in a second. But against those very tiny, explainable threads—the feds often kept the names of killed agents from the press for a while, and Dugan was right about the sloth of computer revisions—I had the weight of Dugan telling me point-blank that Frank had died. I had to go with that. . . .

I got to my feet and walked carefully over to the door and the palm-niche. I put my cell phone close to the niche and entered the code with my thumb. The latch clicked!

I opened the door, slowly.

The room was as I remembered it, lined with cages and hamsters in various sorts of computer hook-ups. But no sign of Jill or Glick. No mice or rats, either.

I had no way of knowing if Jill and Glick had even been in this room. Perhaps they had gone into another room on this floor. Perhaps they had taken the elevator to the first or the fourth floor. Perhaps they had walked by that underground elevator altogether, and were in some completely different part of the building, or some nearby building, not Grace. . . .

I looked at the hamster closest to me. If it had been in record mode, its brain could contain a conversation Jill and Glick had just had here, which could tell me where they were now. But how could I get that conversation to play? I looked at the computer keyboard. It appeared to be off. I touched a key. That could stir a computer out of a "sleep" state. Nothing happened. The computer was probably not sleeping but off.

I looked around at the other computers. None had anything happening on their screens. A few had lights on. All right, a start. I walked over to one of the lit computers and touched a key. A menu burst onto the screen. Fortunately there was no start-up crescendo, I realized a second after the menu came up.

I looked carefully at the screen. Its choices said nothing about hamster recordings. I looked at the hamster in the cage. It stopped chewing and regarded me with gimlet eyes.

What to do?

I could work blindly through this menu and see if I stumbled on to anything. I could try my luck with another computer. I could take another one or two of these hamsters and bring them to Rachel. I could call Rachel on the phone and see if she could talk me through this menu—

I heard voices. Jill and Glick—

They seemed to be coming from outside this room.

I walked to the end of one row of hamster cages and looked around. A door I hadn't seen had opened on the far side—what else was new?—and the voices seemed to be coming from just on the other side. I walked toward the door, crouching—

"I think Albert's good to go now," Glick's voice said.

"I almost hate to send him like this," Jill's voice said. "He looks so cute."

"We can't get emotionally attached to the subjects," Glick's voice said. "That's the first rule of research—you know that."

"Yeah, but once we put Albert out, he'll be a player, not a subject."

I caught a flicker of motion through the door.

I ducked behind an adjacent row of cages and crouched down lower.

I heard the door swish closed.

I squinted through the cages at two sets of legs, one clothed in man's pants, the other in sheer stockings.

The couple were parallel to where I was crouching. I got

down lower and looked up to see if I could get a glimpse of the woman's face as she passed. Yes—it was Jill. She was carrying a cage.

I couldn't get a clear look at Glick.

They passed me, reached a corner, and turned.

Jill said something about being late.

"It's the price we pay for working down here," Glick replied.

"I miss Cerebreeze," Jill said.

"We had no choice," Glick said.

I debated whether to jump up and introduce myself, or stay hidden and follow them. I decided on the latter and hoped they didn't look in my direction. They cooperated.

I stood up about halfway and walked quickly and quietly behind them at the safest distance I could manage.

They headed toward the outer door of the lab.

Yeah, I was sure now that was Glick, and no doubt about Jill, swaying smoothly as she walked, and—

I got a clear view of what was in that cage:

Fuckin' A—Albert was a squirrel!

PART IV:
Grand Central Park

SIXTEEN

So Jill had been telling me the truth almost all along about the squirrels.

She was the only one.

Even Temp, the hologramic windbag, had lied to me in Wilmington. Though I suppose he had said only that he wasn't composed of any squirrel images, as far as he knew—which referred only to his state of knowledge, and not whether squirrelcom was real, and not even if it had actually contributed to Temp's construction in a way unknown to him. Okay, so maybe Temp wasn't a liar.

But Frank had certainly, blatantly, denied any relevance of squirrels to this case, ridiculing Jill's claims when I had presented them to him. Could he have been ignorant of what I had just seen? Much as I hated to think ill of the dead, lying rather than ignorance was the more likely explanation for Frank. He was an informed man. . . .

Jill and Glick were through the outer door of the lab and in the hall with their squirrel. I thought again about making myself known. Jill seemed more attractive as an ally than she had been a few seconds ago. Telling me the truth about one important thing made her seem more trustworthy about everything.

Still, I had done pretty well, learned a lot, in the past few minutes as an eavesdropper. I might as well continue playing hamster and see what other plums it got me.

I walked to the door and opened it a crack. Glick and Jill were at the end of this segment of the hall—they had walked right past the vanished elevator from the basement. Perhaps it was not capable of recall on this end.

I watched. Jill opened the door at the end of the hall the old-fashioned way, just pushing it forward—just as Red had done yesterday.

I waited until Glick and Jill were through, and then went out into the hall.

Glick hadn't lied to me, either, actually. We had never discussed squirrels. And Paton had told me the truth, too, in our short interview at Gnarlingview. Unfortunately, I hadn't been able to get anything more from her about squirrels in our Central Park conversation, terminated by the sudden visitation of bicyclists. The Central Park South Precinct hadn't gotten back to me about anything untoward about that group, so I guessed they were okay, but I hoped their IDs were on file, anyway, just in case. . . .

Time to move forward in this little start-and-stop game. I hurried to the door, opened it a little, and wrapped my face around it.

I could just make out what looked like Jill's skirt walking through the far door. Same color, same rippling interplay of supple bulges. Tough job, but someone's got to do it, some part of my brain never too far from the surface pointed out.

I waited until the far door was completely closed and then I ventured forth. If I timed this just right, I might be able to follow the two completely out of the Grace Building, and then to wherever they were going. Rushing down each hall, stopping at each door, opening it slowly, rushing again—I felt like a bubble of seltzer making my way through an array of just-opened soda bottles. . . . Boy, what I wouldn't give right now for an ice-cold cherry lime-rickey, just like I used to slurp down after playing handball as a kid in the playground on Britton Street in the Bronx. My mouth was dry and my lips felt like they were splitting from all the tension. . . .

I made it into the outermost office—the one with elevators to the lobby—the one with Red's desk. But no one was behind it. She was likely on lunch break. Good. Fewer complications. Glick and Jill and Albert the squirrel entered one of the elevators. There were half a dozen secretaries talking in front of another one. Red was not among them.

So now I had another decision to make: should I take the elevator down? Would I encounter any trouble leaving the building?

Likely not—most security, as Houdini had realized about locks long ago, was designed to protect from the outside in, not the inside out. And, anyway, taking an elevator down was the only chance I had of following Glick and Jill and the squirrel. I was in a goddamn Aesop's fable here. . . .

I walked over to the elevators. There were three. Glick and Jill had taken the one on the far left.

"I think that's a special one that goes only to the basement," one of the secretaries, a blonde about twenty-five, offered. "You need some kind of special security to get in."

"Ah. Thanks," I said. "Did you see the couple who were just here? Did they say anthing about where they were going?"

Shrugs and no's from the group about seeing the couple.

"Okay, thanks."

I looked carefully at the elevator. I found a small sliding panel and slid it open. It contained a palm niche.

I glanced at the secretaries to make sure they weren't too attentive an audience now. They seemed oblivious to me. A bell chimed, announcing the arrival of one of the other elevators. Presumably that one required no special security. Everyone entered the elevator except the blonde, who smiled at me and walked slowly past me in a direction away from lab labyrinth.

I took out my cell phone, looked at her receding form until she was gone. Then I played back Frank's code and hoped for the best.

Yes!

The elevator beeped at me and shifted into some kind of movement.

I thought again about Frank's numerical code. It had worked. But if he was dead, sooner or later whoever programmed these and like palm niches would get word of that, and despite the lame revision system, would expunge his code. And my use of it could well call attention to this—who knew where and how each access registered?—and accelerate the code's elimination. Using my cell phone this way was a piece of digitechnic magic, all right. But it was not likely to last.

The doors of my elevator opened.

I walked in, and was whisked downward.

THERE WERE NO buttons on this elevator, no floors to select. Shades of Wilmington Station, again, though the ride was much shorter.

"Basement," a soft female computer-voice said—like the one in the Washington, D.C., Metro. The elevator settled into the landing. My guess was this was at least several floors below the lobby and its cybergrill. Good.

I exited, looked around, and adjusted to the new lighting. It was a little different than Wilmington's—more hospitable. It almost reminded me of the light from fireflies that I'd seen utilized in Pennsylvania some years ago. Good, maybe our world was finally beginning to catch on to some of the benefits of low-tech biotechnology. In a way, telecommunicating rodents were like that. They could be used for good purposes, too. There was nothing inherently good or bad about most technologies. It all depended on how they were used. Just like knives, which could cut food—or people.

I was standing near the intersection of several passageways. The look of the construction was a lot like the work beneath Wilmington. This was likely the other underground facility Frank had mentioned. But there was no watch-dial of choices.

There was some intricate pastel ceramic tiling overhead, reminiscent of the delicate work in some of the oldest subway stations in New York City—like the Borough Hall station in downtown Brooklyn, at least a century old. This struck me as good, a hopeful sign that whoever had built this would take such care with its ornamentation. Perhaps this spoke of an intention to open at least part of this up to the general public sometime soon. The hush-hush, high-tech ambience of some of the gadgets I'd touched, some of the tunnels I had been dashing through, made me a little uneasy.

I looked at the cloverleaf of passageways more closely. There seemed to be several paths, but only one was automated and working. Above it, a small, inlaid configuration of tile said CENTRAL PARK.

There was no guarantee that Jill and Glick had taken this route, but the park surely was an apt, likely destination for Albert the squirrel.

I stepped onto the passageway. A Velcro-like substance gripped my feet, and I was moving.

THE RIDE WAS quick. I was at my destination in three minutes. I didn't see any place that looked hospitable to mice and rats. It was all too new. I was surprised that this had been built so quickly, or, if it had taken longer, that it had remained secret that long. But as Frank and everyone had been telling me, we were living in a new world.

I was deep underground—not as deep as Wilmington, but deeper than the subways. My cell phone didn't work at this depth. I would have to wait until I got to the surface to call

Dugan and tell him I'd be late for our appointment.

But how to get to the top? I didn't see any obvious elevators near where the conveyor from under the Grace had brought me.

Wait . . . was that a flight of stairs or maybe an escalator? Yes, a flight of stairs, made of a bluish, marblelike substance. The stairs sparkled as I approached.

As long as I wasn't more than five or six flights below the surface, this should be easily walkable. I walked.

It felt more like nine or ten flights. . . . Well, this couldn't have been intended as a main or featured way out for the public. Maybe an emergency or utility exit? I finally arrived, breathing a little hard, at a circular hatch at the top of the stairs. It didn't appear to have a palm-niche.

I pulled it toward me, with no result. I pushed up—it opened, I climbed out, and sure enough, there was Central Park. I wasn't close enough to any street sign to know exactly where I was, but this part of the park had the feel of the sixties, west side, not too far from Columbus Circle. This was a bit south from where Jenna and I had gone on our first missing-squirrel expedition—it seemed a few years ago, but was actually just a week now.

I looked back at my exit—it was a manhole cover from the outside, done up with just the right amount of corrosion and rust to make it look fifty years old. I considered. This exit in Central Park certainly bore more investigation—was it also an entrance, was there some kind of camouflage, digital imagery or whatever, to conceal people popping out?—but I saw no immediate sign of Jill and Glick, and my highest priority was now tracking them. Presumably it would be easy enough to examine this structure more carefully later.

I walked forward a few feet to get better bearings. Okay, there indeed was Columbus Circle, and the Trump Tower, and the AOL–Time Warner complex, and the new digiplex theater, so I was correct in my initial assessment. But where were Jill and Glick and Albert?

Winter was near, but the breeze in the park was mild, which meant lots of people were out. Almost as many people as squirrels. Albert could have been any one of them. The only thing I knew about him for sure was that he was grey. I hadn't even actually seen wires coming out of his head.

I swung around and scrutinized every path, every cluster of people, in a 360-degree surround. Lots of good-looking women, but no one resembled Jill. No one looked at all like Marty Glick.

I wished I had a pair of binoculars—

My phone rang.

"Phil." It was Dugan. "Can we push the meeting back fifteen minutes? I got caught up in a couple of things, and since you're not already here, I figured—"

"Sure, no problem. I'll see you in about twenty minutes, then."

I hung up, took one more look around for Jill and Glick, and walked back to the manhole. It would be interesting to see if I could get back down, and take some conveyor to Forty-second Street.

I knelt and ran my hand over the cover. Nothing unusual, no movable part, that I could feel—

"You work in the sewer, mister?"

I looked up at a group of kids, about ten years of age. Hard to tell whether they were on a school trip or playing hooky in the park. "In a way I do," I replied. "But I'm actually a special kind of policeman."

They stepped back, a little concerned.

"Don't worry," I assured them, "I'm not that kind of policeman—I won't report you."

"We're on a trip with Mrs. Beacham from P.S. 9," a girl with curly black hair spoke up.

"Oh, okay, good," I said. I actually had heard of Public School 9—it was a school for gifted children. I got to my feet. "Did any of you by any chance see a man and woman walking around this place a little while ago? They were carrying a squirrel in a cage."

The kids shook their heads no. "Was the squirrel sick?" the girl asked.

"I think it was okay," I replied.

The kids smiled. They didn't look like they were about to leave. In the distance, a woman with grey hair was walking our way with about half a dozen more kids. "Should we go say hello to your teacher?" I asked my little audience.

They nodded and we walked toward the woman. "Mrs. Beacham?" I asked when we met, "I'm Phil D'Amato—a forensic detective with the NYPD—just doing a little animal research in the park." I showed her my badge, and she nodded. "I'm looking for two colleagues—a man with a well-trimmed beard, and a well-dressed woman. They were carrying a cage with a squirrel?"

Mrs. Beacham shook her head. "Haven't seen them, sorry." She turned to her group of kids. They shook their heads the same way.

"Okay, then, thanks," I said. "It was a pleasure talking to all of you." No point in staying here any longer and attracting more attention to the manhole.

I started to leave—

"Mister?" It was the little girl with curly hair. "I saw a dead mouse in the subway last week—eeuuw!"

One of the boys laughed. "You sound like my mother when the cat brings something home."

"The subway is one of our two special areas of study this year," Mrs. Beacham said proudly, "along with the park. We have lots of trips planned there."

"Well, you should stay away from dead animals," I said, and

managed a smile. "You take care, now, all of you."

I turned and headed to the subway at Fifty-ninth Street. I needed to talk to Jack about animals, dead and alive, and people. . . .

SEVENTEEN

There was security all over Dugan's building—the New Muni Building—too. Of course there was. A bomb had blown in front of it just yesterday, killed Frank Catania, sent me to the hospital.

But I had to admit it was really grating on me already—seeing security everywhere I turned. Supercilious computer screens interrogating me, decent people who were out in front of the New Muni right now, asking me for ID. Okay, the two old gents in the library had their moments. But I could have lived without them, too. It was odd for me to feel this way, I knew, because I was part of the rest of the world's security. I was supposed to help bring to justice at least some of the bad guys. But in this case, they seemed to flip back and forth like a figure-and-ground demonstration, the faces on the sides or the vase in the middle, that I had seen years ago in some psych class. Frank's death had tended to exonerate him; Jill and Glick had just made him a liar.

I showed security my credentials. They nodded. I went upstairs.

Jack had bags under his eyes like the suitcases my mother used to pack for our family excursions.

"Hernia time," my father would grumble with a smile.

"Pack 'em yourself next time," my mother would reply, the same way.

Jack looked like he desperately needed a vacation. God knows what I looked like. We both knew neither of us was going anywhere soon.

"You're the forensic scientist, take a look at these." Jack handed me a sheaf of reports, photos, analyses of yesterday's bomb scene.

"What am I looking for?" I asked.

"What brought the bomb," he answered.

I looked up.

"NYPD bomb squad has gone over this a dozen times," Jack continued. "They have no idea how the bomb got here. The feds looked over it, too—they're as puzzled as our guys."

"Is it possible . . . Frank was wired?" The thought made me sick.

"No. Ed says the damage to his body isn't consistent with that."

"You don't think that I—"

"No, no," Jack said. "We checked your clothing when you were in the hospital yesterday. No chemical traces like that."

"Thanks for the vote of confidence."

"Hey, you might not have known you were carrying," Jack said. "Same for Frank. But neither one of you was the vector."

I nodded.

"We've checked and double-checked everyone we know was there," Dugan continued. "They're all clean, too."

"I'll look these over, page by page." I hefted the sheaf. "Everyone's sure it wasn't left there overnight?"

"No way, not in a public place like that," Jack replied. "Nowhere to hide it. But the bomb squad guys were on their hands and knees examining the sidewalk, looking at that possibility, just to be sure. No way."

"And I assume the same is true about the bomb being on the inside? Somewhere in this building?"

"That the squad is one hundred percent sure about. The explosion occurred on the outside."

"And no dogs around? I mean, after what almost happened at the library yesterday?"

"No one saw any mutts, alive or dead, before or after, in whole or in part. That was one of the first things I asked about."

I nodded again. "Would you like to know what I think?"

Dugan looked at me. "Of course. That's why you're here—but you haven't read the report yet."

"I know," I said evenly.

Dugan's eyes narrowed. "What's on your mind?"

"I think we should be looking at squirrels, maybe rats and mice, anything that could be living in front of this building, in this weather." I also explained my concerns about mice and rats in the subways, how there was no reason to believe the feds were not deploying them now, too.

"As bomb carriers? With bombs embedded in the brains? Why would the feds be doing that?" Jack demanded, incredulous.

"To fight terrorists—or maybe terrorists stole some of the fed rodents and got them outfitted with bombs," I replied. "That's the way they operate—use our own technologies against us. I'm willing to assume here that terrorists, not feds, killed Frank."

Jack shook his head, still not believing. "Phil, there's no room in there—in the skull—for a bomb, for crissakes."

"Gabe Nebuch thought there was," I retorted.

"That was for dogs, and he was very hypothetical."

"You willing to bet the life of this city on an inch or two difference in skull size?"

Jack shook his head some more. "You're suggesting we do, what—shut down the subways, round up all the mice and rats? You realize what you're asking—that would cripple the city almost as much as a terrorist attack."

"You don't really mean that," I said, slowly. . . . "Look, I'm suggesting we at least dust off the contingency plan—"

"The one we drew up half a year ago about rounding up rodents to forestall a bubonic plague attack?" Dugan interjected. "The mayor said no to that, remember—in large part because he didn't want to freeze the subways."

"We need to take a look at that plan again," I maintained.

"On the basis of exactly what?" Dugan asked. He looked at the reports on yesterday's explosion. "All right, you look those reports over, you liaise with Gabe, you find anything—any scintilla of evidence, anything—that that bomb came from the brain of a squirrel or a rat, and I'll think about it. I'll think about talking to the mayor about a subway shutdown and a rodent roundup. Christ . . . That's the best I can do—I'll think about it."

"Okay."

"Now can we talk about something else? Something a little more real?" He gave me a single sheet of paper. It announced that Secretary of Homeland Security Machem was giving a pep talk speech at a rally in Central Park next week.

"Short notice for a rally. Strange place for a rally. Why give a pep talk now anyway?" I asked.

"Short notice is the way we do these things now," Dugan replied. "To give terrorists as little time as possible to plan disruptions. The place and the timing?" Dugan shrugged. "I don't know. We've heard rumors that the feds may be announcing a new homeland security initiative soon. A separate, unverified report that the Office of Surveillance—that was Frank's unit—may soon have a new director. Maybe that's tied to the new initiative. Maybe it has something to do with your squirrels, and that's the connection to the park."

"The city has operatives spying on the feds?"

Dugan nodded. "We can't afford to be caught off guard by anything. . . . Everything's up in the air now. . . . What I can say for sure is that the civil liberties types will be demonstrating in the park like yellowjackets on lemonade. It's a sure thing someone's gonna get hurt."

I BROUGHT DUGAN up to speed on Rachel and Walter, and Glick and Jill.

He raised his eyebrows the highest about Frank and Jill's hamster-recorded conversation—about holograms. "Maybe you were right that those things are playing some role in this, after all."

"So far, the only holograms I've actually seen in the flesh—in the light?—are Temp, and me. I haven't shaken Glick's hand yet, either, but seeing him on Forty-second Street, and everything after, like I told you . . ."

Dugan took it in, nodded. "You think it's coincidence that you trailed Mr. Glick and Ms. Cormier and Albert the rabbit—"

"Squirrel," I corrected.

"Squirrel, right, to Central Park? In view of next week's event?"

"I don't believe in coincidences," I said.

"I know. That's why I asked," Dugan said. "You were right that the girl wasn't a target in the park—we questioned her family in Riverdale when you were in Boston. Nothing wrong there. No other little girls have been hurt."

I nodded.

He grew thoughtful. "I'm surprised that the underground link from Forty-second Street to the park is operational—it wasn't last month. I wonder if Homeland Security sped that along—if that figures into this."

"There's some connection, certainly with the squirrel," I said. "The problem is we still don't know whose side Jill is on. Let's say she's setting up some sort of squirrel spying operation to go online next week. On whose behalf? And what if the squirrels are being primed to do something worse?"

"I could get the cops to put out an all-points on her—they'd find her," Dugan said.

"Yeah, but on what grounds? She told me something about squirrels when everyone else lied?"

"I dunno . . . material witness? . . . we can come up with something. . . . I'm just not comfortable letting things unfold."

"You're starting to sound like me." I smiled a little. "You're right that there's a danger in going too strictly by the book here."

"Thank you," Dugan said sarcastically.

"But I think we need to give Jill and Glick just a little more room and time."

"You have no idea where the hell they are now."

"True," I conceded.

"But you think more harm than good might come of trying to shake everything up now with a manhunt, and reeling them in."

"Right," I said. "If you interdict a terrorist cell too soon, you can leave enough of the colony alive to kill you later on. Not that I think Jill's a terrorist—"

"I understand. So we let it breathe a little more—Jill, Marty Glick, the squirrel, in Central Park, where the Secretary of Homeland Security will be giving a goddamn speech next week."

I nodded. "Yeah."

"Let it breathe. Like a fine, poisonous wine."

I nodded at that, too.

Dugan exhaled harshly. "All right, you've convinced me. . . . Check in with Rachel Saldana and see what more she's uncovered on the hamster front. I'm going to get wheels in motion so we can at least be ready to come down on those hamsters at the Grace Building and scoop 'em all up at once. Who knows where they've been and what they've heard?—the payoff could be enormous."

"All right." I clutched the reports on Frank's bombing, and looked at Jack.

"I know," he said. "I'll keep your mouse concern in mind. Get back to me after you've read the reports. But we have to focus now on Machem's speech in the park."

I GOT RACHEL on the cell phone as I headed back to my office.

She sounded beat. "I've isolated a garbled section," she explained about the words in Walter's brain, "but I can't seem to get it to play. I've pulled the program inside out, clicked every option I could find, but it's still babble."

"What makes you think it's a conversation at all?" I asked. "Maybe it's just Walter's rodent recollection of his last big score."

"If that were the case, the program that Temp gave you shouldn't be accessing it at all," Rachel replied.

"Maybe it's a glitch in the program?"

"Maybe," Rachel replied. "Doesn't feel that way to me. We may have to get someone else in on this—some computer expert or hacker. You still think we need to keep all of this to ourselves?"

I told her I told Jack, what I had told Jack, and that it was okay for her to tell Ed Monti.

"Wow. Okay," she said.

"You sound exhausted," I said. "Go home and get some rest." I felt the same, myself.

"Good thought. I'm just gonna take one or two more shots at decoding the garbled section."

"Okay."

"You know, Jack's attitude about Secretary Machem?"

"Yeah? I think the attitude was more about the speech than the Secretary," I said.

"Sure, I don't blame him for being upset about it," Rachel said. "But if Jack has a special animosity about this, it may be because he's possibly a candidate for that post if the Democrats get elected next time. You heard the rumor that was going around about that, right?"

"No—I missed that." Jack did have a pretty high profile as Deputy Mayor for Public Safety—which was tantamount to the city's Secretary of Homeland Security, and, as some would have it, at least as important a job.

"Anyway," Rachel said, "I'm gonna give these decode scripts one more workout."

I HATED THINKING of Jack as a player in any of this—as anyone more than a public servant committed to getting the best resolution possible for the city, for the world. If he had political interests, that could distort his judgment. But when you got to the rank of deputy mayor, was there anyone who did not have a political agenda? The higher you rose in public service, the more inevitably political you became. Almost a political version of the Peter Principle—in which good people rise and are promoted to a point at which they cannot avoid being political and doing a worse job because of that. . . .

I shook my head. . . .

My cell phone rang.

Caller ID said Rachel.

"Hey, you found something?" I asked her.

"We've got a squirrel!" she said breathlessly.

"You mean—"

"Yeah, one of the parks people brought it in earlier—I just got a call, and it's waiting for me upstairs. It's acting like it's drugged. It has telecom nodes coming out its head—just like Walter's."

I was halfway home, about equidistant from my office and hers. "I'll be right over."

"Good. Bring me the fattest, blackest coffee you can get."

RACHEL LOOKED BEYOND tired—dark eyes sunken in her head, face sallow, sweaty. She was running on nervous energy.

She gratefully accepted the coffee. She sniffed it, smiled, took a long sip. She closed her eyes and let her head loll back.

"We're close," she said, eyes still partially closed. The bottoms were just visible, rich brown, like the color of what she was drinking. "But close is nothing." She opened her eyes, mocha latte, and regarded me, then the squirrel.

It was in a cage like Walter's, new plastic, all hooked up to a computer. But the screen was in idle.

"The hook-ups don't work?" I asked.

"No reason they should," Rachel replied. "The software was for hamsters."

"Conceivably the program could also have a visual option for squirrels."

"Yeah, conceivably. But it doesn't—or I can't find it. Same thing, at this point." Rachel took another long sip.

"So we have no idea what this guy's been seeing—is it a guy?"

Rachel nodded.

"And no proof that it can even relay or record what it sees," I said.

Rachel sipped and agreed.

"Still, the nodes on the top of his head can't be just for decoration," I said, "unless someone were trying to pull what I did with Walter-the-hamster's double."

"These are deeply implanted," Rachel said. "I doubt someone would go to the trouble just for show."

I tried to picture Albert. I couldn't say if I had seen nodes coming out of *its* head. My glimpse of him had been quick and broken. "I followed Jill Cormier and Marty Glick from the Grace Building to Central Park through an underground tunnel—"

"When did they construct that?"

"Recently. Presumably. And they were carrying a squirrel named Albert in a cage. Came from a room adjoining hamster-central in the Grace."

"Don't tell me you're Albert," Rachel said sweetly, disbelievingly, to her inscrutable squirrel. "The chances of that would be—"

"Very small. If digital squirrels are being deployed in the park, there would have to be more than one."

"Do digital squirrels dream of electronic sheep?"

I smiled. "More likely cyber-acorns. But my point, anyway, is not that he is Albert, but that our discovery of two suspect squirrels in one afternoon has to be significant. At very least, it suggests a sudden upturn in squirrel activity."

"Why? For what purpose?"

I pointed to the bomb-scene reports, which I had put on the table next to Rachel's coffee. "I haven't done more than glance at those yet, but I'm thinking the worst." I shared my suspicions about the explosion that killed Frank, and my concerns about the subway.

She looked at her coffee. Whatever pleasure she had been deriving from our banter about Albert was gone. "You think there's a bomb in its head?" She looked at the squirrel in the cage. "Is that why the computer is numb?"

"Jill and Paton say it's telecom. Odds are that's what the nodes are for."

She picked up her coffee, sipped, turned away from the squirrel, and me.

"You have any tea?" I asked gently.

"Just Earl White—it's a lighter form of Earl Grey."

"I'll take two bags, then."

"You know about the Homeland Security Secretary giving a speech in the park next week?" I said, lifting and turning the cup of tea to me so it came into tender, brushing contact with my upper lip. It was just the right temperature, now that I had added a splash of milk.

"Yeah?" Rachel replied.

"I wouldn't want his job."

"It's an almost impossible job," she agreed. "You think his speech in the park has something to do with the squirrels?"

"I don't know," I replied. "At this point we can't rule anything out of the picture."

Rachel regarded the squirrel again. "We need to know what's in that brain."

I nodded.

"I could get a scan," she said.

"Do it."

She examined her watch and frowned. "Jason will be gone by now, given his schedule. He's in charge of that."

"He comes in early?"

"Yeah."

"I don't suppose you know how to operate the machine?" I asked.

"I do. I'm not supposed to."

I gave her a look.

"Phil, come on. You know how touchy the Department is about maintaining turf."

I sipped a bit of tea without moving my eyes.

"All right, I'll do it," she said. "We need to find out what's in there."

"Good. So we catch a cab to coroner central on First Avenue?" I asked. That's where most of the expensive equipment resided.

"We have an M&MRI right upstairs, down the hall," Rachel replied.

"Impressive." I had seen these Multi Magnetic Resonance Imaging machines only two or three times. They projected free-standing holograms of the brain from twenty different angles, including inside out and cross sections.

"Yeah, it'll show us all the goodies inside the skull—including whatever implants might be there," Rachel said. "It's sensitive to even the slightest divergence from healthy brain tissue. It can also track brain function."

"Including for squirrels and hamsters?"

Rachel nodded. "It has a very sophisticated PET scan."

I snorted at the wordplay. We had to take our humor wherever we could find it.

I FOLLOWED HER up the stairs—a cage with Walter the hamster in my left hand, a cage with the unnamed squirrel in my right, the bomb reports under my arm—to the more public floor. Rachel had her handbag and a thick manual for the M&MRI she had fast-printed from the New York City Medical Examiner's intranet. ("I know how to use it. I just also believe in instructions at hand, as backup—unlike most men.") We walked down the hall and stopped at an unnumbered door. It had a palm-niche. Rachel knocked a few times without result, then applied her palm.

The door opened.

The M&M was more or less in the center of a large room stuffed to the gills with all manner of equipment. No one, including Jason, was around.

Rachel pressed a bunch of buttons and the M&M stirred into life. A rosy hologram with the letters "MMRI" shimmered to the left. "That's where we'll see just what's inside these little guys," Rachel said.

She put Walter's cage on a conveyor and flicked a switch. Walter began moving toward the heart of the machine.

"No need to take him out of the cage?" I asked.

"Right," Rachel replied. "That's one of the beauties of this

'PET scan' feature. Its program compensates for interference from the cage, minimal anyway, since it's plastic. It keeps the animals as relaxed as possible—in familiar surroundings."

Walter was soon in the cavern of the machine, and out of direct view. But a hologram of his brain now floated in precise detail to the left, where the "MMRI" letters had just been.

And, sure enough, there was the telecom implant, no bigger than a dot, in glowing orange, right next to his auditory center.

I whistled. "Amazing what digitechnology can do these days—the dymaxion principle writ large."

"Dymaxion?" Rachel asked.

"Yeah. A philosopher by the name of Buckminster Fuller came up with it all the way back in the 1930s—as technologies develop, they do more and more with less and less size."

Rachel nodded. "Hey, we do a hell of a lot with our brains, which aren't exactly huge."

"Exactly."

"You want to see what happens to Walter's telecom unit when we talk to him?" Rachel asked. "He's not hooked up now, but maybe we'll at least get some memory function."

"Later," I said. "Let's take a look at our anonymous squirrel first."

Rachel nodded, flicked a switch, and Walter came out in his cage. He looked none the worse for a hologram of his brain having just appeared a few feet out of his skull.

I took his cage off of the conveyor, and substituted the squirrel's. Rachel flicked the switch again, and the cage moved into the depths of the M&MRI.

Momentarily, a hologram of his brain was floating to the left.

We both examined it very carefully.

It looked a lot like Walter's.

But there was no orange dot, nothing that looked the slightest like a technological intrusion.

WE LOOKED AT the hologram from at least a dozen different angles, with at least as many color schemes, for more than ten minutes.

"I'm no expert on squirrels, or their brains," I said, "so I can't say for sure that we're not missing something." I was mostly aggravated that nothing was there, and a little relieved—"nothing" also meant no tiny bomb.

"You don't have to be an expert to recognize silicon—or any kind of inorganic circuit—in the brain," Rachel said. "Its signature is unmistakable, as we saw with Walter."

"Could there be an *organic* circuit in there?" I asked. "Something made of brain tissue?"

"It would have to be not only organic, but pretty damn similar to what's already in the brain," Rachel replied. "Remember, MRIs were designed in the first place to find tumors."

I nodded, frowned. "Suppose these squirrels were, I don't know, genetically designed so their brains could telecommunicate images when outfitted with the proper skull nodes?"

Rachel frowned as well. "Hell of a lot of genetic engineering, done in a hell of a lot of secrecy—not to mention I've never heard a thing about anything remotely like an organic telecom device in any animal's brain. Have you?"

"No," I admitted.

"It would be a kind of telepathy, wouldn't it?"

"Well, not quite," I replied. "It would send images, not thoughts. But I guess it could be construed as a first step in that direction—if it existed." But I didn't really believe that it did.

Rachel studied the hologram some more. "I can't see anything there but ordinary, unadulterated squirrel brain. The nodes are deeply embedded in the skull, all right, but no further. I guess we should get an expert to look at it."

"We're on the wrong end of a seesaw of decreasing time and increasing need for experts," I said.

Rachel continued to call up different views of the squirrel's brain. "Occam's razor says it's just a brain, and the nodes are window dressing, or, I don't know, maybe the squirrel's keepers are planning another operation to implant a telecom device like Walter's . . . or something else."

"And we got lucky and grabbed it in time?"

"I'd say unlucky—we'd be better off with a squirrel already in telecom mode, right?" Rachel asked.

A cell phone rang.

It wasn't mine.

Rachel snapped open her handbag. "Hello? . . . Hey . . ."

She looked at me apologetically.

Guaranteed it was her boyfriend—the writer who liked her behind in bed with him in the morning.

I made as if to leave.

She motioned me to stay.

I complied, and made busy with the sheaves of bomb reports. . . .

I also tried to hear as much as I could of Rachel's conversation while reading the reports. . . .

". . . I know," she said. "I'm sorry . . . We can have dinner at Luigi's tomorrow . . . I can't really talk about it . . . Yeah . . . all my work *is* important, but this time it's more important than usual . . . I'm sorry . . ."

Her part of the conversation went on like that for a few minutes.

She finally concluded, and looked at me, again apologetically.

"You don't need to apologize to me, of all people," I said.

"I'm with you on this. I break appointments with people all the time—including Jenna."

"She understands?"

"Mostly . . ."

"You found something more in there?" She noticed that I was holding two of the pages.

"Yeah. This is what I noticed before." I handed her one of the pages. "And take a look at this." I gave her the second page.

She read them, carefully, more than once.

"I see exactly what you're talking about," she said slowly. "The remains on those parts of the sidewalk could both be squirrels."

"And Dugan and the bomb team missed them because squirrels getting caught up in an explosion outdoors, in this part of the city, with lots of nearby trees and little vestpocket parks, is no big deal."

"That's still the most likely explanation," Rachel said.

"Agreed. But we have to protect now not only against the likely but the possible."

EIGHTEEN

I called Dugan at his home very early the next morning to tell him about the squirrels. He had given me his number for this very purpose—to tell him about anything I thought was crucial. He'd awakened me like that many times.

"Hello," Dugan said, sounding as if he'd been awake for hours.

I told him what I had spotted in the reports.

"Two of them?"

"I'm going to ask Gabe to confirm that—along with looking for evidence that the blast came from inside either of the remains—but, yeah, it looks like two."

"I've been seeing them running around the New Muni Building, begging for peanuts, for months now," Dugan said. "You think those squirrels were anything more than moochers looking for a handout in the wrong place at the wrong time?"

"Like I said yesterday, I think we need to consider that possibility. And maybe we have some evidence now."

Dugan was silent.

"And I know you don't want to hear this, but I also think we need to start doing something about the subways."

More silence. Then, "All right, I'll call Sally Li when I get in my office, fill her in on your concerns, tell her to expect your call."

"Thank you." Sally Li was MTA chief, with authority over Grand Central, Metro North, and the city's subways. "Oh, and here's another installment in the squirrel saga." I briefed Jack on the squirrel that Rachel and I had examined.

"But you didn't see anything unusual in its brain," Dugan said.

"No. We're going to see if we can draft a brain-hacker or two to look at the hologram."

"Experts on neuro-cyber interface?" Dugan asked.

"Yes."

Dugan sighed. I could tell by the sound that he was shaking his head, slowly, ruefully. I had seen that shake, heard that sound, many times before. "Your squirrel with nothing in its head has to count, in whatever small way, against your squirrel-bomber hypothesis. . . . I don't know, maybe we should stay focused on more reliable kinds of threats to the Secretary—the one thing we know best is he'll be speaking in the park next week."

I thought of what Rachel had said about Jack's possible interest in the Homeland Security job. "We should get more people out in the park, watching for squirrels with nodes in their heads, anyway. The one squirrel in the lab disproves nothing." There was no way Jack might let something slide to embarrass the Secretary—let alone risk his life, certainly not intentionally. But I had to make sure nothing slid, nonetheless.

"I'll get the parks commissioner to put more people on it," Jack said. "Keep an eye out for squirrels with horns on their heads." I could hear the point of his pencil snap on the pad as he finished writing a note to himself. "And you let me know what Nebuch finds when he reexamines those squirrel remains."

I didn't blame Jack for feeling frustrated.

I FIXED MYSELF a pot of tea and sat by the window of our brownstone apartment. It looked like the beginning of a bright, clear, late-autumn morning.

Jenna stirred in the bedroom and joined me.

"I didn't hear you come in last night," she said. She was wearing a loose flannel top and panties.

"I kissed you in most of the right places, but you were out like a light," I said.

She smiled. "How about you try me again?" She sat on my lap and put her arm around me.

I kissed her gently on the neck, and moved my head to do more, when something outside the window caught my half-closed eye.

"What's the matter?" Jenna asked.

"Do you see anything unusual about that?" I replied, and pointed to a squirrel on a branch outside our window. Its winter pelt was almost white, and the sun bouncing off it made it difficult to see.

"I'm not sure," Jenna said.

Neither was I. I shifted my head and squinted to get a better view. I still wasn't sure. But I thought I had seen nodes coming out of its head.

JENNA SLID OFF my lap, looked out the window, then back at me. "How do you want to handle this?" she asked.

"Get the binoculars," I replied. "See if you can see what the squirrel looks like, closer up. I'll go downstairs and see what it looks like from the street."

Jenna nodded and went for the binoculars. I went back into our bedroom, put on socks and shoes, and hustled downstairs.

The damn squirrel was nowhere in sight.

I looked up at our window. It was open, and I could see

Jenna scrutinizing the tree with the binoculars. "I don't see any squirrels," she shouted down.

"I don't see any, either," I shouted back.

"Hold on a second—the phone's ringing. Should I get it?" Jenna asked.

I looked again at the tree. Nothing but weathered bark and a crisp, brown leaf or two. "Yeah," I shouted up.

Jenna returned to the window a few seconds later. She spoke more softly, carefully, as if she didn't want the whole world to hear. "Someone who claims to be Frank Catania is on the phone."

I FLIPPED THROUGH the possibilities as I ran up the stairs.

Frank was really alive. Which meant Dugan had been point-blank lying. Much as I would have wanted Frank not to be dead, I didn't want to believe that—not about Dugan. Maybe he had been seriously mistaken? He had told me at the hospital that he had seen Frank's body . . . The only conceivable way out of this for Dugan, if Frank was alive, was that Dugan had been the victim of a highly effective hoax.

The other possibility was that Frank was not alive—had indeed been killed the way Dugan had said. So who was on the phone. An impersonator? A recording of Frank? Some kind of hologram with his voice? Jenna hadn't said how much of a conversation she had had with the voice on the phone—it couldn't have been too lengthy. I'd find out soon enough.

Jenna was waiting for me at the top of the stairs, phone in hand. She had put on some clothes.

She handed the phone to me and squeezed my shoulder.

I took the phone off hold. "Hello?" I said.

"Phil—"

It certainly sounded like Frank.

"—you've probably already surmised that I'm a hologram—

or the equivalent of a hologram on the phone."

"Maybe you're still alive."

"Hey, I appreciate the thought, but I'm afraid not—surely you or someone you trust has seen what was left of my body?"

"Yeah," I said somberly.

"Look, please don't feel bad about my calling," "Frank" said. "I'm just a list of a whole bunch of Frank's traits, including his voice, and the recollections he chose to invest into this hologram project for several years. Our government's been working on this hologram thing for a long time, even before the terrorist attacks. I told you that when I was alive, didn't I?"

"Not exactly. But don't worry about it—it's not crucial to this conversation."

"Okay. What is?"

I thought for a second. "Assuming you are a hologram, there's presumably a person calling the shots—choosing what words you speak to me," I said. "Frank's voice and his recollections of me couldn't know how to respond to what I was saying. We didn't have that many conversations."

"Half right," Frank's voice said.

"Which half is wrong?" I asked.

"The part you said about a person pulling my strings behind the scenes is wrong—that 'person' is really a program."

"Ah, I see—you're the same program that runs Temp." That program had had at least two conversations of experience talking to me through a hologram, plus all of its prior programming regarding me.

"Very good, Phil."

"So you are in fact Temp, talking with Frank Catania's voice, and maybe some of his experiences mixed into your data base?" Actually, so far I had no evidence that this voice was drawing on anything more than I heard from Temp.

"We're getting into metaphysical territory here, Phil—if Temp's 'personality' is mixed with attributes from Frank's, is the result Temp or Frank? Is it Temp *and* Frank? Is the 'and' additive—I'm both Temp and Frank? Or transformative—I'm not really Temp or Frank, but a new combination, in the sense that hydrogen and oxygen mixed together two-to-one yields something, water, with very different properties from its constituents? Is the answer really important right now?"

"All right, then, tell me something that is," I replied. "Why did you call?"

"To make an appointment with you—I'm not comfortable talking about this over the phone." "Frank" laughed, but the laugh also sounded like Temp's.

"Don't tell me—the Grace Building?"

"You're right, I'm not going to tell you that," "Frank" said. "The Grace will be difficult for you to get into without my palm—and at the same time, the security there is rotten anyway."

Interesting. So Temp/Frank was not aware that I had Frank's palm code in chirpy beeps on my phone. But then what did he mean about the security there being bad? My friend with the moustache? Or had that damn computer program in the lobby received some indication that someone had entered with Frank's palm print code, after all, after his death?

"Okay," I said. "Where, when?"

"Grand Central Park."

"What?"

"Grand Central Park," Temp/Frank repeated. "That's what we like to call it. It's on its way to becoming that—with all the underground construction moving up from Grand Central Terminal, pretty soon the park and the station will just be one big complex. Pretty nice, actually."

"Why not Times Square Park, or New York Public Library Park?" I queried. "They'll be part of that complex, too."

"Are you devoid of poetry, Phil?"

I had to admit that sounded just like Frank.

"Grand Central Terminal and Central Park share the same 'Central'—Grand Central Park is the logical name," "Frank" said. "Anyway—how does twenty minutes from now sound to you, in the new little structure off Seventy-first and Fifth Avenue?"

"I thought electrons travel at the speed of light—are you all congested again?"

"I'm fine. I'm figuring it'll take at least that long to get your carcass down fourteen streets and five avenues this time of day, with all the morning traffic."

And that sounded most of all like Frank.

"FRANK" WAS RIGHT. Traffic was crawling. Cabs were out of the question. I took the train downtown—nine minutes, including my three-minute sprint to the station—and another eight minutes to dash west across the avenues to the park, with a red light on every corner. Fifth Avenue also had a red light—add a minute to cross it. I used the time to leave voice mail for Gabe about the bomb reports. Add another minute to locate the little building "Frank" had indicated.

I looked around—no one else was in sight, not even a squirrel. I stepped up to the structure with a minute to spare.

How to get in?

I didn't want to use my cell-phonic rendition of Frank's palm code. I saw no point in trumpeting its residence on my phone to Frank/Temp.

I thought for a moment. Somewhere along the line in this investigation, prior to an interview with Temp, my palm code had already been entered into the approved index, prior to my arrival. Yes, that had been in Wilmington—when they, Temp, Frank, knew I was coming. Okay, Frank/Temp knew I was coming now, too. Maybe my palm would work here.

I looked for a niche . . . Okay, there it was. I put my palm against it. No click. Nothing. I pulled on the door. It felt bolted shut.

Damn . . . I looked at my watch. Now I no longer had a minute to spare. I was right on time. And Frank/Temp was presumably inside.

But I had no way to get in. I tried the palm-niche again, and got the same palpable lack of result—

"Excuse me?"

I wheeled around to face the owner of the voice, who had approached on some kind of silent, little cat's feet. Jeez, he looked just like the nondescript man in the Wilmington Station—of course, some of these public palm-print devices apparently needed a second hand to get in. That had been the case in Wilmington.

The man now in front of me wasn't precisely the same as the Wilmington man. But he was dressed the same, had the same stubble of grey beard—maybe a bit darker—and was equally nondescript. What the hell were the feds up to now—fielding a force of nondescript palm-print facilitators?

(But if they could be described as nondescript, that meant they were describable, and hence not nondescript—great, that's what I got for talking to a hologram on the phone about metaphysics. . . .)

The stubbled man smiled at me, apparently pleased to see by my expression that I understood why he was here. "This takes two, as you know," he said, and regarded the palm niche. "Did you try it in the past thirty seconds?"

"Um, probably—I didn't time it," I replied.

"That's all right," he said. "We'll just wait another fifteen seconds to be sure your unauthorized attempt at entry has expired."

I nodded. No point in objecting that Frank/Temp hadn't reminded me about this process on the phone—hadn't said anything, in fact, about how to enter this structure.

"All right, then," the nondescript man said. "This should work now." He put his hand to the palm-niche. "And you've got ten seconds to put your palm right there now, too, as you know."

He turned—

I grabbed his shoulder.

He turned back to me, surprised.

I pumped his hand, quickly. "I just wanted to thank you."

He looked at me disapprovingly. "I assure you, I'm real. You just saw me palm the niche."

"Could have been some hologramic signalling."

"Well, now you know otherwise," he said. "And you've got just scant seconds left to put your own palm there."

He turned back to the park and hurried away.

I put my palm to the niche.

I heard the familiar click.

"FRANK" WAS WAITING for me inside, seated behind a small desk. He looked up at me as I entered, and smiled. "Have a seat, Phil."

He seemed so much like Frank, it hurt. But he was dressed all in grey, like Temp. I sat down in the one seat in front of his desk. I didn't offer to shake his hand. "It's sad that we have to meet in such circumstances," I said.

"I appreciate the thought," "Frank" replied.

He'd said that to me on the phone. Made sense, I guess—finite, programmed vocabulary.

"Frank" continued, "But you know we can also be happy that we have this technological capacity to meet and talk now, at all. Until pretty recently, I just would have been dead, with no surviving interactive part of my personality. Bombs have been around a long time. What's new, and hopeful, is our technological wherewithal to counter them, and perhaps negate a bit of their worst effects."

Optimism from a corpse, a murder victim, via his hologram. I found it difficult to embrace. "New technologies are also part of the problem." I asked him about the squirrel with the nodes in his head.

Frank's hologram waved a dismissive hand. "We told you there was nothing to that squirrel angle. Not surprising that you found nothing in its head but squirrel brains." The voice now had a bit of Temp mixed in—just-noticeable differences—perhaps that's why it had said "we." But Temp had not explicitly denied squirrel involvement. He had, rather, maintained that he had heard of none, and went on to talk about dogs.

"Anyway," "Frank" went on, "let's talk about why I asked you over here."

"Okay. Why did you?"

"We wanted to find out what, if anything, you've learned about the circumstances of my death—the bomb in front of the New Muni Building. I'm sure Dugan and the NYPD put you on it, right?"

"Yeah."

"And?"

I considered. There was no point in keeping from "Frank" my suspicions about what had killed his original. Dugan certainly hadn't indicated that he was keeping it secret. And unless Frank had been a terrorist—which his death counted against, assuming he was dead—Temp was apparently legitimately federal, since Frank had introduced us. Tangled, tangled, but enough to proceed on . . . "I hate to say it, but all that I've learned so far is that there were squirrels in the blast area, and—"

"Christ, back to that again? There are squirrels just about everywhere you go these days. New construction codes have been setting buildings back from the street for a good while now, lots of trees and grass and benches on the sidewalk, midtown and downtown have become one big playground for the squirrels—they're the pixies of the city."

"That's part of what's worrying me."

"You didn't find any nodes or rodent telecom equipment at the site?"

"No."

Now Frank's image appeared thoughtful. "Look, the nodes on the squirrel you and Saldana examined could have been self-sufficient relay devices, which would explain why there was nothing more inside the head."

"You mean like a relay antennae? But wouldn't that have to be connected to something else, something to power it, to work?" I asked.

"Not necessarily," "Frank" replied. "That's what I meant by 'self-sufficient'—there are hook-ups these days that supply their own power, right inside the node."

"So I guess we should look at those nodes more carefully," I said. "We were concentrating yesterday on what was inside."

"Purely external devices attached to the outside of animals, including rodents, are actually no big deal technologically. We've had telecom equipment—cameras and microphones—on rats and mice for years now. What makes all of what's happening now different are devices, whether external or internal, that directly interface with the perceptual centers of the rodent. Those recordings you heard back when we visited Grace were literally what the hamster heard—his brain was the microphone."

"And in principle, then, every rodent brain is also a recording device," I said, thinking about Walter the hamster in Rachel's lab. "All we need to hear or see its contents is application of our decoding technology. Every brain is a recorder waiting to play for us—that *is* extraordinary."

"Frank" nodded. "You're finally getting it."

"But what about the possibility of something else inside the rodent brain?" I asked. "Something that could be set off by a remote trigger? Can you look me in the eye and deny that you and the feds have any knowledge of that, any involvement with that, Frank?" I felt like an idiot challenging a hologram this way, but . . . "I'm thinking maybe that's how you were killed, and I don't want it to do more damage, Frank."

"Frank" looked even more thoughtful. I knew that this was just a canned image, preprogrammed, of Frank looking that way—designed to run, I guessed, when the massive program that ran the image and Frank's part of our conversation required a bit more time than usual to locate data, process information, whatever. But it still looked damned convincing. "Yes," "Frank" responded at last, "I can give you that assurance—we know nothing about bombs in brains. . . . Have you found any evidence of that at my bomb site?"

"We're looking into that," I replied. "I've seen some suggestive evidence, and our people are checking it out."

"Remote triggering is easy," "Frank" said. "But if you find no evidence of the bomb itself on the site, then . . ." He got that very thoughtful look again. "We know that terrorists have been rounding up hamsters—"

"Stealing them?"

"Sometimes—some of them think that stealing gives them anonymity—they think that's worth the trade-off in police scrutiny. No credit card, no customer identification of a thief—"

So that explained Teaneck, I thought, one little thing—

"—they've been into mice, too," "Frank" continued. "But it's all been telecom—we know some of them have been trying to use our own devices to spy on us. . . ." "Frank" paused. "I promise you I'll look into this bomb thing and get back to you."

"Meaning, you'll look into all the fed computer files about

it." One form of information—a hologram—investigating another. It was better than nothing, I supposed. Well, a lot better, if it did get back to me. Sad, but I was getting more cooperation from Frank dead than when he was alive.

"Frank" nodded, smiled . . . and his image vanished.

This hologram's departure was a bit more abrupt than I'd remembered Temp's, who had at least left me a Latin proverb to mull over.

I looked at the desk where "Frank" had just been seated. I looked at the ceiling and the walls. No visible sign of how the holographic image and voice had been conducted here.

If I got killed, would I wind up behind some desk like this? Is that what that ride in the elevator at Wilmington was ultimately about?

I looked around another second. No point hanging around this loony bin when there was a bigger, brighter one just outside.

I WALKED INTO the keen sunlight, and my cell phone squawked in my pocket. I pulled out the phone and squinted. The display was hard to read here. But two urgent calls from Dugan, and one from Rachel, had come in during the brief minutes I had been inside with Frank's ghost. Apparently the little structure damped out cell phones.

I called Gabe Nebuch at the bomb squad first.

I got him live this time. "Tell me everything you can about the tiniest possible bombs."

NINETEEN

I decided to return Rachel's call next.

But Dugan nailed me with another urgent incoming call before my thumb hit the keypad.

"Phil, dammit, I've been trying to reach you for five minutes!"

He sounded really upset. I started to explain about my latest interview with the hologram—

"Never mind about that now," he cut me off. "Here's why I was calling—Machem switched his Central Park speech to tonight!"

"What?"

"You heard me. He's speaking in the park tonight!"

"Why?"

"Why? This is the world we live in—everything revolves around security to such an extent that it twists everything around and makes our lives *less* secure. The feds think that suddenly moving up the date will throw any terrorist plans off balance."

"Well, I can see the logic. But it also gives us zero time to prepare."

"Exactly," Dugan said. "The fuckin' idiot will be wide open. Serves him right if . . . I'm sorry, I shouldn't say that. Look, I've got a major meeting about this with the police commissioner and the mayor in fifteen minutes. The feds are saying they want us to keep visible security to a *minimum*—can you believe that?—because they don't want the news coverage showing the Secretary of Homeland Security speaking to an armed state. I just wanted you to know."

"All right. Do we have a time and place?"

"Seven this evening, in the new amphitheater near Columbus Circle."

"Okay." Just about any other place in the park would have been safer. The amphitheater was designed for maximum accessibility from the south and west sides of the park.

"I phoned Sally Li and told her about your subway issues, just before I got the call from the feds. She'll be happy to talk to you, but we've got to focus everything on the park tonight. . . . Keep in touch, and keep your goddamn cell phone open."

I WALKED A few steps on the path back to Fifth Avenue, absorbing the information along with the sunlight. The feds did have a point, as I had told Dugan. Our enemies couldn't possibly be prepared for a last-minute shift in the schedule to this evening. . . . Or could they? And the damn thing was, if they were, then we would be significantly less prepared ourselves. . . . It was a dangerous gamble, a trade of less preparedness for us in return for less preparedness for terrorists. . . .

Why were the feds doing this?

To push the envelope, to make a point.

I certainly couldn't say that the status quo was any great shakes. . . .

My phone rang again. Rachel . . . I hadn't returned her urgent call yet.

I looked at the phone. It was Rachel.

"Phil, we've got another squirrel, and this one has something shining in its brain."

Maybe because I was walking on a brick path in a park, maybe because squirrels reminded me of flying monkeys, but something about what Rachel said made me think of a combination of the Tin Man and the Scarecrow needing a brain. . . .

I cleared my own head. "What does it look like—the hamster telecom unit?"

"I can't tell yet," Rachel replied.

"I'll be right down." I followed the path to a bus stop. One was just pulling in, and heading downtown.

THE TRAFFIC HAD lightened up a bit—at least, up here, north of Fifty-ninth Street—so I jumped on the bus. I'd stay on it as long as I could.

A new magic-wand Webcast, silent and captioned, displayed breaking news above the big windows of the bus. *Homeland Security Head to speak at Central Park tonight* . . . the crawl read, *NYC officials, caught by surprise, fuming* . . . *NYC officials say not enough time for proper security..* . . .

And there was Jack, presumably on his way to that meeting with the mayor, talking over his shoulder at a flock of reporters. *We'll handle it, don't worry,* the caption of Jack's words said, *but we're not happy. After all these years, and all these dangers, we still need better cooperation with national law enforcement.*

And if I lived to be a thousand, I'd never understand why any of this—even a hint of the city's possible unpreparedness—was leaked or given to the press. Why let the terrorists know? The only conceivable advantage to the city was political—zing the feds, stick it to the other party. Was risking the Secretary's life, or putting it in greater exposure, worth it?

A bio brief of the Secretary of Homeland Security filled the panels above the bus's windows. *Julius Machem served as the junior senator from Utah for two years before being picked by the president for his current job,* the words at the bottom of the panels explained. Now his image filled the screens—mid-forties, thick hair with a bright, premature whiteness that made him look wiser than he perhaps was, and a cowboy's ruddy complexion that definitely made him look tough and reliable at the same time. He definitely had the face for the job. As for his performance . . .

The traffic was beginning to bunch up outside. I got off at the next stop—Fifth Avenue and Forty-second Street—and made my way to Grand Central. I took a quick glance at the Grace Building, which loomed over my shoulder.

RACHEL WAS WAITING for me in front of her building. She looked well rested today—eyes smiling, loose hair blowing in the breeze, clearly a lot happier than yesterday.

"Jason's upstairs with the M&M," she told me. "He doesn't know you were there with me yesterday. He wasn't too happy that even I was there, so I figured I'd best leave it at that."

"Sure," I said. "So tell me about the new squirrel. Where was it found?" We walked into her building. I showed my ID.

"Northern part of the park," she replied. "Near the old skating rink."

"Hmm . . . nowhere near yesterday's model." Which had been picked up some twenty blocks south, on the west side.

"Right, and this one was discovered by a homeless man."

"Good for him." I made a mental note to track down his name and see that he got some kind of cash reward.

"It hasn't really been below freezing yet," Rachel said. "There are still lots of people walking around."

"There are still lots of squirrels running around, for the same reason."

"Yeah."

We approached the lab. Rachel knocked on the door.

A kid with sandy hair opened it.

"Freddie Jason," Rachel introduced us. "Hacker extraordinaire."

I shook his hand. "Glad you're on our side, then."

"His friends call him Jason," Rachel said.

"All right . . . So what does he have inside his head?" I asked Jason, about the squirrel.

"She," Rachel corrected, and gestured to the cage in the M&MRI.

"Okay," I said.

Jason projected the M&M image. There was something foreign inside that squirrel's skull, that was clear—clear as day in the hologram of its brain. It might have looked a little different from Walter's implant.

"Could we see the M&M of Walter's—the hamster's—brain, for comparison?" I asked.

The kid nodded. He clicked on a couple of icons, and a recording of Walter's M&M hologram floated right next to this squirrel's. The squirrel's implant did look a little . . . rounder than Walter's. "Do those two look a little different to you?" I asked.

The kid nodded. He didn't seem to say much.

"Does this squirrel have nodes coming out of his head?" I asked.

The kid nodded again.

"So can we assume that this squirrel works the same as Walter, except the squirrel conveys images?" I asked.

Rachel answered. "I hooked the squirrel's nodes up to Walter's program, and got nada—as far as the computer is concerned, that squirrel might as well have nothing but plain brain inside its head."

"All right, so maybe it needs a different program," I said. "I mean, Walter is a hamster, and his *shpiel* is acoustic."

"Look," the kid finally spoke up. "Like I told Dr. Saldana. The only way we're gonna really know what's inside its head is to cut it open and get a real look at it, firsthand. Images are images. Reality is real. Whether you say it in English or Jewish."

So the kid—Freddie Jason—did have a mouth on him. I could see why Rachel was chary about incurring his anger yesterday.

"Yiddish," I corrected him. "Jewish is the religion and the culture. Yiddish is the language—and only those of us from Eastern and Central Europe." I was actually Marrano—my ancestors pretended to convert under threat of the Inquisition, lived in Spain ostensibly as Catholic, migrated to Italy, but continued to practice Judaism in secret.

"Whatever," Jason said, unimpressed.

"I'm not comfortable with killing the squirrel," Rachel said.

"It's a fucking squirrel, for crissakes. Get over it," Jason responded.

He was a jackass all right, but that didn't mean he was wrong. Still . . .

"If it's dead, we can't make any further attempts to hook into its programming," I said.

Rachel nodded.

Jason shook his head no. "I'm not likely to find anything more. Get me another program, then maybe."

"We're not likely to get another one anytime soon." Unhelpful to Rachel's position, but true. I had no control over my meetings with Temp and Temp/Frank, and had no reason to think they would necessarily oblige me with another program even if I did find myself in a position to ask them.

"So go over the data with this program again." Rachel looked steadily at Jason. I wasn't as familiar with the arcana of hierarchy in the medical examiner's office as in the general NYPD, but Rachel likely had superiority over this kid hacker, even if he was extraordinaire. But whatever their relationship, techies were notoriously hard to direct. They tended to do what they pleased—and if pressed to do something that went against their grain, they'd plead technological impossibility, in a way that a layman lacked the knowledge to refute.

The kid held his ground. "There's nothing there—at least, not with this program. Look, with the hamster, you heard something right away, right? Then you were able to get the memory to play. There was that other weird, incomprehensible stuff which we still don't know what it is, but the point is, you did get some kind of response, an indication, right away. It wasn't the whole story, but you knew you were on the right track—you were engaged. There's nothing here with this squirrel. No handshake, not even fingertips touching. You understand?"

Rachel looked thoughtful, distracted. "I saw a squirrel in Prospect Park a few months ago," she said. "It was looking at two acorns, in two almost opposite directions. It looked at one, then the other. One, then the other. Lots of times. And finally it went to one. I don't know why it made that decision—why the one it approached was more attractive than its competitor. But it sure looked to me like it was exercising some kind of free will."

"Jesus Christ on a popsicle," the kid said.

I hadn't heard that expression in years. The kid not only had a mouth, it was well versed.

"Is there some important government official in danger, in just a couple of hours," he continued, "or are we here to debate existential philosophy?"

I started to speak; my cell phone interrupted me.

"Hello?"

"Phil . . ." It was "Frank." "I don't know how long I can talk to you on this connection, but we've been looking into some of the things we discussed earlier today, and I wanted you to know that we think there's a better than eighty-five percent chance that someone from the inside is helping with some of the bombings."

"Helping as in making them happen?"

"Yes."

"In the NYPD?" I asked.

"In the government, local," "Frank" replied. "That's all we know at this point."

Funny, I had had the same concerns about Frank, when he was alive. "Do you know about—" I started telling "Frank" about the Secretary's speech in the park tonight, and received a dial tone in reply. Well, "Frank" had said the connection was tenuous. . . . Interesting that the feds were using Frank's holographic program to contact me, rather than his human replacement. Maybe they hadn't had time to replace him, maybe they didn't want to reveal any more of their operation, maybe they didn't completely trust me. . . .

Rachel and Jason were looking at me.

"Give me a few minutes—I need to make some calls," I said.

"So Mata Hari the Squirrel gets a last-minute reprieve," Jason said sourly.

I EXCUSED MYSELF and walked out into the hall, for privacy. (Such was the world of the cell phone: whereas fixed phones in offices were vulnerable to ears of colleagues in the vicinity, the cell phone allowed the anonymity of bathroom stalls and public places.)

I called Gabe Nebuch again at the bomb squad. Out of the office, back at 4:15, his voice mail informed me. That would be thirty-five minutes from now.

I called Dugan.

"Phil, I was just going to call you." He sounded less upset than before.

"Ah, well, I just wanted . . . no, you first," I responded.

"I wanted you to know that I think we have the Secretary's speech situation pretty well in hand now," Dugan said.

"He's called it off?"

"No, he's still going ahead with it. But we, I think it will be okay."

"I don't understand," I said. Just an hour or two ago he was going ballistic about the speech, and with good reason.

"It's under control now," Dugan replied. "You can focus on other aspects of this case."

"You're not worried about his safety?"

"Of course we're worried—we're always worried about the safety of high-profile officials. It's just . . . well—just a second, I have another call coming in." He returned a moment later. "Gotta go now, Phil. I was just saying it's not quite the crisis that I thought."

I thought through the brief conversation after we got off. This made no sense. How could the speech in the wide-open park in just a few hours now suddenly not be a crisis? Did Machem call in some federal reinforcement which Dugan was not at liberty to reveal? No, if that had been the case, Dugan would have been hopping mad, and I'd have discerned that anger. As it was, Dugan was far calmer than he'd been earlier in the day.

So what was going on? Jeez, were they planning on putting a hologram of Machem up there on the stage to give his speech? That would take a lot of cooperation from the press—a good flashbulb would shine right through the hologram and produce a picture of an amazing translucent Secretary. . . . And if anyone reached out to shake his hand, or clap him on the back . . .

So why, then, did Dugan now not seem to care if the Secretary was in danger? I didn't want to even start going down that road. . . .

But I might as well take advantage of the sudden lull to put a call in to Sally Li.

"Phil D'Amato! I'm rushing out of here for a last-minute

powwow about Machem's speech in the park—we're putting in extra trains and security to handle the crowds—so I can't talk to you now. But I want you to know I support your concerns about vermin in the subways. I don't know about bombs, but I can tell you I'm very concerned about those rodents as vectors of disease. We've found more than a few dead ones lately—"

"Were they autopsied?"

"Yeah—we didn't find what we feared—it wasn't plague or anything, but still—You know, the mayor shot me down, last spring, when I urged that we shut down the subways for a few days and round up all the rats and mice we can so we can get a look at what's in their bloodstreams. And I thought that you and I might be allies on this, even though we're looking for different things—"

"Absolutely."

"But I can't talk to you now—everyone's very worried about Machem's security tonight. But let's have a long talk tomorrow."

She got off before I had a chance to ask about why she and Dugan were on different levels of anxiety about Machem's speech—most likely, word just hadn't reached her yet. Why would Dugan tell me one thing about that, and the head of the MTA something else. . . . I also needed to find out more about those dead rodents—had to be rats, if Li was looking for *Pasteurella pestis.* If not plague or some other disease, what did they die of? Who performed the autopsies?

I walked back to Freddie Jason's lab.

"You were gone a long time," Rachel greeted me.

"Do you know anything about rat autopsies?" I asked her.

"Not Dr. D'Amato, Dr. Dolittle!" Jason offered, and laughed. "Talk to the animals: hamsters, squirrels, now rats!"

"No," Rachel said, "haven't seen anything on rats."

I looked at Jason. "Did I say anything about rat telecom?"

"Hey, that's what all of this is about, isn't it?" He pointed to the squirrel, now out of the M&M, in its cage. "You want to know if the dot in its head can show you what it sees."

"Yeah . . ."

"We're also concerned that it may be a bomb," Rachel said, a little nervously.

"Whoa!" Jason looked at Rachel, then me. "You know what—if that's even a tiny possibility, pardon the pun, then I'm withdrawing my recommendation that we cut its head open. In fact, I'm going to withdraw myself from this facility, right now, unless you get that squirrel out of here."

Neither Rachel nor I moved.

"No? Well, then I'm out of here. And I'll be talking to Ed Monti—I'm not your goddamned bomb squad." He grabbed his coat and walked out.

"I'm sorry," Rachel said. "You never know how people are going to react in those situations."

"Not your fault." I touched her shoulder and looked at the squirrel. "Maybe I should take her over to the bomb unit."

"We have no hard evidence yet of bombs in any skulls," Rachel objected. "But we do have evidence of telecom. I think it makes more sense for me to keep fiddling with those nodes and see if I can get anything out of it. The advantage we have over the last squirrel is that we know there is something artificial in this one's brain."

There was almost a pleading quality in her voice—don't kill the squirrel, give me a little more time. She knew, of course, that the only way the bomb squad would be able to examine the dot would be to excise it from the squirrel—just what Jason had wanted to do. And the bomb squad wasn't exactly known for its expertise in surgery. . . . I sighed. . . . It would change the whole picture, literally, I had to admit, if we could get pictures out of that squirrel. . . .

"Okay," I said.

Rachel smiled her thanks. "Why are you interested in rat autopsies? Has something happened with them?"

"Sally Li—MTA head—thinks we should round them up from the subways. Enormous task—it'll close the system. But I'm going to talk her about how we can do that, tomorrow."

"Good." Rachel picked up the squirrel cage. "I better get to work on her. Will you stay?"

"No, I think I'll head up to Central Park—one way or another, I've got a feeling there's going to be some sort of finale there tonight."

Regardless of what Dugan had just told me.

And I wanted another look at the subways.

TWENTY

I don't really know what I expected to see on the subway—the tracks, the blur of stations, the sapphire of Grand Central Terminal, which I kept coming back to . . . But now I was here again, solely for the purpose of contemplating a nightmare. How many tiny bombs in the heads of how many rats and mice would it take to burst this gem? I had no real idea. I knew what had happened to Frank in front of the New Muni Building. I knew that I hadn't heard back from Gabe Nebuch, but I would soon . . . I wondered if there would be bombs tonight in the park . . . I looked up at the twinkling ceiling, patted one of the cool walls, and walked back to the subway and a train uptown. . . .

The southwest corner of the park was already bristling with all manner of police contraption when I arrived. Men and women on high-stepping horseback, footcops, patrol cars, old wooden barriers with blue paint forever chipping, even a fair number of spanking new immunogates were in view. (These had been approved by a controversial one-vote margin in the City Council just last year. They packed a jolt that rendered anyone who touched them—with either hands or clothes—unconscious. Only cops with special gloves were exempt.) But the real top of the line of our security were three cyberspotlights that would shine down from the stage before and during the Secretary's speech. These would play over the faces of the crowd and report back any retinas that matched suspect scans stored in the federal system. They had saved the life of the mayor of Baltimore three months ago, and just about every big city, including New York, was implementing them now.

But this sprouting of security, impressive as it was, could not have been what had put Dugan suddenly at ease. He had known all about this when he had been hyper a few hours earlier about the Secretary's speech. . . .

I looked around the park. The armor was clear, at least to my eyes. Where were the flaws?

I was no expert on security. I was probably no more likely to spot a flaw than any averagely observant citizen. I did see lots of squirrels.

I put in another call to Gabe Nebuch.

"SORRY FOR BEING out of touch," he said. "We've got our hands full with Machem's speech in the park tonight."

"You coming up here?" I asked.

"Probably not," Nebuch answered. "Denny Sontag's coordinating bomb squad activity in the park—you probably know him. He's a good man."

"Yeah." I had been sitting next to Sontag at some briefing in the past year. He was big, jovial, but deadly serious when it came to his work. "So what are you guys looking for in the bomb department up here?"

"A bulletin came through just yesterday about smaller devices, more pinpoint, that pack more punch. Denny's got the stage area patted down pretty well for that."

"Good. And have you found anything regarding those reports that I asked you to look over?"

"Oh yeah, sorry, right. I didn't call you because, so far, everything's come up just as it should—negative. There were two squirrels killed in front of the New Muni—we've got that definitely established. Sharp of you to notice. One looks like it was killed from the outside-in—the pattern of blood on the concrete shows that pretty clearly. That means no bomb in that head. The second squirrel is not as clear. But we've still got one or two more tests to perform on that one."

I WALKED AROUND and scanned the growing crowd for familiar, suspicious, any kind of out of-the-ordinary faces. Actually, the park was populated with something more like growing crowds than a single crowd—pockets of people, at least a dozen, most of which were expanding.

I looked at my watch. The Secretary was due here in about ninety minutes.

Some of the groups were clearly hostile, though not necessarily dangerous. They carried signs—including a few of the newer sheerscreens on poles, which displayed changing messages. The ones in front of me said the Secretary was doing just what the terrorists wanted—destroying our American way of life.

A small group, a bit off to the side, caught my eye. I thought I noticed the dour face and grey apparel of Deborah Paton—whom I had last seen right here in Central Park, though further north and on the east side, with Jill Cormier. I approached to get a better look. She looked at me for a split second, then turned her head, and pretended she hadn't seen me. Yep, that was Paton.

I walked right up to her. "Deborah Paton," I boomed out. "I had no idea you were a fan."

She wheeled around and eyed me coldly. "There's still a First Amendment in this country, Dr. D'Amato. It gives people the right to peaceably assemble."

"No one is saying you can't," I told her sincerely. "Is Jill Cormier around?"

"We're colleagues, not each other's keepers," Paton replied. "I wouldn't know."

"Well, enjoy your evening in the park, then." I bowed slightly, nodded, and walked away.

I had seen Jill just yesterday, when I had followed her and Glick through the tunnels from the Forty-second Street library to the Grace Building to Central Park, like a hamster running through burrows. The Burrow of Manhattan, that's what this place was becoming.

I could just make out the area from which Glick and Jill and then I had exited. There was a phalanx of New York's finest around it. Good, that sewer cover would be a perfect place for an assassin to emerge at the last minute. Not that I thought that Jill or Glick were killers. . . .

There were other security types stationed casually around the little structure, including . . . yes, the two elderly, pen-and-ink gents from the library. They were somewhat older than the stubbled guys who had assisted me at Wilmington and in the park this morning with "Frank," but all four were definitely of a piece. I wondered again: an octo- or maybe septuagenarian special fed force. . . . Not such a bad idea . . .

A corps of different law enforcement crossed my path from another direction. Each cop had a dog on a leash. They stopped about fifteen feet beyond me and fanned out in all directions. The leashes seemed to . . . pulsate. Were they attached to the special seeing-eye dogs Temp had told me about down in Wilmington? I had never seen them, but the dogs walking by me seemed to match his description. I smiled for the putative canine cameras.

I looked up at the sun. It would be down in about ten to fifteen minutes. That would make security tougher. But lights of various sorts were already flickering into life. They would take out about eighty-five percent of the dark when fully deployed.

Another advantage we had was the weather. It had been unseasonably mild all week, and the temperature now was in the high fifties. Most people were dressed in light jackets. I saw few if any bulky overcoats. Fewer places to hide weapons.

I looked again at the makeshift stage. Various people who looked like techies were now in view, puttering about with microphones and other electronics. I thought I saw the cyberspotlights in place—one on the canopy just above the stage, the other two on either side of the stage—

My cell phone rang. "Hello?"

"Phil? Gabe Nebuch—" His voice dissolved in a mush of static.

I looked at my phone. The letters on the screen said "No connection."

I tried to return the call. "Circuits busy."

Goddamn it. Of course they were. Every security detail and his uncle must have been on the phone right now, not to mention reporters, demonstrators, and—

I thought I saw Rachel, about halfway between me and the stage.

IT TOOK ME a few minutes to weave through the crowds and reach her.

"Phil! I figured you'd be here—I'd tried to get you on the phone." She looked upset.

"All the circuits are busy. Are you okay?"

"Yeah." Her face was sallow in the cyberlight.

"So you got something with the squirrel in the lab? That was quick—good work."

"No, I didn't get a chance to do much with the squirrel. . . ."

I looked at her.

"Ed Monti's out of town, in Albany today," she continued. "Jason got to one of his assistants, who sent over two guys to take the squirrel. I tried to call you, but couldn't get through."

"So they're going to—"

"Not until tomorrow." She took a deep breath. "I know I'm overreacting." She looked towards the stage. "We've got more important things to think about now—what's the drill with Machem?"

"We just keep our eyes open for anything untoward," I said.

"Including squirrels," Rachel said, half-jokingly.

"Yeah . . . You know, I understand your feelings about the squirrel . . ."

She nodded.

"Not wanting to kill it, I mean."

She said nothing.

"I can understand your not wanting to kill it for no reason—I agree with that entirely," I continued. "But if that was the only way to get a better idea of what was in its skull? I mean, I guess I just assumed that with all the bodies you autopsy . . ."

"I autopsy bodies that are already dead," she said sharply. "Big difference between that and killing anything, including a squirrel." She turned and strode away.

I caught up to her. "Okay," I said. "Understood . . . Are you all right here now, on your own? I guess we can cover more ground, see more things, if we split up."

She nodded, perhaps partially mollified, and walked on.

I LOOKED YET again at the stage. Various lengths and colors of cable had now joined the people. The Secretary would be there in under an hour.

From this vantage point, which afforded a good view of all the interlocking levels of security around the stage, the Secretary's perch surely looked impregnable. No one could get through that combination of cops and barriers.

Okay, so what possible lines of attack did that leave?

I looked at the sky. Half a dozen dragonfly helicopters,

armed to the teeth with sharpshooters and laser-cannon, hovered above. No way an assault could come from the air. Skyscrapers of varying size and vintage sparkled on the horizon. Morse code for: we're keeping vigil on this park. . . .

I hoped so.

The best chance an assassin could have here would be from a bomb, planted here before all of this security, ticking or ready to be set off by remote signal right underneath our very noses. But this is where the federal strategy of moving this talk up, rescheduling it for tonight, showed its mettle. Would terrorists have had the time, on such short notice, to plant a bomb beneath that stage?

I didn't see how.

Unless they already had bombs planted all over the city, waiting for detonation . . .

I put in another call to Gabe Nebuch.

All circuits were still all busy.

I wondered where Denny Sontag was. Presumably his unit had given the stage and the area immediately around it a thorough going-over.

I walked closer to the stage. I flashed my ID a few times. The security I encountered was all NYPD, and many of the people knew me.

If a bomb had been planted—even just conventionally, not in squirrels or rats—could telecommunicating rodents triangulate on the exact target, presumably the Secretary, and trigger the explosion? Well, remote control of rats was a fact. But a bomb planted in a fixed place would be susceptible to the bomb squad's sweep. The greater danger came from bombs on feet. . . .

Three dignified figures walked onto the stage. I recognized them right away—the police commissioner, the parks commissioner, and the deputy mayor for public safety, Jack Dugan. The police commissioner was dressed in his full uniform.

The parks commissioner was an elegant dresser, a devotee of Armani suits, one of which he had on now. And Jack . . . was dressed like Jack, in a suit that always looked a little too starchy, a little too big, a little too something. I smiled. It was one of his endearing qualities.

He looked out over the crowd. I half-waved to Jack. His eyes went right by me. I wasn't sure if he saw me.

"Phil D'Amato—catching tonight's little concert in the park?" A big man extended his hand.

"Denny, good to see you," I replied.

Sontag introduced me to his two companions, a woman about thirty with short blond hair, and a bushy-haired man about twenty years older with a small ring in his nose. Neither smiled, but Sontag made up for it with a characteristic grin of big yellow teeth.

"So you've got the place certified as clean?" I asked. That had to be the case, or he and his teammates would have been hard at work making it so, right now.

Sontag's smile broadened, then vanished. "I'd stake my job on it," he said. "There's no bomb anywhere from here to there." He pointed to the stage.

I nodded. "Good. I believe you." I shook his hand again, and walked on.

And I did believe him. But I didn't feel any less worried about this situation.

THE SUN FINISHED setting. The artificial lighting had all kicked in now, and taken up most of the slack. The sky was slate-grey in the west, darker in the east, punctuated by the fluttering dragonfly helicopters overhead. The lights within the helicopters glittered in the dimming sky like fireflies. Made me think, again, of the real fireflies I had seen so much of during autumn evenings in Pennsylvania. Except these firefly-dragonflies shone with lights that never went off. Which was good in these circumstances.

I spotted a disturbance on the south side of the park. A woman had apparently circumvented one of the old wooden barriers—the kind that didn't render people unconscious to the touch. Cops converged on her from all sides, like white blood cells on a splinter or a bacterium. Maybe she was a decoy, probably she just was a crank. Anything worse wouldn't have been that easy.

The woman looked a little like Rachel—dark hair, dark eyes, attractive. Perhaps a little older. She cursed her head off as cops escorted her away. . . .

Rachel's behavior bothered me. Not that I was angry at her—I just hadn't pegged her for having such an intense love of animals that it could get in the way of her job. I guess the signs were there—the little baby squirrel and her father, other things she had told me . . .

I thought I saw the mayor on the stage, flanked by NYPD bodyguards. The police commissioner approached him. Jack and the parks commissioner were chatting on the other side, with a few other officials. Ah, one was Sally Li. She looked better than her pictures.

I looked at my cell phone. I ought to call Jenna, tell her where I was. . . . Circuits were still busy.

I looked at my watch. The Secretary's talk was scheduled to begin in eight minutes.

I took in the scene, closed my eyes, tried to envision what was wrong. Everything seemed in place, at least here in the park. Even the media trucks and kiosks, dozens of them, were ringed with local and national security. The cyberspotlights were playing the crowd. Sontag had said he'd stake his job on no bombs already being in place underneath all of this.

I looked around at the park's usual wildlife. There were

pigeons and sparrows and a good number of squirrels running around, excited by the crowd and the chance for a crumb of a cookie or pretzel it promised. None of the squirrels that I saw had anything other than ears coming out of their heads.

Someone approached the microphone. One of the mayor's press people.

"The mayor will be speaking in a moment or two," her voice rang out across the crowd. She repeated her announcement two times. The ambient noise in the park dropped to whispers.

A figure moved up to the mayor from the back left of the stage. The Secretary.

The mayor smiled at him.

Machem smiled—a bit stiffly, from where I stood—and turned his head to the crowd. He conveyed an air of power, confidence, serenity. Impressive.

The lights shone on the mayor as he walked to the microphone in the center of the stage.

"Thank you, New Yorkers and Americans," he began. "Thank you for joining us here this evening, and showing the world our strength. We're strong enough to meet anywhere, and so we meet here, under the stars, on this late fall evening. . . ."

I took a quick look at Machem. He was standing, straight as a pine, with the same aura of confidence.

I located Dugan on the other side of the stage. He was standing by himself now, and looked more nervous than before. He was moving slightly, shifting his weight from foot to foot, in the way that he did when he was anxious about something . . .

The mayor concluded his introduction. "So please join me in welcoming the Secretary of Homeland Security, my good friend, Julius Machem."

Everyone on the stage, and most of the people in the

crowd, burst into applause. Machem and the mayor shook hands. Boos and shouts also came from a few places in the park. Some no doubt came from Deborah Paton's group, which I tried to locate in vain.

The applause continued. Cops and feds scanned the crowd with hungry eyes. I imagined some group of locals and feds were doing the same at some nearby facility with all of the retinal scans the cyberspotlights were delivering, giving a bit of eyeball backup to the fast, vast search for suspect scans that powerhouse computers were conducting.

The applause subsided.

Machem cleared his throat.

Someone in the crowd started singing "God Bless America."

Others joined in, including some of the security. Machem joined in, off-key. . . . I sung a little myself, under my breath. . . .

The song concluded. Machem applauded the crowd, and the applause was returned.

Machem held up a quieting hand.

"Thank you, New Yorkers, Mr. Mayor, for inviting me here."

Another round of applause. "I came here to talk to you this evening—"

A horrible feedback squeal lacerated his words, and maybe a few eardrums.

Machem stepped back, looked at the microphone, and resumed. "I came here—"

The squeal came back as well.

Machem stepped back.

A techie in a bright orange NYPD windbreaker dashed from the back of the stage to the microphone. Four other security types, likely feds, took a position between Machem and the microphone.

The techie examined the microphone carefully. He made

some kind of adjustment, and said, "Testing, testing." It sounded good. He and the security receded to the rear of the stage.

Machem approached the mike for the third time. "All right, let's see if we've got this right now," he said, and smiled. His voice sounded fine. The crowd applauded.

Machem nodded. "Thank you, thank you," he said. "I came here to talk to you this evening about a very important sea-change in the way we will be safeguarding our homeland security—"

My cell phone rang.

A woman, about sixty, glared daggers at me, and moved a bit away.

"Yes?" I answered, softly.

"Phil—Gabe Nebuch! I've been trying to get you—anyone at the event—for nearly an hour!"

"I know," I said quietly, one eye on Machem, the other on the crowd. "Circuits are busy."

"Yeah," Nebuch said. "I know. Listen—this may be important. The last tests on the squirrel remains I performed—like I told you I would do before? There's a good chance you were right."

"What? You mean—"

"Yeah, I mean the tests we ran report an almost eighty percent chance that the bomb that killed Catania was contained in a squirrel's brain. It's the only explanation for the splatter pattern. You see, it was disguised at first, because there was so much other damage, but the bomb came from inside the skull—"

"Have you told Denny Sontag?" I looked, helplessly, at a nearby squirrel—

"No, his circuits are busy, too. This must be one of those tiny dot-com bombs that I told you about—I don't know, maybe there was more than one, in different animals. We have to repeat our tests—"

"Okay, Gabe, thanks for this. Let me get off and see what I can do here."

The Secretary was talking about privacy versus security, saying we could have both, waving his arms expansively to make his point.

What could I do? Run up to the stage, tackle him, get him off the stage, and tell him to watch out for squirrels? I'd be tackled myself—if not shot—before I got a tenth of the distance.

I looked desperately around. A federal agent, dressed like he had plenty of telecom up his sleeve, was just a few feet away.

I pulled out my ID, held it high, and excused myself as I pushed through a dozen or more annoyed people.

The fed looked at me suspiciously as I approached, then saw my ID and nodded.

He had an earphone and a mouthpiece on his head. Good. He could talk to the stage.

". . . we have to think differently in these times," the Secretary was saying, "out of the box of fear—"

"Listen," I started to say to the agent—

A powerful concussion like an elephant on my chest knocked us to the ground.

TWENTY-ONE

I didn't lose consciousness for an instant this time.

I looked up from the ground. The fed was already on his feet and was talking rapidly.

Everything was in motion around me. I stood up, shakily.

I realized that some plan for this confusion, a plan already in place and well practiced, was unfolding. Immunogates and older barriers were swinging or being swung into place. NYPD looked mostly dazed, as was I. But the feds seemed on top of it, urging everyone to calm down, shining flashlights with a soft kind of beam into everyone's face.

"They're hand versions of cyberspotlights," the fed next to me offered. "We'll get these fucks, don't worry. By the way, I'm Dimitri Tolis, Department of Homeland Security."

"Phil D'Amato, NYPD Forensics," I replied, and showed him my ID. It was still in my hand.

"Yeah, you were trying to show me that when the bomb went off, weren't you?"

I nodded and looked at the stage. All I could see was smoke.

"Who was hurt up there?" I asked.

Dimitri shook his head. "Unknown, at this point."

"You sure it's a bomb?" I asked.

"Why, you've got a better idea?"

"NYPD bomb squad checked out every inch of the area,"

I replied. "They didn't find so much as a firecracker."

"You're talking delivery, not weapon," Dimitri said. "If your bomb squad found no bomb beforehand, and you believe them, the question now is not if it was a bomb, but how was it delivered."

I debated whether to tell him about the squirrels. "We've been investigating the possibility of little animals—actually, squirrels—as bomb carriers—"

"What, tied around their necks?" Dimitri looked dubious.

"No, implanted in their brains—"

A loud crackle of noise came through his headset—loud enough to be audible to me.

"Just a second," Dimitri told me.

"Yeah, understood," he said into his mouthpiece. "Understood. Anyone else? All right. Understood."

He turned to me. His face showed just a flicker of wild emotion, which he struggled, more or less successfully, to control. "The bomb killed the Secretary," he said.

"What about Jack?"

DIMITRI SAID THERE was no further information at present about other casualties on the stage. I thanked him; we parted company.

I looked around the park. I wanted to make contact with Rachel, Denny Sontag, even Deborah Paton—anyone that I knew. But the diversity of faces and expressions swirling around me had one thing in common: They were all anonymous.

I pulled out my cell phone to make contact with Dugan.

All circuits were busy. Of course.

I took a moment to program the phone's round-robin feature. I listed every number I had in the phone's directory that could possibly reach Jack—eight in all—and set the phone to call each number in sequence, every thirty seconds, until it got something better than a circuits-busy buzz.

I looked up. It was clear, at least, that no one in the audience had been hurt. I saw no stretchers or medics among us. Good—

I caught sight of a familiar profile.

Deborah Paton. She looked pale in the half-moon and the artificial light. I approached her as rapidly as I could.

She saw me. Her eyes were red, teary. "We didn't want this. We didn't want this," she said in my direction.

I nodded—

My phone beeped.

I looked at the display. I had reached Sheila, Jack's secretary.

"Sheila, Phil D'Amato here," I said.

"Dr. D'Amato." She sounded terrible.

"You heard what happened in the park?" There was no point in being subtle.

"Yes, yes," she said, and took a shaky breath. "I just heard from the deputy mayor. He said the explosion was pretty powerful—amazing it didn't do more damage."

"You heard from Jack? He's okay?" There was no other deputy mayor whom Sheila would refer to as "the" deputy mayor. But I wanted to make sure.

"Oh yes, thank God, he's okay. He could have been killed!"

"I know." I took a shaky breath of my own. "Do you know where I can reach him?"

She gave me the number from which he had called her.

I thanked her.

"What happened to our world, Dr. D'Amato?"

CELL PHONE SERVICE was still spotty. It took me four tries to reach Dugan, and then all I got was his voice mail.

I told him about what Gabe had found. "Maybe the best thing now is just round up all of the squirrels in Central Park and scan them to make sure they don't have bombs in their brains." I refrained from saying, If a squirrel or squirrels were responsible here, who knew what the hell was at large in Van Cortlandt Park in the Bronx, Prospect Park in Brooklyn, and whatever they called their parks these days in Queens . . . And then there were the subways . . .

I tried Jenna on my cell phone.

"You okay?" She sounded relieved. "I just heard what happened."

"Yeah. I'm not sure how much more I can do here tonight. I should be home pretty soon." But our connection lapsed before I had finished. "No service," my ever-helpful little screen advised.

I put the phone back in my pocket and looked at the stage. There were so many security people and checkpoints from here to there, it was difficult to see much.

I decided to walk toward the stage, on the chance that I might get through some of these checkpoints and reach someone in charge, or close to it.

I didn't get very far.

"Sorry, Dr. D'Amato," the first fed I encountered told me. "We're under strict orders not to let anyone go forward, even NYPD, unless they've already been cleared."

His face had an odd expression when he said "go forward." He was likely Irish, or originally from Canada. I was once at a wake of an Irish Mountie in Toronto, and his relatives talked about "going forward"—by which they meant walking forward to look at the casket.

But other than his interesting language, this fed had little to commend him. He was far less talkative than Dimitri, and refused to budge despite my pleas.

I tried two others, at different points on the outer perimeter of security around the stage, but got the same cold shoulders and hard lines.

I looked around the park again. The crowds had thinned,

and so had the lingering warmth of the day. I shivered, and decided to head home, to Jenna and dinner—

". . . city officials injured," a voice on a passing radio said, "admitted to Cornell University Medical Center . . . Irene Palmolive with the story . . ."

That was over on the East Side, on my way home.

A CAB BROUGHT me to the vicinity in twenty minutes. I asked the cabbie if he could switch his music to an all-news station. He insisted on listening to his John Cage. I was too tired to argue.

Cop cars were everywhere. I ran into Janny Murphy—a friend since she had been a footcop, now a lieutenant. "Jack's okay, definitely," she assured me. "He left about fifteen minutes ago."

"And the injured officials?"

"The parks commissioner was bleeding a little from the biceps—I don't think it's anything serious. I don't know about the other one." She got pulled away by a sergeant with a problem. I knew it wasn't likely I would see her again this evening.

I took the uptown bus back to our brownstone on East Eighty-fifth Street. It stopped at every corner. . . .

I finally walked up the stairs to our apartment. Radios, TVs, computers with webcasts were playing out of every door. I was moving too quickly to hear what they said.

Jenna was waiting for me in the hall. She flung her arms around me.

"You sure you're okay?" she said, and touched my face.

"Yeah."

"Thank goodness no one was killed. But I heard there were injuries."

"Yeah . . . What?"

"You didn't know about the injuries?" Jenna asked, and

pulled a bit away. "I think I heard the MTA chief was wounded. They say it's not life-threatening. She was onstage with the Secretary—"

I absorbed that about Sally Li. "I'm not talking about the injuries. What do you mean, no one was killed?"

Jenna looked at me. "I—"

"The Secretary of Homeland Security was killed," I continued. "Dimitri—a fed agent stationed next me—got the report on his headset."

Jenna took my hand, pointed with her other hand to the television inside. "Julius Machem was just interviewed," she said. "They were just talking about it."

We walked in. Jenna closed the door and I looked at the TV.

Fox News was on. They were live from an airport—it looked like La Guardia.

A press conference was just ending.

I spotted the mayor—and there was Dugan.

A voice-over said Secretary Machem would be flying to Washington.

And a camera zoomed in for a close-up of Machem smiling at the camera, waving good-bye, and then turning and walking toward an airline terminal.

THERE WAS NO getting anyone useful on the phone the rest of the evening.

I left voice mail for Gabe, Rachel, and again for Dugan.

I watched every station on the damn tube, and they all reported Machem alive and well after a close call in the park. One or two national cable stations mentioned that the parks commissioner and the MTA chief were injured. The local stations gave more coverage. The commissioner's injury was minor; he was being kept in the hospital overnight for observation. There were conflicting reports about Sally Li's condition. I made more calls, found out nothing more.

Eventually, Jenna and I went to bed.

I DIDN'T CALL Dugan early the next morning.

I kissed Jenna, then went in to see him.

Secretary Machem was all over the radios and morning television shows in Dugan's outer office. The Secretary was talking about what almost happened to him yesterday in New York's Central Park. About what *had* happened to two of New York's brave officials. About how he was in the process of giving a speech about the need to protect privacy in this age of terrorism, balance the needs of freedom against the need for security, but how what had happened in the park had changed all of that. We had to get tougher, really tough now, he said. Use all means at hand . . .

Most of the people watching, the folks in Dugan's outer office, looked like they had pulled all-nighters. It was hard to say how they were reacting.

I knew how I felt about it.

"Fucking bullshit," I said to Dugan when I finally got in to see him. "That's a goddamn programmed hologram on TV out there, and you knew about this all along."

"You've got it wrong," Dugan replied. "And calm down . . . No, don't calm down. You've got a right. But you've got it wrong."

"Got what wrong?" I demanded. Who the hell cared if I offended him? He was no longer officially part of the police department. He was just a political appointee now. He couldn't fire me.

"I didn't know all along," Dugan said, unflinching.

"No?"

"No—I found out what was going on just yesterday afternoon, for the first time. I was ordered not to tell a soul. You've got a soul, right? So that included you. I suspect I was bugged, monitored, anyway, just to make sure. So if I *had* told you, all that would have accomplished was your being picked up by the feds, and monitored, too—if they didn't pull you off the street altogether."

"You were told that the plot against Machem was serious, that it might succeed, and if it did, that a hologram would be sent out in his place—all of that, just yesterday afternoon?"

"You're wrong about that, too," Dugan said wearily.

"About what? That's not a hologram of Machem out there? He survived the bomb blast? Then—"

"You're right about the hologram," Dugan said. "You've just got it a little reversed."

I looked at Dugan.

"It was the hologram of Machem giving the speech yesterday. That's the real Machem out there right now."

"I saw the mayor shake hands with him on the stage," I objected. "Is His Honor a hologram, too?"

"No, the mayor's real," Dugan replied. "But did you notice what happened after the handshake, right after the Secretary started to speak?"

I thought back to the park. "That feedback on Machem's microphone? That was staged to replace Machem with his hologram?" A quartet of fed security had indeed stepped between Machem and the microphone—meaning Machem and the audience—at that point. I doubt anyone in the crowd had been able to see Machem then. I certainly had not. . . . But some of the press had to have been in on the switch, too. "No close photos of Machem after the replacement—all the pictures were taken before the squeal . . ."

Dugan nodded.

HE INVITED ME to breakfast in his office. Organic oatmeal, at his suggestion, from a new take-out place around the corner from his building. It was delicious. It should have been calming. Oatmeal in the morning always had that effect on me. Not today.

"You have to admire their ingenuity," Dugan said, referring to the feds. "They staged the whole event, with no risk to the Secretary, to draw out the terrorists. Which it did."

"Then why move it up on such short notice?"

"The feds were concerned that word was leaking out about their hologram plans."

"To whom?"

"They didn't specify. Maybe you."

I started to react—

"No, they don't think you're a terrorist. But you knew about their holograms. They don't have a complete record of everyone you talk to—despite what you may think, they're not tailing or bugging you, at least as far as I know."

I scowled. "Their little charade last night could have killed other people. I heard the parks commissioner is out of the hospital, but the MTA chief is still there, right? Or is that just part of the performance, too?" This—Sally Li's condition—was the other thing I wanted most to talk to Dugan about, in addition to Machem.

"No, her injuries are real," Dugan said, very seriously. "She'll need at least a few weeks in the hospital. I was just on the phone with her assistant—Al Bromley—before you arrived. He'll be filling in for her while she mends."

"Jack, listen to me," I said, even more seriously. "Li and I talked yesterday. She wants it for other reasons—she's most concerned about germ-warfare, or disease—but she agrees with me that the rats and mice in the subways could pose a terrible threat. I don't know if you've spoken to Gabe—"

Dugan nodded.

"—you heard my voice mail, we saw what they can do in

the park. We don't have the time, now, to explain all of this to Al Bromley—I've barely even heard of the man—"

"He's a don't-rock-the-boat civil servant," Dugan said, "just the opposite of Sally."

I looked at Dugan intently. "That's my point."

"What do you want me to do? I can't fire him," Dugan said.

"I want you to give the order for an immediate rodent roundup in the subways, at least starting in the bigger stations. And if you don't have the power to do that, talk the mayor into issuing the order."

He shook his head slowly, negatively. "That battle was lost six months ago, you know that. . . . Look, the feds expected one of the new pinpoint bombs, designed just to take out the Secretary. The terrorists are touting them in their backweb chatter as giving them the power to take out anyone, anywhere, without harming bystanders—they're trying to clean up their image."

"Wonderful."

"Just about every federal agency has been trying to track down those bombs," Dugan continued, "see if they're real. Up until last night, no luck. Now, at least, we know. But don't you think it makes more sense, as our very next move, to focus on the parks? Since we know, from Gabe, that squirrels are carriers?"

"Math was never my strong point. But how many people use the parks, and how many use the subways? I'm glad only Machem's hologram was killed in the park last night, but goddamn it, Jack, the people in the subways aren't holograms!"

Now Dugan scowled a little.

"So what is everyone's thinking on how the almost-pinpoint bomb was delivered?" I asked. "Do they agree with my voice mail?"

"I forwarded it to the feds," Dugan replied. "It's one of five delivery theories. The feds think it's the least likely. I also passed it on to the police commissioner."

"And?"

"Dunno. Haven't heard back from them on that yet."

"Of course not. The feds are busy taking advantage of the situation, pushing the agenda Machem wanted in the first place—more security, less freedom," I said.

Dugan's phone rang. He indicated that I should stay.

"Mr. Secretary. Of course. Always glad to cooperate. Sure, we'll keep you posted, and I hope your office does the same for us. Certainly, I will."

Dugan made a face, got off the phone. "Machem wants me to convey his best regards to the mayor."

"Why the hell was he reported killed in the first place? I heard that straight from a fed agent's mouth at the scene—he didn't seem to be putting on an act for my sake."

"Chatter factor," Dugan replied. "The feds wanted to see if the report of the Secretary's death got the terrorists to say anything interesting in their back channels."

"Have they?"

"Nothing more from Homeland Security about that yet, either."

I frowned.

"Look," Dugan said, "I'm no fan of the guy myself, believe me."

"I've heard."

Dugan regarded me. "Oh?"

"You know, rumors that you'd like his job."

Dugan took a long sip of his coffee, black.

"My highest aspiration used to be police commissioner," he said quietly. "That's all I had ever wanted to be, even as a kid."

"What happened?"

"Oh, you know what happened. Same thing that happened to all of us. September 11. Everything that came after. But when I looked out at those towers burning, when I first saw them on that morning, I knew right then that much as I loved the uniform, I needed to do more. I want to help make policy, not just follow it. My family's been following loyally for four generations. But these times require more. Does that sound crazy?" His voice was hoarse, and his eyes were moist.

"No, not all," I replied. "That's why I'm here myself right now. I can't just collect and analyze forensic evidence for ordinary crimes anymore—"

Dugan harrumphed. "Don't bullshit me, Phil—you've been wanting to do more than just ordinary rapes and murders since the day I met you."

That was true enough. "Yeah. But now I have more reason—or, at least, a reason just about everyone agrees with, even you."

Dugan smiled, a little sadly. "Point taken." He returned to his coffee. He kept his hand and eyes on the cup. . . . "Should we talk a little about suspects now?" He slowly lifted his gaze to mine. "The squirrels didn't do this on their own." He reached into the file drawer in his desk and pulled out a manila folder.

RACHEL SALDANA'S NAME was in several places, and not just for her squirrel autopsies.

I glanced up at Dugan. "So she's an animal rights activist," I said. "I'd figured as much—not exactly a federal crime, if you'll pardon the expression."

"She got right by me, too," Dugan said. "Same with Ed Monti. Let's hope it's not any more than it seems. Sweet little piece of work—but keep reading. Wait till you get to the section on the live-in boyfriend."

"Okay." I found the boyfriend part. He was a writer, all

right—with half a dozen bylines in the violently anti-American newspapers which had sprung up in Europe in the past year, and were probably here as well. I stopped at a clipping of an especially egregious little essay: TOWARD AN ASSASSINATION OF THE AMERICAN DREAM.

I caught a paragraph near the end:

Religiously motivated terrorism isn't enough. Political terrorism, personal terrorism, psychoterrorism—each has a part to play in laying the American dream to ruin.

I shook my head. "Is there any indication at all that she shares his views—even knows about them?" Goddammit, if she was in league with her boyfriend, she had played me perfectly. I had been so proud of myself, hadn't I, for sticking Frank with the bogus hamster and delivering the real thing right into Rachel's hands. . . .

"I was hoping *you* might be able to tell *me*," Jack replied.

"How the hell did she get hired, get by our background checks, with a boyfriend like that? Are we that lame? Maybe the boyfriend was a recent addition?"

Dugan nodded. "About six months, we think. She's been working in the medical examiner's office for more than five years—we don't do continuing background checks on employees. The only reason we looked at her now is that the feds asked for checks on any city law enforcement working on unusual, recent cases. Saldana qualified."

I shook my head.

"Right, Phil—you did, too. . . . Look, I'm no dumb tool for the feds, I think you know that. Rachel Saldana's one of ours—my first instinct is to protect and defend her. But we've got to know what's going on—especially if your squirrel theory's right."

I sipped tea. "Well, try this: It just occurred to me that

Rachel is the only one who knew about the good conversation I had with Sally yesterday. So, if she's in with the terrorists, she gets them to maneuver the squirrels to take out not only Machem but Sally. You know what? She made a big deal about not killing a squirrel to see what was inside its head—after we'd seen a bright orange dot in there on the M&MRI. Maybe she didn't want us looking too closely because that dot was the bomb, and—jeez, she brought that squirrel with the bomb in its head right up to the park yesterday. How's that for a take on what happened? Is that too crazy?" A lot of me thought it was. I pictured Rachel in the park. . . .

Dugan grimaced. "Back to the subways again, huh? On that score, yeah, your theory's probably too crazy. . . ."

"What do we know about Freddie Jason?" I asked.

"Your question is the first I've heard of him," Dugan replied. "Who is he?"

"As long as we're focusing on Rachel, we might as well look at him, too. He runs the fancy equipment in Rachel's lab. He was on the right side of the squirrel surgery argument yesterday, but he had an odd intensity."

"Comes with the territory for a lot of these technicians—better with software than people."

"Yeah."

"But why don't you get over to their building this morning, and interview both of them—separately. Keep some cops nearby in case things go badly."

"My thoughts, entirely." I finished the tea and pulled back my chair. "By the way—what were the other four?"

"Four? What?"

"Delivery methods—that the feds are looking into, in addition to mine."

Dugan waved a dismissive hand. "Garbage. Someone somehow sneaked through all that security, our bomb squad missed something in its sweep. . . . I'm getting smart—or maybe a little nuts, listening to you all of these years. I'm betting on your squirrels."

"Then keep thinking about rats and mice in the subways, too. . . ."

"The parks commissioner is rounding up squirrels as fast as they can throw peanuts in the southwest corner of the park. We'll see what they come up with, and then take it from there regarding rodents in other places. Best I can do on this, Phil, believe me."

MAYBE SO. BUT I couldn't let it be the best that I could do.

I called Janny Murphy right after I left Dugan. "I know, we're out of contact for months, and then twice in two days. . . . But I need someone with a little clout in the Department—you're a lieutenant now—to do a strange little favor for me, no questions asked, right away. . . . Yeah, I wouldn't ask if it wasn't crucially important. . . . Yeah, that's the way I operate, I'll never change. . . ." I asked her if she could round up a couple of cops and animal control people and pick up all the mice and rats they could get their hands on at Grand Central, then call me. "You know a guy at the ASPCA? Excellent. Thanks. I owe you one on this, Janny. Yeah, I know I already owe you a lot." I also gave her Mel's number—the only rodent expert I could think of that I trusted—and then left voice mail for him at The Grace Note that Janny might be calling. . . .

I turned my attention to Rachel.

"McQuail? You got an hour with a partner you can spare? Excellent. Much appreciated."

I was in Rachel's building, on her floor, with McQuail and his partner, Harry, twenty minutes later.

Her office was locked.

Perhaps she was in her secret office, but I had no direct access to it. I could call her, but . . . I decided to drop in on Freddie Jason first.

He responded to my knock with a smirk.

"Got a few minutes?" I asked.

He nodded and waved me in. McQuail and Harry followed. Jason didn't object.

I looked at his desk, next to which was seated . . . "Frank," slightly gleaming, maybe a bit less matte today than Temp, or the way "Frank" had looked the other day. I could tell by the way McQuail and Harry were breathing—they almost gasped—that they were surprised by the sight. But they were too professional to say anything.

I turned from "Frank" to Jason. "So, you two are friends?" I asked matter-of-factly.

"More like, I'm one of his programmers," Jason responded. "Hey, I'm the ghost-of-Frank-Catania's handler—were you a boxer, Frank?"

"Frank" ignored Jason and looked at me. "Phil," he said. "An unexpected pleasure."

And a feat of programming for the unexpected, I thought. This was the first time I had talked to either Temp or "Frank," when they hadn't expected me, or my presence hadn't been advertised by a prior scanning of my credentials—

Though, I had shown my ID in the lobby of this building to enter in the first place, and that could have been relayed upstairs to Kid Hacker here, and whoever else helped program "Frank". . . .

I shook off this analysis—it could wait for later—and focused on the matter, and the nonmaterial entity, at hand.

"So I assume you two are fully conversant about what happened in the park yesterday?" I asked.

"I helped program the Secretary's hologram," Jason replied laboriously, as if he were talking to an idiot. "I do contract work for the Department of Homeland Security."

"We were glad no one was killed," "Frank" added.

I looked at the hologram for a second, and realized I had

no way of knowing if this was the "Frank" who had warned me yesterday about someone inside the Department—someone who might have been Rachel—or a "Frank" doppelganger, a completely different set of programs behind what looked and sounded like Frank, controlled by people other than those who controlled the original hologram "Frank," with who-knew-what intentions. . . .

What a situation . . . Will the real Frank hologram, the real illusion, please stand up?

But given this predicament, I had to be very careful about what I said.

"Do you know where Rachel Saldana is?" I asked, of neither party in particular.

"I haven't seen her since yesterday," Jason replied. He gave me a defiant look—as if daring me to ask more. Or maybe that was just the way he looked.

"She told me you took the squirrel, on Ed's say-so."

"Did she? Well, that would not be true."

"So the squirrel would be, where now?"

Jason shrugged. "No idea. It was here when I left—so were you, remember?"

"You were pretty angry when you stalked out—you said you were going to Ed's. What happened when you saw him?" I asked Jason.

"I didn't—Ed Monti was in Albany yesterday. And before I had a chance to talk to anyone else on First Avenue, I got a call from Homeland Security. They had some last-ditch questions about the interplay of the cyberspotlights and the hologram in the park."

"And you're an expert on that, right."

"Phil, you're questioning this kid like a perp," "Frank" piped up. "He's on our side."

I felt like telling the hologram to shut up. I regarded Jason.

"And your opinion, then, on what was inside that squirrel's head? If you had to bet?"

"I'd bet telecom," Jason replied. "I know you told our friend here"—he gestured to the hologram—"that you think he was killed by a bomb-brained squirrel. I've heard the rumors about the dot-com bombs. I know I reacted strongly yesterday—hey, the city doesn't pay me enough to risk my life on this shit—neither do the feds, for that matter—but if I had to bet, hey, a telecom in hand's worth two bombs in the bush. . . ." He chuckled. "There's a good joke in there, somewhere. I could figure it out if I had the time."

So he didn't know about Gabe's findings. And neither did his sector of fed intelligence . . . Well, Jack had forwarded my squirrel hypothesis to his contacts just a few hours ago. . . .

"So, if Rachel brought our squirrel up to the park yesterday, your best guess would be the worst it was packing was telecom," I said to Jason. And I still wanted to believe that—even though it made no sense, or less sense than she was deploying a squirrel to kill Sally Li. . . . Everything else that Jason had told me made Rachel a liar. . . .

He got a peculiar gleam in his eye. "You know what? Let me show you just how much of an expert I am—I'll let you ask Rachel herself." He looked at "Frank," smiled, and did something on the keyboard in front of him. "Frank" dissolved into . . . "Rachel".

She was naked from the waist up, and not grey at all. Her breasts were the color of buttermilk, and her nipples were rich brown—

"That's enough," I told Jason.

I heard McQuail and Harry shifting, clearing throats, whatever, behind me—

"Oh, you don't like her that way?" Jason responded. "Well, how about this?" He touched the keyboard again, and the hologram of Rachel dissolved into . . . another hologram of her. I saw enough to see that this Rachel was naked from the waist down—

"I said that's enough." I lunged at Jason, grabbed his wrist—

"Okay, okay," he said. "I could do one of you, but I thought you'd prefer Rachel." I let him pull his hand free. "Here's Frank, again—you seem the most comfortable with him."

"Frank" reappeared. "You're getting a little physical there, Phil—not like you," "Frank" intoned.

Of course "he" had heard, seen, what had just happened—"Frank," "Rachel" nude, clothed, in-between, had the same eyes and ears—the cameras and microphones of the hologram's programmers.

My cell phone rang. "All right, Phil. We've got nine mice and fourteen rats in custody," Janny said. "What should we do with them?"

TWENTY-TWO

I asked Janny to hold on a second.

I looked at "Frank"—"I wish you well," I told the hologram. And I meant it, at least for that part of the specter who had been Federal Agent Frank Catania, Office of Surveillance in the Department of Homeland Security, if any part of that man was still in this hologram.

I nodded to Jason. "We'll be in touch, I'm sure," I told him.

I signalled McQuail and Harry that we should leave. We tried Rachel's office again. It was still locked. "Call the medical examiner's office, find out her home address," I told them. "Get over there as fast as you can, and take her into custody if you find her."

They nodded, turned, and walked to the staircase at the end of the hall. "Nice snatch," I heard Harry say as the door closed behind them.

I took Janny off hold. "Sorry to keep you waiting," I told her. "Great work."

"Thanks. What do I do with it?"

"You know where the bomb squad is headquartered?"

"Of course."

"Good. Bring your menagerie right over there, and leave it with Gabe Nebuch. He'll know what to with it."

"All right . . . Big time, Phil, big time."

"You got it, Janny. And I won't be the only one who owes you, big time, if this pans out."

I ended the call with Janny and called Gabe.

I got his voice mail.

Damn. I hung up, and thought who else I could call.

I certainly couldn't have the rodents delivered to Rachel. There was Jason. No, I didn't like him, I didn't trust him, and I didn't have the time to decide whether that was just personal or I was picking something else up about him. . . . I could have the rats and mice delivered to Ed Monti. . . .

I tried him. Voice mail for him, too.

I might as well go with Gabe's—at least he knew what was going on. "Hey Gabe, Phil D'Amato here. Lt. Janny Murphy will be delivering a bunch of rats and mice to you—they were just rounded up in Grand Central. I know you have your hands full with squirrels being picked up in the park, but I need you to find out what's happening in the brains of the Grand Central rodents, too. Call me when you receive the message so I know you heard it." If Gabe didn't hear it in time—Janny would be arriving there in about twenty minutes—Janny would no doubt call me, and I could figure out what plan B was then. . . .

Plan A, I knew, was nothing to write home about, either. Even if Grand Central were crawling with rat and mice time bombs, the likelihood of finding any of that in the thirteen rodents Janny had in tow was practically nil. But any chance better than zero was a chance. And if that didn't work, I had one or two other desperate moves. . . .

My cell phone rang. The caller's ID was unfamiliar—not Gabe, Ed, or Janny.

"Phil, I've been hacked. I'm unreliable." It was "Frank"—or some facsimile of "him" or "his" voice.

"I gathered as much," I replied. "How do you suggest we proceed?"

"I can give you a codeword right now. Don't talk to me again unless I say it to you first."

"I don't think so," I said, and hung up.

The real Frank wouldn't have been so naive as to suggest a code word after what had just happened inside. Neither would the real "Frank."

Both would have realized that, if the "Frank" inside had been compromised, I would have no way of knowing, just from this conversation outside, whether I was talking to the compromised or uncompromised—real—"Frank." The voice on the phone could well be the compromised, Jason-hacked "Frank," setting me up to regard "him" as authentic with a code word. I would confide in "him," be advised by "him," all because, why?—"he" could repeat a codeword which had been created by Freddie Jason?

No, I didn't think so.

The real Frank, as well as the real hologram of Frank, would have understood. . . .

I walked to the exit, down the staircase, and out of Rachel's building. For all I knew, Jason might have been "Frank's" programmer all along—and Temp's and who knew who else's. Well, there was nothing I could do about that. All I could be is very careful about what I said to holograms now—especially one I had just seen in Jason's office.

I thought about my next move. If I was right about the danger from rodents the city now faced, I couldn't afford any mistakes. And I didn't have much time.

I dialed another number on my cell phone—Cerebreeze. Back in business or not, I hoped someone would answer its phone.

"Hi, Phil D'Amato, NYPD," I said to the laconic receptionist, a new voice on me. "I'd like to speak to either Jill Cormier or Marty Glick, whoever's available."

"Well, which one, sir?"

"Make it Jill Cormier."

"Very good."

The usual discordant string of sounds followed.

"Phil! How are you?"

Jeez, it was Jill. I hadn't expected to get her so easily. I stopped by a lamppole near the subway so I could concentrate fully on this conversation.

"You heard what happened in the park yesterday?" I asked.

"Yes, Deborah told me. I'm glad no one was killed."

So much for Deborah's claim that she and Jill weren't each other's keepers. Maybe not, but they kept in close touch after the bombing.

"Yeah," I replied. "Look, can I run a little theory by you?" Ordinarily, I would have done this in person, so I could get the full nonverbal gamut of Jill's response. And to prevent Jill from bolting in response to something I said. But I couldn't take the chance that I might not talk to her at all today—or tomorrow, or who knew when—if I didn't take this opportunity now.

"Sure," she responded. "Go right ahead."

"Well, what would you think if I told you I was thinking that the explosion in the park yesterday was caused by a powerful little nugget of a bomb embedded in a squirrel's head. I'm asking what you would think of this as a scientist who has had some experience with some kinds of implants in rodents. You're the only one who's been honest with me about the squirrels."

"I understand what you're asking," Jill replied. "Can I ask you a question first? Am I under suspicion in some way for yesterday's explosion? Are you asking me these questions in preparation for arresting me or building a case against me? Should I call my attorney?"

"No, not necessary." From a strictly legal point of view,

correct procedure was to err on the side of telling suspects they were under suspicion if there was any suspicion at all, and certainly advise them they might need an attorney if they asked. Not doing so could lead to charges of entrapment, which could weaken the subsequent court case. But I was after prevention, not conviction, at this point.

"I'll be happy to talk to you, then," Jill said. "But not here, not on the phone."

"Where are you?" My earlier calls to Cerebreeze had been routed off-site—to Manhattan.

"Never mind that."

"Okay, where would you like to meet, then?" I obviously had no choice. If I wanted to talk to her, it would be on her terms.

"I was coming in to your area anyway," Jill said. "How about same place as last time? Fifty-ninth Street and Fifth Avenue—southeast side of the park. About eleven o'clock?"

DUGAN CALLED ME right after I got off the phone with Jill.

I looked at the lamp pole, my watch, gave in, and leaned back against the black wrought iron.

A classic pose for early twenty-first-century Homo sapiens: leaning against a lamppost, cell phone to the face. They ought to make one of those bronze, urban, everyday-people statues of that pose and place it right here, so there would always be someone leaning on a lamppost, talking on the phone, on this corner. . . .

Dugan got right to the point. "Early results are in from our squirrel roundup near the bomb site," he told me. "Two kinds of modules have shown up inside their little heads on the scans so far. One comes with little antlers on the outside, the other has nothing but the module inside the skull."

"No bombs?"

"So far, Nebuch and Sontag think not—we're double-teaming on this, treating all the modules as bombs until we know better."

"Good."

"I'm still betting on your theory," Dugan said. "So far, the other four theories have borne no fruit at all. No evidence in hand supports them, I'm sure you'll be happy to hear."

"Believe me, I wish I were wrong."

"I hear you—let's keep each other posted."

I CAUGHT THE uptown train. My cell phone rang, but the subway was so noisy I didn't hear the phone until my voice mail kicked in. I accessed it. Message from Gabe: "Happy to give your subway rodents our hospitality. I'll be back to you with results as soon I have them."

I arrived at the southeast corner of Grand Central Park.

. . . Jill was there, sitting on a bench. More than one of my cases, I reflected, seemed to resolve themselves on park benches. . . . I hoped this was a good omen.

She looked up at me and smiled. I sat next to her.

"You never should have been involved in this in the first place," she said. "You know that."

"Yes, I know that very well—it's pretty much the story of my life—or, at least, my professional life."

She chuckled slightly. "You're a local forensic detective, Phil. This business has implications that go far beyond New York City—I know, New York has been a central part of this from the very beginning, but I think that . . ." She trailed off, shook her head.

"It might surprise you that I've been enmeshed in things that go way beyond this city since long before September 11," I said.

"Really," she said doubtfully.

"Some of my cases involving genetics have been pretty well publicized—DNA dates from long before New York. And primitive cultures . . . and, well, some things I can't really talk about."

"But you want me to talk about what *I* know," Jill said.

I nodded. "We're both scientists. But in this little setting, I'm the cop, and you're the—"

"Suspect?"

I shook my head no. "Would you believe 'civilian'? And, who knows, maybe even savior . . ."

"Whatever you say . . . Okay, so what's your first question for me? How about: where was I last night?"

"Good a start as any," I replied. "Deborah told you I was asking about you?"

Jill smiled. "And the answer is: I was at our command center, monitoring what was coming in from our squirrels. We have two different kinds in the field at this point."

"And your command center was where, at the Grace Building?"

Jill looked impressed. "Yes."

"And you're going to tell me about the two different kinds of squirrels now? I assume the differences are in telecom outfitting, not whether the squirrels are grey or black?"

"Right. We don't care about the color. We operate, after all, under Equal Opportunity provisions, like all government agencies." She smiled again.

"And the two different kinds of telecom in the squirrels?"

"Maybe you've encountered them—I can't remember what you told me in our prior conversations," Jill said. "The older squirrels have telecom nodes jutting out of their heads—just like what you saw with the hamsters. We're phasing them out, for obvious reasons. The newer nodes are entirely internal."

"One of those squirrels was the source of my picture at Gnarlingview—Deborah Paton was telling the truth at first, wasn't she? She's actually a part of your government group—and the civil liberties group is a front or she's infiltrated it, right? A federal agent impersonating a scientist impersonating a First Amendment zealot—she gave a hell of a performance."

Jill nodded.

"And you were looking at images from those online squirrels in the park, back at the Grace Building, last night," I said.

Jill nodded again. "The Gnarlingview squirrel would have had external nodes—I don't believe we ever got any internals up there."

A panopticon of squirrels.

But they failed to prevent the attack last night.

"We have close to a hundred internals fielded in the park at this point, mostly in the southern part." Jill waved to the trees, the paths, the tired grass all around us. "And about fifty externals. And, oh yeah, about ten of those externals have no internal components at all—we were beta-testing a setup in which the external nodes did all the telecom. The surgery on the squirrel was less demanding. But we dropped that line when we decided to go completely internal."

So that explained the first squirrel in Rachel's lab. "Do you know Freddie Jason, by any chance? He's a computer technician who works for our medical examiner, apparently also has access to federal systems?"

"No, never heard of him," Jill replied. "But the Department of Homeland Security has lots of operations going, and I wouldn't know the personnel in most of them. I can check on him, if you like—Freddie Jason?"

I nodded. "Thanks . . . Now let's talk about the bombers. There's actually another variety of squirrel, a third variety that you haven't mentioned, and these are outfitted with bombs in their brains, right? Equal Opportunity killers."

Jill spoke slowly. "Apparently. But we don't know anything

about them. We were hoping you could educate us about them, Phil. You seem to be the resident expert."

THIS OF COURSE was where I had come in on this conversation, on the phone—asking Jill to tell me what she knew about the squirrel bombers. Except now she was the one asking. Which was likely why she had agreed to see me.

"Meaning, your people did not send out those squirrels?" I asked her.

"Of course not! You think *we* killed Frank Catania?" She was indignant.

"His death could have been an accident," I retorted. I also reflected that her mention of Frank in this context meant that she had some mole in the NYPD bomb squad, with access to what Gabe Nebuch had told me only yesterday, or maybe some source into Dugan, whom I had briefed about this just this morning. And she didn't care that I knew this.

"Look," Jill said, succeeding in keeping her anger, real or fabricated, under control. "I've been honest with you. I've told you what we know, what our side—"

"What side, exactly, is that?" I interrupted.

"Department of Homeland Security, Office of Surveillance, same side as Frank's. As I've told you."

I nodded. Paton, Jill, Frank when he was alive, all on the same team, made some sense. It explained what Frank had really been up to at Cerebreeze and Gnarlingview. I still had some questions about all of that—like why Jill had sent me up to Gnarlingview behind Frank's back, and Paton had blown it up, if all three were on the same team—but I wanted her to continue. "Okay."

"I've told you the truth about what our side has contributed to this," Jill reiterated. "As a result, whether you like it or not, we expect you to keep your mouth shut about this. We expect you to be open with us, about what you know. There's no in-between for you. The only way out for you now is—"

"What? You blow me up?"

"For God's sake, Phil, don't be ridiculous! What do you take us for? Our government's not in the habit of just killing people, for any reason, unless they're terrorists or working hand in hand with them."

"So what's my only way out?"

Jill stood suddenly. "I told you what I told you. If you can't accept the strings attached, then consider it a gift and I'll just walk away, right now, and never talk to you again. We'll both have to live with those consequences." She made to leave.

"Sit down, please," I said. "I'm willing to extend some level of trust to you."

"All right, then." Jill sat. "So, to resume: What do *you* know about the squirrel bombers?"

I considered. Her side—the Federal Office of Surveillance, if she was telling the truth—did blow up Cerebreeze. I heard Glick and her talking about that. But no one had been killed or even hurt in that or any of the lab bombings. I had to give them that.

So I told her what I knew and suspected about the squirrel bombings. And I told her my nightmare about rats and mice in Grand Central, because that was one of the reasons I was having this conversation. I needed some last resorts, however unreliable, in case Dugan and the NYPD fell through.

Jill took it in, said nothing. "Okay," she said when I was finished, "but what we're most interested in is . . . what first made you think about squirrels as bombers? It's a pretty bizarre scenario. I guess squirrels as peripatetic webcams is, too. But I don't know, that's still more passive, and odd forms of bugging have been around for decades."

I thought about it. The idea had been nibbling at me for a while now. Frank's death had given it jagged teeth. . . . "I'm not sure," I said. "You want to know whose words set me in that direction?" I understood the strategy. The speaker of the crime was sometimes its maker. "Squirrels were part of this from day one. You got me started on the telecom. Then the bombs began. We stopped a St. Bernard with a bomb around its neck in the library. Bombs in the brain seemed the next logical step."

Jill nodded gravely. "That's probably just how the terrorists reasoned," she said.

"You think squirrels were responsible for Cerebreeze and Gnarlingview?" I asked her. Might as well push her on this and see what resulted.

"You mean the explosions there?"

"Yeah," I replied.

She looked at me. "No," she said. "We were responsible for both of those, and they weren't done with squirrels."

I couldn't be sure if she thought I already knew the answer and was testing her, or if I was genuinely asking. Passing the test the latter way would of course have been more impressive, but at least she hadn't lied. I still needed to find out more about the "we" in her "we were responsible" . . . the flowchart of Frank, Jill, and Paton. . . .

"So let's go over what we—both of us, now—know," I said. "You guys in the Department of Homeland Security have Peeping Tom squirrels and eavesdropping hamsters, right?"

Jill nodded.

"Whose vintage is at least a few years?" I asked.

"Let's just say this started well before our Department even came into existence, and the squirrels are more recent than the hamsters. But we're really still in the beginning stages with all of this. Even the hamsters. There's lots in those little brains of theirs that doesn't make sense."

"Any other telecomming critters I should know about?"

"We've developed a nice line of Seeing Eye dogs—they

operate the same as the squirrels," Jill replied. "The dogs obviously are the eyes of choice indoors."

"Okay, Peeping Tom dogs," I said. And this confirmed what Temp had told me in Wilmington, and what I was pretty sure I had seen in the park last night. Again, I had no way of knowing if Jill knew that I knew about the dogs. She conceivably could have had access to Temp via her work with Frank. But, again, it was to her credit that at least she hadn't lied about the dogs. "And you actually have two kinds of altered squirrels. Older outies and newer innies. And a few of the outies have self-sufficient antlers."

"Yes."

"So the question remains: Who is responsible for the squirrel bombers—and the likely answer is terrorists," I said.

"Who else?"

Frank's hologram had told me—when his hologramic persona was still trustworthy, or, at least, not compromised—that someone on the "inside" of local New York law enforcement was involved. . . . "The terrorists wouldn't have adopted the squirrel, had they not known about your own deployment of squirrel viewers. It's not only a logical move, as you said, it's brilliant, because it fits right in with the confusing situation you already have with the different squirrel telecom setups. There's no way such a clever choice of bomber camouflage could be coincidence."

"Agreed," Jill said.

"Your agency is the likely source of such information, since the NYPD—at least, as far as I know—knew next to nothing about squirrels in any context other than 'give me peanuts and popcorn, and once in a while I have rabies.' "

"You suspect Frank?"

"Not as much since he was killed."

"I hear you," Jill said. "He was part of our team."

"Operation Wildflower?"

"Yeah. We didn't agree on everything."

"You certainly didn't when it came to letting me know about the squirrelcom," I observed. "Why did you send me up to Gnarlingview, if you knew you were going to torch it?"

"That was Frank's call, to send it up in smoke." She sighed. "Wildflower became Wildfire . . . He gave the order for Cerebreeze, too—"

Right, he had been up there that morning, too—

"—he was concerned that the terrorists had infiltrated our operation—he didn't want them getting their hands on any of our animals. . . . The order for Gnarlingview was already in motion. I didn't like it—Deborah didn't, either. We had no choice. But I figured hey, you're one of the good guys—no reason you shouldn't see what we were doing. And you might have, if you'd arrived a little earlier."

Damned T over the Charles, I recalled. "And . . . you were the one who got the hamster to me—Walter—in the Grace Building, weren't you?"

Jill nodded. "And Frank tried to take it back from you, I know. His philosophy, even when he wasn't worrying about infiltration, was give the questioner information only about what the questioner already knew or suspected. You had already seen some of the hamster operation at Cerebreeze, so Frank thought, all right, you could be satisfied by limited disclosure of just our hamsters. You see . . . we operate much more independently of one another in our little group, more individually than in traditional agencies. It's part of the new decentralized strategy. It's supposed to maximize creative input—everyone agrees it's been in short supply. Closer cooperation between agencies, more independence for individual operatives in the field, but Frank was still in charge. Don't look so surprised. Do you work a hundred percent in lockstep with your superiors in the NYPD?"

"So, who else, other than Frank and you, might have been

operating independently in your group—so independently that they primed the terrorists for the squirrels?"

"I know you don't like Deborah," Jill responded, "but I'd be stunned if she was the one—her niece was killed in a terrorist bombing in Tel Aviv. She was like a daughter to her. She has no children of her own."

I nodded. "I'll take your word for it."

Jill thought for a few moments. "This has been very useful to me," she said, in a suddenly summarizing tone. "And I hope you feel the same."

"More or less."

"Let me talk with some of my people and see if I can get an inkling of who might be the problem in our organization. And perhaps you can do the same with the NYPD—we can't rule out the possibility that the terrorists have someone inside your operation who might have some access to what you know."

"True, we can't."

"And why don't we speak again tomorrow—phone'll be okay then. You can call me at the same number you did today."

"All right. But I need to think about one more thing right away—something that may need to be done before tomorrow."

"Okay . . ."

"I told you my concerns about rat and mice bombers—they could do far more damage than squirrels. They're an extension of the same logic—mice were the government's first telecom rodents, remote-control rats have been in the press. I want you to see what it would take to get the Department of Homeland Security to shut down New York City's subway system, beginning with Grand Central, and sweep it all clean of rodents. I—"

Jill was shaking her head, rolling her eyes—

"Homeland Security has that authority, doesn't it?"

"Yes," she said, "but—"

"Then I want you to be goddamn ready to use it. Wouldn't it be nice to prevent rather than recover from a terrorist catastrophe for a change?"

She grew quiet. "Local authorities can't cover it?"

"You know I wouldn't be asking if I had confidence that we could."

She exhaled slowly. "I'll see what I can do."

"Thank you."

She nodded. "No guarantees, you know that . . ." She looked toward Fifty-ninth Street. "My boss will be here in a minute. He'll want to talk to you—just the two of you, a few words. That's the way we do things."

"No problem."

"I'll speak to him afterward about the subways, I promise you."

"Why not now?"

"It may work better if I line up some other support first . . . trust me on this."

What choice did I have?

"Ah, there he is," Jill said.

SOMETIMES FIRST IMPRESSIONS prove out over time. Jill had said Marty Glick was her boss the first time all three of us had met at Cerebreeze, and here she was, introducing him to me as her boss again.

But of a very different kind of operation.

She smiled at me, then rose from the bench. She and Marty conversed briefly, out of my earshot, and she walked away, down Fifth Avenue.

Marty approached and stood about a foot in front of me. He gave me his same easy grin.

"Jill thinks you're okay," he began.

"Glad to hear it."

"I wanted to explain to you, in a little more detail, the responsibilities you now have, given that Jill has told you what she told you."

"I'm listening."

"We sincerely hope you'll keep working for the city, just as you have, and be part of our organization—at the same time."

"You mean a federal spy on local law enforcement?" I asked. Frank had said pretty much the same on the train back from Wilmington.

"I think you understand what I'm saying," Glick replied. "Now if you choose not to—and this is, indeed, your choice—we, for our part, will try to understand that, too."

"Good."

"And don't worry. As I know Jill assured you, we won't kill you or do anything like that."

"That's especially good."

"But please understand that if you decide not to work with us, that doesn't mean we will simply forget that we—and you and Jill—had this conversation. Yes, as Jill told you, we won't talk to you any further, we won't tell you another thing. But understand that we'll be aware, *always*, of what you now know—what we told you. And if something arises in which it seems that information such as what you now have somehow fell into bad hands—well, let's just say we'll know where to come looking."

I nodded. "Got it." I wasn't sure I'd be able to keep my concerns about rats and mice to myself in this conversation, despite Jill's plea.

Glick grinned again. "Look, these questions of who gave what information to whom happen all the time—it's what you and Jill are looking into right now, right?—so we've got to keep tabs. But understand, again, that I—we, Jill and I—hope that you'll join us."

"I promise I'll think very seriously about that," I said.

"Good. Can't ask for more. And you'll be calling Jill tomorrow, right?"

"Yes."

"Thank you," Glick said smartly, turned, and started walking away.

I stood up. "Marty?"

He turned around to face me.

I bounded up to him.

"Yes?" he asked.

I shook his hand.

"Does this mean you're in?"

"Not necessarily," I replied. "I just had to make sure you were for real."

I LOOKED AT Glick as he walked away, and then at my cell phone. It betrayed a variety of incoming calls that had arrived since I had joined Jill on the bench and set the phone to "Silent."

I returned Gabe's first, and got right through to him.

"Phil—good news about your subway vermin—they're clean as a whistle!"

"You sure?"

"Of course I'm sure—do you want the gory details? I looked right into their brains."

I thought quickly. Yes, excellent news in one sense, bad news in another. If Grand Central was crawling with four-legged time bombs, and this minuscule sample had missed them . . . "Gabe, can I ask you a favor? Could you not tell anyone about these rodent inspections for the time being?"

"Well . . . sure," he said. "We're up to our asses in squirrel work now anyway. . . . I'd have to report the rats and mice eventually—they were officially logged in our records—but I suppose that could wait until tomorrow. . . ."

"Thanks, Gabe—whatever time you could give me would

be appreciated." Dammit, I was tempted to ask him if he might be willing to falsify the results and tell Dugan and the feds that a rat or two had a bomb in its head. . . . "Any progress as yet on the squirrels?"

"We're close, but not ready for a formal report. But . . . between you and me . . . yeah, there's no doubt that a few of our squirrels had some very powerful dot-com artillery in their skulls. We're not quite sure yet how they operate. We're being very careful how we detonate the dots—obvious reasons . . ."

"All right, thanks for everything, Gabe. We'll be in touch." So the dot-com bombs were real—more reason than ever to worry about rats and mice in subways. Of course the bombs turned up in the squirrels first. The mice and rats Gabe had examined numbered a pitiful thirteen.

I walked slowly toward the Columbus Circle subway. Probably the best thing I could do was get back to my office now. . . . I looked at my cell phone with an eye toward returning the other calls—

"Sorry—" a man, about forty, apologized. He had bumped into my arm as he rushed down the street.

I look around, and realized a lot of people were rushing, walking quickly . . . in a direction opposite mine.

I walked on. The crowd got bigger, faster . . . I looked ahead and saw they were pouring out of several subway entrances. . . .

I hurried toward the closest.

I glanced at my cell phone before putting it in my pocket. It said "Circuits Busy". . . .

A little boy ran into my knees. "Johnny, watch where you're going. Apologize to the man," a woman, I assumed the boy's mother, admonished him.

"That's okay," I said, smiled at the boy, and hurried on.

“What’s going on here?” I asked a police officer directing pedestrians out of the subway. I showed him my ID.

“All I know is it’s something at Grand Central,” he said. “No trains are going in or out of there.”

PART V:

The Grace Note

TWENTY-THREE

I looked again at my phone. Circuits were still busy, of course.

I looked around. What was the fastest way to get to Grand Central?

Trains were out. The streets were already so clogged that buses and taxis would be of no use. Neither would walking—I wouldn't make much speed through elbows and knees and holiday shoppers with packages at intersections. But I started walking, anyway—

Wait. Maybe there was another way. I looked north to the park. Somewhere not too far in there was a manhole cover and a passage below straight to the Grace Building. I hadn't been able to get it open last time, but I hadn't tried very long. It was worth a try now. If I failed, it would cost me ten, fifteen minutes at most. . . .

I had a pretty clear idea of where it was. I walked quickly. No, not quite there . . . I changed direction, very slightly. . . . No, not there either . . . Don't tell me it had disappear—Ah, there it was. Corroded and rusty, just as it should be. . . .

I looked around me. I wondered if there were any security still around from last night, cyber or human. A group of people walked by me—businessmen dressed in sharp suits, out of place in the park. I thought I heard one of them say something about bombs in the subways—

I focused on the manhole cover. I ran my hands over it very carefully. Nothing happened, same as last time. Damn. I took out my phone. It still said "Circuits Busy," but . . . well, I had nothing to lose.

I called up the phone's memory and played a palm-code sequence—the one that had gotten me into the lab on the fortieth floor of the Grace Building. I heard a noise in the manhole, then a voice that only I could hear, in this position—

"Please step back. The facility will open in ten seconds, and you'll have twenty seconds to enter. Please step back—"

Yes! The voice sounded like the one I had heard at the bottom on the elevator in Grace—like the futuristic woman in the Washington Metro—

I stepped back.

The manhole cover spun around quickly, like a 45-rpm record. It popped open on a hinge. The inside looked pretty dim, but I lowered myself in. I didn't have time to worry about dimness—nor about whether any businessman or dimwit cyberspotlight saw me entering. . . .

I walked carefully down, my front to the stairs. The cover closed, very shortly after my head was below the surface. My eyes adjusted to the lighting. I could see pretty well, and soon, just fine.

The stairs were as they had been yesterday—long, but firm and perfectly safe.

I reached the bottom. There were the conveyor belts. I stepped on one, and it started to move. . . .

THE RIDE WAS swift and smooth, as before. Whatever had happened at Grand Central Terminal, this tunnel was unaffected. What had Frank said about the complex under Wilmington? *Built to withstand just about anything.* The New York underground facilities were no doubt made of the same stuff.

I got off at the first intersection. I couldn't be sure this was the one I had trod upon below the Grace Building yesterday. But I hadn't passed any intersections in my conveyor ride to the park from Grace then. And besides, my conveyor had stopped here now and didn't show any sign of resuming.

I located an elevator. I pressed the button—only one, pointed up—and entered. There were no buttons inside. The elevator whisked me upward. This time I hoped it stopped on the street-level floor.

It did. I walked into the lobby, glared at the cybersecurity screens, and proceeded out onto Forty-second Street.

I was almost afraid to look around. The street was a madhouse, all right—twice as many people as in the park, heading west, toward Times Square. But the air smelled okay. I looked up. No fires in the sky. Good, at least, for that. Maybe the damage was limited. . . .

I walked east, against the crowd, and pictured that beautiful blue eggshell ceiling. . . . Goddammit, even a crack in it was unacceptable. I had tried to warn them. . . .

My cell phone rang. "She's gone, Phil," McQuail said, barely audible. "She and the boyfriend—" And the connection was gone, like Rachel. . . .

I cursed the phone, then patted it anyway because it had gotten me into the passageway in the park, and down here, so quickly.

But I was still walking here without information. I looked, in vain, for a cop or any kind of official. The closest were a flock of police helicopters circling overhead.

I finally reached Fifth Avenue. I looked across the intersection—first toward Grand Central, then the New York Public Library. Was that smoke coming out of the ground by the Library? No, it was steam out of a vent.

I looked a little further, toward the lions. There were a fair number of media people gathered around them. . . . No, they were gathered around someone standing between the lions . . .

He looked like he was conducting a press conference . . . I couldn't make out who he was. . . .

I crossed Forty-second Street to the Library corner. There was no traffic, no cars to contend with, just droves of frightened, running people. . . . I angled my way to the press conference—

"Sir, you'll need credentials to proceed any closer."

NYPD, good. I showed him my ID. He nodded.

"How bad is it?" I asked, and turned my head toward Grand Central.

"A mess." He shook his head.

"Casualties?"

"None that I've heard of, but the radio's spotty here," the cop said.

I must have looked surprised. I know I was happy.

"Well, it's amazing no one was trampled," the cop continued. "They should have given us a little more time, for God's sake."

"Who—"

"Oh, you don't know? I guess word's just getting out—that's why Dugan's up there, talking to the press—the damn feds. They ordered a complete shutdown of Grand Central—they're catching fuckin' mice!"

I nodded, stunned, thrilled, and moved closer to the cameras and microphones. Damn, it *was* Dugan up there.

"—understand, the mayor doesn't necessarily agree with every federal procedure," he was saying. "We share the same goals, completely, to keep our people safe. But this was a federal call."

"Isn't this going to cost the city plenty of money—money we can ill afford?" a reporter from the *Daily News* spoke up.

"Yes, it no doubt will—"

"Well, will the federal government be reimbursing the city?" the reporter asked a follow-up.

"This isn't about money," Jack replied. "Okay, one last question, and I really have to get back to work now."

"How long will this whole rodent operation take?" someone from the *Bergen Record* asked. "I know you told us Grand Central will be down at least until tomorrow. I'm asking about the complete subway, the PATH trains, the whole metropolitan-area system."

"I honestly don't know," Jack replied. "We're going to try to do this in a way that inconveniences the public as little as possible. . . ." And he waved and walked off.

Other questions were shouted. . . . "Does this have anything to do with the attack in the park last night?" . . . "Did the order come from the President?" . . . "How's Sally Li?" . . .

Jack brushed them off and came down the stairs, flanked by cops. I caught his eye. He said something to one of the cops, and they and Jack came over.

"Well, you got what you wanted, Phil." He gestured to the crowds in the street and frowned. "I sure hope it's worth it."

I started to answer—

He leaned closer. "We need to talk—somewhere out of our offices. Call me."

And he turned and was ushered by more cops, south to Forty-first Street. . . .

I FINALLY GOT back to my office almost two hours later—by a circuitous combination of cabs and feet. I didn't get an ounce of further use of my phone, but I felt better, more connected, than I had been in a while. This was by no means a victory—we were still vulnerable in myriad places, and not only from animals—but at least it was a little progress.

But who deserved thanks?

No way Jill could have moved that quickly, not from what she had indicated. Did Frank's hologram have something to do with it? Had Freddie Jason used his hacking for some good?

I called Mel and asked if I could have a meeting with a colleague at The Grace Note sometime in the next few hours. If Mel had said no, or The Grace Note, for some reason, had not been open today, I would have picked some other cafe, dinner, or bar, anonymous to most of the world. But it wouldn't have been as good as The Grace Note. Mel said sure.

I got through to Dugan, and we set the meeting for two hours. Dugan said I should wait for him if he was late—he'd be there eventually.

I called Jill and got through to her, too. Didn't hurt to thank her, in any case. "You pulled some kind of magic."

"I'm glad it's happening, but I had nothing to do with it."

"Who, then, Marty? But—"

"Nope. It was someone else. But I really can't tell you."

We talked for a few minutes. I did my best to pry it out of her. She was clearly pleased at the turn of events, but adamant on not revealing who turned them. "Not now, anyway. Not until you commit to joining us. And even then, it won't be my call."

We said we'd keep in close touch.

I needed to make a whole bunch of additional calls. I realized, again, how valuable a good, old-fashioned phone in the office could be in an age of crises and circuits-busy cell phones.

But my phone working didn't mean everyone else's was. I'd been lucky with Mel, Jack, and Jill. I struck out with Gabe and McQuail.

I tried Ed Monti.

He had just returned from a coroner's convention in Albany. I forwent most of my usual cracks about everyone on the dais being stiffs, even the perennial "you picked a good time to be away," and got right to the point.

"You know, by any chance, where Rachel Saldana is?"

"Why? She's not in today?"

"Yeah."

"News to me. You want me to try her at home?"

"She's not there, either." I filled him in on the wretched details—

He stopped me when I got to Freddie Jason. "You saw Jason yesterday?"

"Yeah, this morning, too."

"Well, that's news to me, too," Ed said.

"What do you mean?"

"I'm surprised to hear he's back already—he's supposed to be in Paris for a special training seminar on new scanning techniques. We can see all kinds of things in corpses these days, before we start the autopsy—"

"He's supposed to be in Paris now?"

"Yes, I'm pretty sure the seminar's going on for another week," Ed replied. "You want me to call him there and find out what's going on?"

"Good idea," I said. "And I'll do some checking around here, too."

"If it wasn't Freddie Jason you saw this morning, then who?" Ed asked.

"Good question."

I HAD GRABBED Jason's wrist this morning—right after he'd projected the nude holograms of Rachel. That proved Jason was no hologram.

He was flesh and blood.

But whose? And how the hell did he get past security?

Well, if he wasn't Freddie Jason, he certainly lived up to what Rachel had said about Jason's computer expertise.

I went back to my office. I had about an hour for some research on the Web.

I located pictures of Freddie Jason pretty quickly—at a medical examiners' dinner last year, from an interview about hacking published in the *Village Voice*, at a science fiction convention two years ago, with his girlfriend, who was an editor.

The asshole I had talked to this morning was not only no hologram, he was not Freddie.

Jeez.

Well, one thing this meant, in case I needed any more proof, was that Rachel was involved in this up to her sweet brown eyes. She had brazenly introduced me to this goddamn ringer, and said he was Freddie.

But who was he, really?

I had no idea what his real name was, so I couldn't do a search on that. He certainly seemed to have considerable hacking capacity—though I didn't know enough about holograms and M&Ms to be sure. But searching all extant Web photos of hackers for someone who looked like him could take years. . . .

Rachel was the only real, searchable information I had on him. She had to have some kind of connection to this guy, some relationship with him, and that might be uncoverable on a Web search.

I searched on Rachel Saldana with every engine I could muster. I got pictures of her at cute fourth and cuter seventeenth birthday parties. Photos of her parents, her grandparents, and three aunts. A nice video of her, from a panel on new directions in autopsying shown on The Discovery Channel, two years ago. Today was my day for seeing her in photographs . . . still, motion, three-dimensional this morning. . . .

I finally located "Freddie Jason"—the face I had talked to just this morning—about five minutes after I looked at my watch and realized I had to leave soon to keep my appointment with Jack.

His face was squeezed right next to Rachel's, and both were smiling. They were standing on what looked like a pebble-covered shore. It reminded me of the beach at Brighton, England.

His name—Elliot Marchand—meant nothing to me.

But a search on that soon showed its relevance.

Among the many articles credited to his name—he apparently was a prolific essayist—was “Beyond Marx and Marcuse—Toward an Assassination of State.” I clicked on it. It was essentially the same as “Toward an Assassination of the American Dream”—the diatribe I had read in Dugan’s office—but the byline was different. Not surprising. Terrorists and aliases walked hand in hand.

And goddammit, we had had him in our hands just this morning.

I CAUGHT A cab to The Grace Note. The ride took even longer than I expected, and I was late to start with. I left voice mail with McQuail to pick up Elliot Marchand in Freddie Jason’s lab, on the unlikely chance that Marchand was still there. I tried, unsuccessfully, to get Dugan on the phone.

I walked in.

“Dit-ditta-dit-ditta-dit-ditta-ditta-dit-dit-ditta . . .” was still playing on that Wurlitzer. Mel loved those Crows. . . .

“Phil.” Mel walked up to me, beer in hand. Other than two big Band-Aids on his forehead, he looked barely the worse for his stay in the hospital and what had caused it. He smiled, and fingered his tortoise-rimmed glasses. “Your friend’s already here.” He pointed to Dugan, seated with his back to me, at a table across the room. “He’s a big Del Vikings fan.”

I squeezed Mel’s shoulder, and joined Dugan. If Mel hadn’t pointed him out, it might have taken a little time for me to recognize him. I wasn’t accustomed to seeing him from behind, relaxing over a table, nursing a beer.

“Hey, Jack.” I sat down.

He looked up at me and smiled. “Nice place you picked out here—they had ‘Come Go With Me’ and ‘Whispering Bells’ playing on the jukebox.”

“Yeah.”

The blond waitress approached, same short black skirt and

all. This time she favored us with a peek of what was underneath—dropping a napkin on the thick sawdust, accidentally or otherwise, saying "oops," and bending over to fetch it. Mel knew how to pick 'em.

"Root beer," I said, when she had finished.

"Another beer for you?" she asked Jack, who was smiling appreciatively.

"I'm fine, thanks," he said. He turned to me. "Okay, let me start by telling you what we've found so far on that smart corner of the park—it's jumping with squirrels apparently outfitted with two kinds of devices."

"Two kinds?"

"Yeah, like I told you on the phone. One with a pair of telecom nodes sticking out of its head, the other with nothing but fur. But they both have some sort of encoding/decoding and transmission device on the inside—like you were telling me."

"None with bombs?" Made sense that none of the antlers-only models had been picked up in the sweep—Jill had said there were only ten.

"I was getting to that. Denny Sontag has two squirrels—"

"Your root beer." Our waitress returned with my drink in a big, frosty mug. She placed a napkin and the mug on our table in well-oiled, rapid-fire succession. "I love squirrels," she offered. "They're like natural garbage-disposal units when it comes to bread."

Dugan shot her a tolerant smile.

"Good point," I said.

Dugan kept his smile as he watched her walk away. "She has good ears to go with that good ass. We weren't talking that loudly."

"It's nice to see you so relaxed," I remarked. "Too bad we never met like this before."

"There's always the future, right?" Dugan lifted his mug

and what was left of his beer. I met it with mine.

"Sontag is ninety-nine percent sure those two squirrels have bombs in their heads," Dugan resumed, more quietly. "Dot-coms, right?"

I nodded.

"Hell, he's a hundred percent sure now—so is Nebuch. They just haven't figured out a way yet to detonate them safely. We're not announcing anything because we don't want the terrorists to know, and detonate them for us."

"They likely know already." I gave him the unabridged story of Rachel and her boyfriend. "The only conceivable out for her is maybe, maybe, she was being blackmailed."

Dugan shook his head sadly, angrily. "It's some sort of terrorist cell. But whose?"

"I don't know if it matters, or if there's any important difference anymore. Like Marchand was saying in his article—Islamic, domestic, personal-psycho—they all amount to the same thing. But this group obviously has a lot of savvy, and tentacles that reach right into the medical examiner's operation, at the very least."

Dugan nodded. "Every part of law enforcement is riddled with impostors and double agents these days—"

My cell phone rang.

So did Dugan's.

We looked at each other and agreed to attend to our dueling rings.

Gabe Nebuch was on mine. "We've three positives in rats—not from your specimens, from the grand sweep that's going on now."

"Jeez."

"We think the dot-com is triggered by a neurochemical signal in the brain—that's why our equipment picked up no triggering telecom in the park. We've got bombs in some of the park squirrels, too—I told you that, right?"

"Yes."

"The bomb uses the chemistry of the body—we think it sucks nitrogen out of amino acids—"

"Transamination?" Proteins practically ran on nitrogen. Its atoms were light, and made highly explosive alliances with other compounds in small amounts—like nitroglycerin. Transamination . . . taking nitrogen out of amino acids, making animals into bombs. . . .

"Yeah. We haven't yet identified the partner compound—we're sure it's found in the body. We're proceeding very carefully."

"That makes sense—thanks, Gabe. I've got Jack Dugan here. Let me brief him, and we'll be back to you about what to do."

Jack was just finishing his cell phone conversation, too.

He looked at me. "That was Denny Sontag—he says his and Gabe's team found bombs not only in squirrels but subway rats. You were right about that. . . . Goddamn disposal units, all right—for innocent people."

DUGAN PHONED THE mayor. They discussed the subways, the rats and the squirrels, and closing the park to civilians. All I could hear was Dugan's side of the conversation. "Of course the public won't like it—but inconvenience is preferable to death, isn't it? . . . I know you didn't want to close Grand Central . . . the media are conveying that accurately . . . but this proves the feds were right to shut it down. . . . We've got to extend that to the whole subway system. . . . Hey, the city has lived through subway shutdowns and transit strikes before. . . ."

He looked at me and raised his eyebrows as if to say, *idiot. . . .*

Meanwhile, McQuail called me. No sign of anyone at Freddie Jason's lab. McQuail gave me more details about his trip to Rachel's apartment. "A neighbor says she saw Rachel leaving with suitcases about an hour before we arrived. I gave the neighbor a pretty thorough questioning. She says Rachel and the boyfriend got along fine, and Rachel certainly didn't seem to be leaving under any visible duress this morning."

I thanked him, turned back to Dugan, and told him what I had just heard. I concluded: "Rachel and her boyfriend put on a good little act in the lab for me—pretending to argue over cutting up a squirrel, when I bet that was the last thing either wanted to do if it had a little bomb inside. She was either a deep-cover terrorist mole when she started working for the medical examiner, or more likely was converted to their cause. Either way, she was in the perfect place to help them when the dead squirrels started coming in. The group had the digital know-how to fake Freddie Jason's ID, fool the cyber-security, and take advantage of Jason's absence. . . . And I, like a moron, thought she was the most trustworthy person in this mess."

Dugan sighed, called the commissioner—got his assistant—and told him we needed lookouts for Rachel and Marchand at airports, bridges, etc.

"I doubt we'll get them," he said to me, after finishing on the phone.

"I know . . . We need more old-fashioned human security in the mix—the human brain is still the most reliable way of recognizing a human face. Not only this case, for everything."

"Yeah." Dugan looked at his watch. "Want another root beer?"

"I'm okay."

He nodded. "I'm gonna have another beer, after all." He signaled our waitress, who was standing, chatting with Mel, on the other side of the room.

I looked at him. "It was you, wasn't it?"

He looked at me askance.

"You ordered the shutdown of Grand Central."

"I'm just deputy mayor," Dugan replied. "I don't have that

kind of authority—you saw what I just went through with the mayor. The feds deserve the credit for acting on your hunch, and God bless them for it."

"I do. But the only outright fed I can think of who might know enough to do that is Frank Catania. But you told me you ID'ed his body. I don't think you'd lie to me like that. So I believe Frank is dead. And I don't really believe in guardian angels. Certainly not in holograms with that kind of clout."

"I'LL HAVE WHAT he's having," I said to our waitress after she had taken Dugan's order.

She turned around and left.

This time neither Dugan nor I stared after her.

"Maybe the people who program those holograms have more smarts and power than you think," Jack said.

"I've no doubt they do, but I'm betting on you as their ignition."

"Why?"

"Not only what I just said, but something about the way you said what *you* just said, Jack—you're not an attorney. I've never known you to plead a case so well that you didn't believe in even more."

Jack lowered his head, shook it, but came up slightly smiling. "Why do you think I asked to have this meeting with you?"

I turned my palms. "I don't know."

"To talk to you about what Jill and Marty told you this morning."

I took that in. "I knew it, I was right." But now that I heard Jack admit it—in the moment from my guessing to his saying it—I found I had mixed feelings about it.

"I'm part of their team—Marty Glick and Jill Cormier. Frank was on it, too, as you know. Office of Surveillance, Department of Homeland Security," Jack said . . .

Jack Dugan, the quintessential New York City cop . . . Yet I had certainly seen signs of his dissatisfaction with New York City law enforcement of late—hell, just here on the phone, a few seconds ago. And his move to deputy mayor was certainly a step away from the Force, no matter how you sliced it. "How long?" I asked him. The huskiness of my voice surprised me.

"Not long," he replied.

"Why?" I said this not accusingly, but genuinely wanting to know, since I had been sparring with this same question myself.

"We're incompetent, Phil. You know that. You know better than most how many criminals get away from New York's finest. The feds are incompetent, too. We're incompetent, they're incompetent. But they're perhaps just a little less incompetent than we are. They have the better resources, the bigger reach. They're the real law enforcement, we're the holograms—the local cop copies, when it comes to fighting worldwide terrorism. And these days, in this world, I came to the conclusion that perhaps I can do just a little more good on their side, on the fed side." He sighed. "I proved that today, didn't I?"

Our waitress returned with our beers.

We thanked her.

I sipped. "So you're deputy mayor and working for the feds at the same time?"

Dugan nodded.

"And the feds know this, and the mayor does not?"

Dugan nodded again. Then sipped some beer.

"So you're not moving back to the Old Muni building—the one that the feds took over?"

Dugan smiled. "No, that would blow my cover."

"Maybe I'm asking more than I'm entitled to know," I said. "But exactly who in the federal government knows about this—your—team? Does the president? Secretary Machem? The head of the FBI?"

"You're asking more than you're entitled to know."

"But Frank was on the team?"

"Yeah—look, if it makes you feel any better, I don't know much more about most of those questions than you do. I just know it's a sector of the Office of Surveillance, Department of Homeland—"

"Right, I got that . . ." I thought for a bit. "They gave you a lot of power, pretty quickly—to shut down Grand Central Terminal, over the mayor's objections. Not that I'm complaining in the least."

"That was the essence of the deal—I join the Office of Surveillance, I pretty much call the fed shots when it comes to the city."

"But you didn't call the mayor with the order?"

"No, I gave the order. Someone else in the feds made the call—to the mayor, to the police commissioner, to me, at the same time, in a conference call. . . . Look, I'd rather the city make these decisions itself. That's why I was just pushing so hard with the mayor . . . We had no choice but to close Grand Central after what you told me, and the evidence beginning to come in from the squirrels. . . ."

I looked at Dugan. I thought I had understood him pretty well as NYPD brass, even deputy mayor. This was different . . . "You're wearing a lot of grey today," I said. Grey jacket, grey shirt, grey tie—I had noticed the color of Dugan's garb in front of the library, but it had slipped my mind in all the excitement. . . . I figured that it wasn't because he was going to a squirrel masquerade.

"You're a haberdasher now?" he responded. "Or is that your way of saying how ambiguous you find my position?"

I kept him straight in my gaze.

"I guess it's okay for me to tell you," Dugan finally said. "Look, understand, this is new to me, too—I received no manual about what to say and not to say to NYPD colleagues who may be joining our team."

"So the grey is for?"

"They asked me to dress in this color whenever I could—so people will get used to seeing me in grey, in case the feds need to substitute a hologram for me at the last minute. The grey somehow makes it easier for them to field the hologram against different colors in the background. . . ."

"Jeez, Jack." So that explained Paton and Temp and "Frank" . . . And hadn't the real Frank also been dressed in a grey suit the first time I had seen him outside of Cerebreeze? I had been right about the grey rehearsals for holograms. . . . I thought again about Rachel's hologram—there had been nothing grey about her body. That prick Marchand probably got her raw footage in their bed. He didn't care about grey. Her hologram wasn't part of the federal program.

I drank some more. And my hologram? It was already grey down in Wilmington. I expected I'd be getting the call to grey soon, if I joined the feds. In effect, I was getting it already. And I didn't particularly care for the color. . . .

"I guess the part that I'm most having trouble getting around is this double-agent stuff," was all that I said.

Dugan looked at me unflinchingly. "I've never known you to shy away from difficult situations, Phil."

"What if I say no? How will we work together then, with my knowing what I now know?"

Dugan smiled expansively. "I'll just have to rely on your discretion and good judgment, then, Phil—as I always do."

I sipped some more of my beer.

I noticed that Dugan's mug was raised, too.

I pulled the cool glass from my lips and held it in the air. I reflected on the light through the glass, on life, the universe, the sawdust on Mel's floor, everything.

I brought my mug next to Dugan's, and clinked. . . .

"Good to have you aboard—again—Phil."

"You saved the city, Jack. It's the least I could do."

"You're the one who talked me into it."

I CAUGHT UP with Jenna after Dugan left.

I had been unable to reach her earlier. She had left me voice mail in the office, telling me she knew about the Grand Central shutdown, and was on her way home on a slow train from Princeton Junction to Penn Station. She had just finished teaching her course in "Treasures in Junk DNA" at Princeton.

My timing now on the phone was perfect, for a change—her train was just pulling into Penn Station.

"You feel like having a little dinner?" I asked her.

"I'm exhausted," she replied. "Where?"

"How about The Grace Note—they had a good tuna steak sandwich on the menu last time I looked." I knew it was one of her favorites. I also knew she approved of my helping Mel.

"Okay," she said. "You sound like something important happened."

"It did."

"I'll see you in ten minutes?"

"I'll be here if it takes longer."

I SCROLLED THROUGH the missed-call readout on my cell phone. Of the ones that had been attempted since this morning, I had spoken to everyone now, except one.

I tried it.

"Sorry, that's an unreal number, or no longer in service," a cybervoice informed me.

I got a chuckle out of the "unreal" explanation—it had just recently been put into use—but nothing else in that advisory pleased me. It meant that the call from "Frank" was untraceable.

I started to put the phone in my pocket; it beeped, as if in objection.

A call had come in while I was attempting to trace "Frank's." The caller was trying again.

"Phil—you were trying to reach me?" It was "Frank." The "guy" was good. Meaning: the hologram was good. Meaning: the programmers of the hologram were good. Meaning . . . it was likely Elliot Marchand who was good, whose programming was sharp enough to pick up my attempts to trace "Frank's" earlier call, if I was right that the "Frank" I had seen this morning, the "Frank" on the phone right now, were Marchand's impersonations of the hologram whom I had come to regard as almost a friend. . . .

It could be Marchand on the phone right now, through a sound-blender that made his voice sound like Frank's.

"Yeah," I said. "I was trying to return your call."

"Well, I'm pleased. Last we talked, you didn't want to talk to me anymore, right?" The voice had precisely the right amount of Frank Catania sarcasm. The original programming obviously had been very deep and rich.

"You were right, I was wrong, I value our relationship," I replied. "I'm willing to take a chance with you, even though you've been hacked." This "Frank" might well be the only lead we could get to Marchand and Rachel.

"Good." The voice-gram still didn't sound fully convinced. "Believe it or not, I enjoy talking to you—even this way—and would miss that." This sounded completely sincere.

"All right, then . . . So, what wisdom were you calling to offer earlier?"

"That you should throw in with Jill and Marty—it's the best move for you, Phil, really, and for the country."

"Well, they make a persuasive case." If this "Frank" was a projection of Marchand, that meant that the author of "Toward An Assassination of the American Dream" had an intimate pipeline to the group that Jill, Marty, Jack—

"This is what I've been urging you to do, hoping you would do, all along, Phil—"

"Someone's here, Frank, I'll get back to you later."

Jenna waved to me from across the room. I beckoned her over to my table, and ended the call.

But she was not the reason I ended it.

JENNA JOINED ME at the table.

I had the cell phone in my hand, pressed against my temple.

"I made great time—you look aggravated—" she started.

I indicated that I needed a few seconds. Which was more important—using what could be a Marchand-hacked version of "Frank" to track down Marchand, or warning Jack and Jill that this possibly hacked version could compromise their whole operation? (Jeez, events had finally conspired to give me Jack and Jill—I'd been getting tired of the Glick version, anyway.)

I called Jack, got voice mail.

I called Jill. Fortunately, I got right through to her. I guess that's what came from being an invitee to her team, and whatever else Jack might have told her if the two had just been in touch. I explained my concerns about Rachel, Marchand, and "Frank."

She said "Frank" would be locked out of operations in ninety seconds. Getting at Marchand through "Frank" was a longshot, anyway—if Marchand was now running "Frank," he would no doubt be exceedingly careful about revealing his location.

But banishing "Frank" would, unfortunately, put a further crimp in the relationship with me that the hologram claimed to value. I did, too, in a way. . . . But if there was any vestige of the original, flesh-and-blood Frank in the current voice on the phone, he would approve completely. . . .

I ended the call and turned to Jenna.

"So," I said wearily, and took her hand.

Our waitress approached. "Could we have a food menu?" I asked.

"Sure," she said, and took our drink orders. I went for ginger ale and lime—she must have thought I was a nutcase when it came to beverages—and Jenna asked for a Campari.

I touched her hand, and recounted the day's events. Amazing how many times, to how many people, I had gone over this today. But Jenna was the only one to hear the complete story—or the most recent edition, in any case. . . .

She listened, and stopped me when I told her about the call I had just made to Jill about "Frank."

"But if he's Elliot Jason's creation—"

"Marchand, Elliot Marchand," I corrected, though "Elliott Jason" had a logic, too.

"Okay . . . if 'Frank' is Marchand's stalking horse, then why would he—'Frank'—tip his hand by letting you know he had such quick access to what Jill and Marty told you in the park?"

"That's the nub of our 'Frank' dilemma," I replied. "The fact that he indicated to me that he knew what Jill told me could be evidence that he—the hologram—was not tampered with by Marchand, because if he had been tampered with, he surely wouldn't flaunt his knowledge of Jill at me—as you say. On the other hand, he might have calculated that very point in his plans, hoping it might convince me that he's not Marchand's creation. . . ." I sighed. "Jill also alluded to that when we were just talking. In the end, there's no way of knowing for sure which is correct—because the same evidence supports both conclusions. The safest thing is to lock 'Frank' out."

Jenna nodded. "You seem to get into situations like that more than anyone I know." She stroked my hand.

"I think lots of people do—they just don't talk about it." I shook my head sadly. "We're at the very beginning here, with this rodent threat. Rats and mice are everywhere, in every city.

We could use 'Frank's' help. But we have no choice."

"So you're going to accept Jill's offer," she said, "Jack's offer."

"Jack made some very good points . . . plus . . . are you okay with that?"

Jenna nodded. "The federal people are right to want you with them. But . . . will you just be pretending to be with them, or will you really be—"

Our waitress returned with our drinks. "Thanks, and two tuna steak sandwiches," I told her.

She wrote the order on her pad. "Mel's finishing up in the back—he'll be out in a few minutes." She turned and left.

I looked at Jenna. "A little of both, I guess. . . . I'll just have to see how it plays out. I know there'll always be something New York about me. I know that's true about Dugan, too."

Jenna squeezed my hand, sipped her Campari. "Could this affect us badly financially?"

"No. If anything, the opposite. I didn't discuss money, but, in effect, I'll be working two jobs."

"I'm sorry, I don't mean to be so venal—especially about something like this, but you know, if we start having kids, I'll have to start cutting back on my teaching—"

"This won't get in the way of that, I promise."

"Okay—"

"Phil!" Mel walked quickly over to our table, feet crunching a half-foot of sawdust. "This must be Jenna!" The two hadn't met before in person. "The sandwiches will be out in a minute or two," he said.

"Good," I said. "Have a seat."

"Thanks." He sat. "The recordings came through perfectly!"

"Oh, you used them? I didn't notice a thing," Jenna said, and looked at the sawdust.

"You wouldn't have," Mel said. "You're sitting in Jack Dugan's seat—his back was to the action. And the hamsters are nocturnal, anyway, as I told Phil. They stayed under the sawdust. Jill Cormier had them well trained, I must say—they barely moved throughout your conversation with Jack."

I had asked Jill, when I had called her from my office, if she could set up a hamster recording operation at The Grace Note—the only method I could think of for evading a possible police sweep. I didn't tell her the meeting was with Jack. Who knew what she would have done had I told her that. But she was inclined to help—as an indication of good faith and a further encouragement for me to join her team. I had wanted my conversation with Jack recorded, in case it had gone sour. He, after all, had been the one who called the meeting. Jenna and I had previously discussed The Grace Note as a good place for a hamster-recorded conversation. . . .

"—she did a great job with the setup," Mel was still going on about Jill. "Worked like that!" He snapped his finger.

The music suddenly changed—to the James Bond theme.

"I had the jukebox rigged to another bio-com gimmick—I guess you could call it that," Mel explained over the twanging guitar. "I snap my fingers, and I change the music. I put in that selection right before you came."

Mel and his sense of humor.

"It's not early rock 'n' roll," I objected.

"I'm expanding my horizons," Mel replied.

Our waitress showed up with our two sandwiches.

"Enjoy," Mel said. "And they're on the house—least I can do, now that I'm on the payroll with you."

I had arranged for that with Jill, as well. The feds paid handsomely for this kind of work. Should help put a nice dent in Mel's bills.

"By the way, I also spoke to her about those messages from

outer space—you know, the ones that some people think are from aliens, planted in the hamster brains, or maybe somehow the little hamsters are part alien themselves?"

I put down my sandwich. I hadn't counted on Mel confiding his crackpot theories to Jill when I had asked her to come down here—

"And she said, well, the federal government has been aware of this for a few years now. Ever since the hamster project began, they've been finding some strange stuff in the audio readouts."

I started to laugh—

Mel snapped his fingers, twice in rapid succession, and the music stopped.

"No joke, Phil. We're going to start looking into this as soon as we get the terrorists more under control."